THE
RED POLE
OF
MACAU

THE
RED POLE
OF
MACAU

AN AVA LEE NOVEL

IAN HAMILTON

SPIDERLINE

This edition published in 2012 by
House of Anansi Press Inc.
110 Spadina Avenue, Suite 801
Toronto, ON, M5V 2K4
Tel. 416-363-4343
Fax 416-363-1017
www.houseofanansi.com

Distributed in Canada by
HarperCollins Canada Ltd.
1995 Markham Road
Scarborough, ON, M1B 5M8
Toll free tel. 1-800-387-0117

This is a work of fiction. Names, characters, businesses, organizations,
places, and events are either a product of the author's imagination or are
used fictitiously. Any resemblance to actual persons, living or dead, is
purely coincidental.

House of Anansi Press is committed to protecting our natural environment.
As part of our efforts, the interior of this book is printed on paper that
contains 100% post-consumer recycled fibres, is acid-free, and is processed
chlorine-free.

16 15 14 13 12   1 2 3 4 5

Library and Archives Canada Cataloguing in Publication

Hamilton, Ian, 1946–
The red pole of Macau / Ian Hamilton.

(An Ava Lee novel)
ISBN 978-0-88784-254-2

I. Title. II. Series: Hamilton, Ian, 1946– . Ava Lee novel.

PS8615.A4423R432012   C813'.6   C2011-907006-5

Cover design: Daniel Cullen
Text design and typesetting: Alysia Shewchuk

*We acknowledge for their financial support of our publishing program
the Canada Council for the Arts, the Ontario Arts Council, and the
Government of Canada through the Canada Book Fund.*

Printed and bound in Canada

For Chloë Hamilton, Matthew Howell, David Hamilton,
Oliver Howell, Gabriella Moniz, Scarlett Hamilton-West,
and Lucas Moniz — collectively, the future.

TRIAD ORGANIZATION

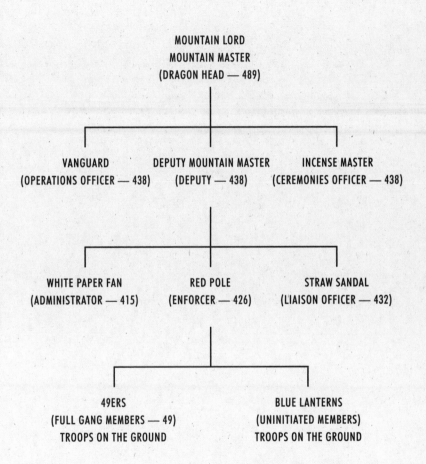

MOUNTAIN LORD
MOUNTAIN MASTER
(DRAGON HEAD — 489)

VANGUARD
(OPERATIONS OFFICER — 438)

DEPUTY MOUNTAIN MASTER
(DEPUTY — 438)

INCENSE MASTER
(CEREMONIES OFFICER — 438)

WHITE PAPER FAN
(ADMINISTRATOR — 415)

RED POLE
(ENFORCER — 426)

STRAW SANDAL
(LIAISON OFFICER — 432)

49ERS
(FULL GANG MEMBERS — 49)
TROOPS ON THE GROUND

BLUE LANTERNS
(UNINITIATED MEMBERS)
TROOPS ON THE GROUND

AVA LEE WOKE TO THE SENSATION OF LIPS KISSING her forehead. She opened her eyes to semi-darkness and saw her girlfriend, Maria, hovering over her, her face in shadow. Ava extended her arms, but Maria shook her head and passed over the phone. "He says his name is Michael and that he's your brother," she said.

"I didn't hear it ring," Ava said. "And he's my half-brother, from my father's first wife. The one I told you I met in Hong Kong."

"I think he first phoned half an hour ago. I didn't answer it then. He's called back every ten minutes since."

Ava glanced sideways at the bedside clock. It was just past eight a.m., eight in the evening in Hong Kong, where she assumed the call originated. She reached under her pillow, pulled out a black Giordano T-shirt, and slipped it over her head. Then she held out her hand for the phone. "I'll talk to him out here," she said, rolling out of bed and walking to the kitchen. "Michael?"

"Yes."

"This is an early call."

"I'm sorry. I spoke to Dad last night," he said, his voice strained. "He said he met you at the Toronto airport and explained that we are having some problems here. He said you were going to call me."

"I was, later today."

"I have to go out in about half an hour and I won't be available for the rest of the evening. I didn't want to wait until tomorrow for us to talk."

"Daddy said there was an issue in Hong Kong. He didn't say any more than that, and he didn't tell me it was so urgent."

He sighed. "I'm sorry."

Ava sat at her kitchen table and looked down onto Yorkville Avenue. Her condo was situated in the very heart of Toronto, and the Yorkville district was one of the city's trendiest, but at eight on a weekday morning the streets were devoid of shoppers and restaurant goers. Farther away she could see that Avenue Road, a main north–south artery, was jammed with commuter traffic. "What's going on?" she asked.

"We're in a bit of a mess."

"Who is *we*?"

"My partner, Simon To, and me."

"Explain what you mean by a mess."

The line went silent. All Ava could hear was deep breathing, as if he were trying to gather together his thoughts and his emotions. "We own a franchise operation: some convenience stores and high-end noodle shops. We were looking at putting one of each into a large new retail mall in Macau, either renting the space or buying it. We were midway through negotiations when the developers asked if we'd like to up the ante, if we'd like to invest in the entire project. It's something we'd always thought about, accumulating some real estate. Simon didn't see how we could go wrong putting money into Macau. So we did."

"How much money?"

"A hundred and fifty million."

"U.S. dollars?" Ava said, shocked.

"No, Hong Kong."

"So about twenty million U.S.?"

"Yes."

That's still a lot of money, she thought, *but in Macau it won't buy much land.* "So you took a minority share?"

"Yes. As I said, it's a large project."

"So what's gone wrong?"

"The development has run into all kinds of delays and we've been trying to pull our money out. They won't let us. In fact, we're getting leaned on to put in more."

"And you don't want to?"

"We can't, and our bank is all over us about the hundred and fifty million."

"The real estate developer is from Hong Kong?"

"No, he's Macanese."

"You obviously have a contract."

"We do."

"Have you spoken to lawyers?"

"Do you have any idea how time-consuming and money-eating a process it is for a Hong Kong company to pursue one based in Macau?" he said, a trace of impatience in his voice.

Maybe you should have considered that before you did the deal, she thought. "So what do you think I can do?" she asked.

"Communications between them and us have been getting more difficult by the day. My partner can't talk to them without losing his temper, and every conversation I have with these people just seems to make things worse. We need a fresh set of eyes and ears. We need a new perspective."

"Michael, what did Daddy tell you I did for a living?" Ava asked.

"He said you were a problem-solver."

"All I do is collect bad debts."

"If things keep going the way they are, I'm afraid this could become one," he said, his voice heavy.

"You don't mean that," she said.

"No, not really. We just need to find a way to negotiate ourselves out of this situation."

"And you think I can do that?"

"Dad says if anyone can, it's you."

"It isn't my usual line of work."

"I don't care, and we'd pay a fee."

"I couldn't charge one," she said.

"Ava, please, whatever it takes to get you here, I'll do it. We're at an impasse."

How strange is this? Ava thought. She had met Michael Lee exactly once, and then for only a few minutes in a Hong Kong restaurant, and now he was inviting, almost begging her into his life.

Ava was the younger daughter in their father Marcus Lee's second family. He had married three times, and in the tradition of wealthy Chinese men, supported and loved each of his families. His first wife had given him four sons, of whom Michael was the eldest. It was understood that Marcus's business and the bulk of his wealth would ultimately reside with the first family, and that Michael would become head of the entire clan if anything happened to Marcus.

Ava's mother, Jennie, had given Marcus two daughters and a volatile relationship. It had become so fractious that Marcus eventually moved them to Vancouver, a city Jennie Lee couldn't abide. She'd lasted two years there before taking Ava and her sister, Marian, to Toronto, where the girls were raised and educated. Marcus eventually had taken a third wife. She had given him two more children, a girl and a boy, and they now lived in Australia.

Jennie Lee had never worked. Marcus bought them a house and cars, paid the bills, and looked after the girls' educations. He still talked to Jennie every day, and he visited Canada every year for a two-week stay. This year had been unusual. He had joined Jennie, Ava, Marian, and Marian's husband and two daughters on a two-week cruise through the southern Caribbean, and then returned to Toronto to stay for another week with Jennie. He was still at her house, in the suburb of Richmond Hill to the north.

Ava's mother had never been jealous about the first family. She knew that the first wife and her family would always be pre-eminent. All she asked was that Marcus be fair in his treatment of her and the girls. And he always had been. He talked to Jennie about his four sons from the first marriage, so she knew about them and had made their names known to Ava and Marian. But none of them had ever met until the week before.

The thing that Ava didn't know was how open Marcus Lee was about her and Marian with the rest of his extended family. She would have assumed that Michael knew they existed, but it was still a surprise when he approached her in the Hong Kong restaurant and said he recognized her from pictures their father had shown him. He had known exactly who she was, and he seemed eager to start a relationship.

Ava found it unsettling. It was one thing to understand and accept the complicated layers of Marcus Lee's life and to know where you fit among them. It was another to confront the physical reality of someone who until then had been just a name, just a shadow.

"Michael, I got home only yesterday. I've been on the road for more than a week. Is there anything I can do from here?" she said.

He hesitated.

She sighed. "Email the contract to me and I'll look at it right away."

"It's all very basic stuff. I don't see how that can help."

"Michael, let me be the judge of that. After I've gone through it we can talk."

"Okay," he said, still sounding reluctant.

"And by the way, how much does Daddy actually know about your problem?"

"Why do you ask?"

"I expect I'll be talking to him today. I don't want to be indiscreet."

"He knows about the size of it but I haven't discussed all the details."

"Then neither will I."

"Thank you."

"Look, I promise I'll read the contract as soon as I get it, and then we can talk," she said.

"I'll email it right away and I'll call when I get back from this function. It will be around midnight."

Ava closed the phone. The sun was glistening off the windows of the condos across the street, taking, she imagined, the chill out of the spring air. It was her favourite time of year in Canada: the world coming to life, full of promise. The last thing she felt like doing was getting on another plane for Hong Kong. After scurrying around Wuhan in China, London, Denmark, Dublin, New York, and then London again, chasing money and forged art, she felt she deserved more than one day in Toronto.

She thought about going back to bed, but Michael's problem was now bouncing around in her head. She turned on her laptop and scanned her email. As she did, a message arrived from Michael with the heading Contract. She opened the message and the attachment and scrolled down. Michael was right; it was a standard agreement.

They had partnered with a company called the Ma Shing Realty Corporation, which had secured a reasonably large plot of land on the Cotai Strip of Macau, the so-called Las Vegas of the East, with casinos such as the Venetian and Wynn. The plan was to build a shopping centre to service the casino customers. Michael and Simon would be given space for a convenience store and a noodle shop and thirty percent ownership of the complex in return for their investment.

On balance, Ava thought it looked like a well thought-out deal. Macau was booming, its sixteen casinos generating more income than Las Vegas's hundred or more. She knew Chinese gamblers. Their money would be pumped into the tables, not hotel rooms, big-name boutiques, or expensive restaurants. Convenience stores and noodle shops were more their style, so the concept seemed sound. She checked the timeline. Ground should have been broken more than a year ago. Michael and Simon should already be occupying their spaces.

She went over the contract a second time, examining the wording, which was quite loose. There were no penalties if Ma Shing did not meet specified dates. There was also no exit provision for Michael. It didn't say that his money was locked in, but there was no clause in the contract to trigger taking it out.

If her father hadn't asked her to help and if Michael hadn't been her brother, she probably would have told him that his best option was to be patient and wait for the centre to get built. But they both seemed so distressed that Ava wondered if something else was in play.

And then a thought occurred to her: *Whose money is really at risk here?* She reached for the phone to call Richmond Hill and then paused. Her father had been vague the day before, saying only that Michael had a problem. What more was he likely to say? *Well, all I can do is ask,* she thought, as she punched in the number.

Her mother answered on the fourth ring.

"You're up so early?" Ava asked.

"Daddy has gone for a walk. I made him coffee and toast before he left."

"I wanted to talk to him about Michael."

Jennie Lee sighed. "Such a mess."

"Has Daddy told you what's going on?" Ava asked, realizing that maybe she didn't have to talk to him.

"I'm not sure that —"

"Michael just called me and then he sent me some information."

"So you should have everything you need."

"Except I can't make much sense of it."

"You need to speak to your father."

"I can't imagine that he'll tell me any more than he did yesterday."

"And that's not enough?"

"No. For one thing, I want to know if he's involved in this investment."

She could hear her mother inhaling and wondered whether she was holding a cigarette to her lips or airing out some tension. "He's not involved — at least, not directly."

Ava felt a door opening and barged through. "Michael said he borrowed the money they put into it. Did Daddy secure the loan?"

"No, but he might as well have."

"What do you mean?"

"I don't know how much I should tell you."

"You should tell me absolutely everything if you want me to help."

"That's what I told your father, but he's a little embarrassed about the situation."

"Why?"

"He doesn't think Michael and his partner did proper due diligence. He said that on his own, Michael is quite conservative and not much of a risk taker. His partner, Simon To, is another story. He's aggressive, rude, and at times too greedy. Your father thinks that Simon talked or pushed Michael into this thing."

"If the shopping centre gets built, it isn't that bad a deal," Ava said.

"But they don't have time to wait."

"What do you mean?"

"Your father said they've breached a loan covenant at the bank. The bank is demanding its money back. If they don't come up with it, the bank will put them out of business."

"Businesses go under all the time. If Daddy didn't secure the loan then they have no recourse with him."

"You don't understand," Jennie Lee said slowly. "They used Daddy's bank to get their loan. Even though he hasn't guaranteed anything, he expects the bank to start squeezing his business very soon. At the very least he thinks they will restrict his working line of credit. They could even refuse to renew the line of credit, and it's scheduled for a review in three months."

"He can find another bank."

"Yes, he probably can, but that doesn't address the depth of obligation he feels towards Michael," Jennie said, and paused. "Ava, there's no way that Marcus Lee will stand back and let his son's business go under. It would bring so much shame upon the entire family. He's spent his life building a reputation, and he couldn't bear to see it sullied. He'd sell everything he owns and give it to Michael rather than let him fail in such a public way."

Ava was taken aback by the passion and certainty in her mother's voice. She also noticed a tinge of anger. Michael Lee had no fans in Richmond Hill. "You do know that we're talking about twenty million U.S. dollars?" Ava asked.

"Enough money to ruin your father," Jennie said.

"And his ability to support the family?" Ava said.

"I don't want to think about that. Your father will do what he thinks is best. It won't change how I feel about him."

Ava thought about her mother and about the two aunties and half-siblings she had never met. "I guess I'm going to Hong Kong," she said quietly. "Even though I'm not sure there's anything I can do."

"You'll figure out something when you get there."

"Let's hope."

"Ava?"

"Yes, Mummy?"

"I am very proud of you."

Ava paused, not sure how to respond. "Look, tell Daddy I called and that I spoke to Michael and I'm heading over there."

"Will you phone him before you leave?"

Ava felt a presence behind her and turned to see Maria standing naked in the doorway of the bedroom.

"No, Mummy, there isn't any need."

"But if he calls you, you won't tell him —"

"I won't say anything about what we discussed."

"I love you."

"Love you too," Ava said, and closed her phone.

"And I love you as well," Maria said.

Ava stared at her and smiled. "Isn't it time you got dressed for work?"

"You're leaving?"

"Yes, I'm going to Hong Kong. It's family business that I can't avoid."

"What time?" she said, her disappointment rippling across the room.

"Tonight."

Maria shook her head of thick, curly black hair. "Then I'm going back to bed," she said. "Join me."

2

AVA WOKE WITH A START, KNOWING WHERE SHE WAS
but for a moment not sure where she was headed. There had
been too many planes in recent weeks. She looked out the
window and saw the South China Sea shimmering under
an early spring sun, sampans and fishing boats skirting the
armada of huge ocean freighters waiting to be escorted into
Hong Kong's container port.

She stretched and made a quick bathroom run, then
organized her papers and closed the Moleskine notebook
that detailed the job she had just completed. Ava kept a
separate notebook for every case she took on. When the job
was finished, successfully or not, the notebook went into a
safety deposit box in a bank a few blocks from her condo.
This notebook was now ready to join the others.

Before leaving Toronto she had received an email from
Roxanne Rice, a go-between, advising Ava that the money
she had recovered for her previous clients had been deposited, as agreed, into a Liechtenstein bank account and was
waiting for Ava's transmittal advice. Ava had sent it immediately, and an hour later she received confirmation that a

wire transfer had been sent to the bank she and her partner, Uncle, used in Kowloon. The money would be there
within two days. Ava had used the time on the plane to
review all the numbers and the expenses attached to the
job so she could know how much of the money arriving
in Kowloon would be forwarded to the clients and how
much she and Uncle would keep as their fee. It was their
largest fee ever — more than twenty million dollars — but
Ava was an accountant by training and didn't like dealing
in round numbers. She didn't close the notebook until she
had figured out their cut to the last cent. While Uncle didn't
care about that level of detail, Ava knew the clients would.
Changxing and May Ling Wong were the most powerful
business team in Wuhan City, in the province of Hubei,
and May Ling was a numbers woman. They hadn't been
easy to work with, and Ava wasn't going to give them —
particularly May Ling — any reason to come back at her
over a few dollars and cents.

The Wongs had hired Uncle and Ava to pursue the
people who had foisted more than a dozen forged Fauvist
paintings on them, paintings with a value of close to $80
million. Ava's sole interest had been to find the perpe-
trators so she could persuade them to return the money
they had stolen. Her and Uncle's fee was thirty percent of
everything they recovered. The Wongs, it turned out, had
conflicting priorities. They wanted the money all right, but
almost as important to them was taking revenge. Three
innocent people had been killed at their instigation, and
Ava had almost walked away from the job. She'd finished it
on her terms, saving another life in the process. Still, even
that act and the size of the fee didn't make Ava feel any

better about the way the job had gone. It had also left a rift between her and May Ling. Initially Ava had felt almost a kinship between them, an emotion May Ling felt even more keenly. But when the job turned sour, Ava had abandoned any thought of a relationship. May Ling had not, and she'd made it clear that she wanted to repair the damage that had been done. Ava was not interested.

Well, now it's officially over, Ava thought as she put the notebook into her Chanel purse. She looked out the window and saw Chep Lap Kok, Hong Kong's international airport, on the horizon. Built on Chep Lap Kok Island, near Lantau Island on Hong Kong's southwestern perimeter, it had been the world's largest land reclamation and construction site before it opened just over ten years earlier. It had replaced Kai Tak, an airport with a single runway situated in the middle of Kowloon. There were those who still missed the romance of Kai Tak, the sight of the planes flying low over Kowloon Bay, their wing tips almost touching laundry that hung from the balconies of apartments that flanked the airport. But with the romance of the old, overburdened airport had come flight delays and slow customs and baggage lines. Ava much preferred the efficiency of Chep Lap Kok; as the plane touched down, she was thinking she could get through Customs and Immigration and claim her checked bag within fifteen minutes of reaching the gate. It took twelve.

She walked into the cavernous arrivals hall, with its great arching glass-and-steel roof, and looked quickly towards the Kit Kat Koffee House. Normally Uncle would be waiting for her there, an unlit cigarette dangling from his lips, the racing form or a Chinese daily newspaper open in front of him. He had been her partner and mentor for more than ten years. They had met in China, where they'd found themselves chasing the same thief for different customers. They joined forces to run the target to the ground. After the job was done, Uncle asked Ava if she would consider a merger. He was then in his sixties, maybe even seventies, a small, wiry man not much taller or heavier than her, with close-cropped hair that was still streaked with black, and dark eyes that conveyed more emotion than the actual words he spoke. He said that he had contacts all over Asia and more business than he could handle. What his business lacked was the accounting skills and the finesse she could bring. After working with the goons he had employed in China, Ava knew he wasn't overstating things. And there was something about him that immediately appealed to her, a simplicity that was reflected in the black suits and white shirts he wore buttoned to the collar, and the direct manner in which he spoke.

People gossiped when they became partners, certain that the union of a sixty-year-old man and a twenty-something young woman had to be about more than just business. There were also rumours about Uncle's former career, rumours that never ceased. He had been triad, people said, and the most senior of triad. She never asked him if it was true, because he was a man she thought she could trust. Ten years later, there was no one on earth she trusted more than Uncle.

Ava had debated the day before about telling Uncle she was coming back to Hong Kong, and decided in the end not to. She was there strictly on family business, she reasoned. He would probably understand that if she had told him, but knowing him as well as she did, he would still have insisted on helping her. She was uncomfortable with that for practical reasons. In the past he had involved her in jobs for personal friends, jobs for which he had waived his recovery fee. Ava had collected her share, though, and her fear was that if she brought Uncle into Michael's business there would be a question of quid pro quo. He might not have asked, but she would have felt obligated to return the favour anyway. She could have lied, of course, and told him she was in Hong Kong for a holiday. But she never lied to Uncle.

So instead of climbing into Uncle's Mercedes and riding with him and Sonny, his driver and bodyguard, she took a cab from the airport to the Mandarin Oriental Hotel in Central, the business centre of Hong Kong. The trip took an hour, about half an hour longer than usual in rush-hour traffic. Her agent had arranged for an early check-in, and Ava was showered and dressed by ten thirty. She travelled light: slacks, skirts, and Brooks Brothers shirts for business, Giordano T-shirts and Adidas training pants for downtime. When she last saw Michael, she had been in casual mode. Now she put on a pair of fitted black linen slacks and a white shirt with a modified Italian collar. She fastened the French cuffs with a pair of green jade cufflinks she had paid a fortune for in Beijing, and then pinned her shoulder-length raven hair into a bun and secured it with an ivory chignon pin, her lucky charm. She added the lightest touch of red lipstick and black mascara and then stepped back to look in the mirror. She was five foot three, and there wasn't an ounce of fat on her 115-pound frame. Her friends couldn't understand how someone who ate like a horse could stay so lean. But she jogged regularly and had a job loaded with stress. And then there was bak mei, the martial art that Ava devoted herself to.

Ava had started practising martial arts when she was a teenager. She was quick, agile, and fearless. She'd soon surpassed those in her age group, and when she began to challenge her teacher, he pulled her aside and asked if she had an interest in learning from a true master. She said yes, and he sent her to see Grandmaster Tang in downtown Toronto. He taught a range of martial arts, but when it came to bak mei he had only two students, Ava and her friend Derek. Bak mei was always taught one-on-one: historically a father passing its secrets to a son, and in this case a mentor to his student. It wasn't a pretty discipline — it was meant to cause damage. Its practitioners were taught to fend off attacks with short, power-laden hand strikes to eyes and ears and nerve endings, and kicks that never went above the waist. It had taken years for her to perfect her technique, to take all the energy and strength she could generate from her shoulders, arms, torso, legs, and twisting hips and focus it into the middle knuckle of one hand, a blow called the phoenix-eye fist. It was the most lethal strike in bak mei, and Ava had mastered it.

She began to prepare herself to call her half-brother. She hadn't told him exactly when she would arrive because she wanted to take the time she needed to get settled. She turned on her computer and opened the Moleskine notebook, which had Michael's name written across the top of the first page. She had found that she retained details — names, numbers, leads, observations, all neatly recorded in pen — if she wrote them by hand. It had felt strange, though, writing Michael's name.

In Toronto she had done what research she could on the Ma Shing Realty Corporation and had come up short. Neither English nor Chinese websites could give her more than a name and a Macau address. That was disappointing, though it was not unusual for a privately held Chinese company that had no need for self-promotion.

The Millennium Food Partnership, on the other hand, had spent a lot of money on their website. There were pictures and extensive biographies of the two founders, Michael and his business partner, Simon To. In one photo they stood side by side. Michael was tall, lean, wearing what looked like an Armani suit, his full hair slicked straight back. Simon To's head barely reached his partner's chin, and his suit may have been as expensive but it hung badly on a pudgy body. They had both been educated in Australia, graduating the same year from business school at the University of Melbourne, and had formed their company immediately thereafter, with the intention of buying up Hong Kong and — if they could — Chinese franchise rights to up-and-coming U.S. fast-food companies. All the big names were long taken, of course, so they were dealing on spec, trying to identify new firms they might sell to. After a couple of unsuccessful launches, they had regrouped and decided to create their own chain of noodle shops. So far, so good. They were running ten in Hong Kong and had about twenty franchises in China. When they'd accumulated some cash, they bought a string of 7-Eleven stores and now owned nine. The foray into Macau was the first time they had tried to combine both of their business models and also invest in real estate.

There were several videos on their site. One focused on the noodle shops, and was jammed with customers only too happy to offer rave reviews of the restaurant chain. Another featured Simon To pitching to potential franchisees in Cantonese. To Ava he looked overeager, stretching the benefits to the maximum and not bothering with caveats. The pitch in Mandarin was a touch more low-key but still aggressive, and it seemed to be targeting companies that could take on a licence for a province. To Ava he didn't come across as trustworthy, but then she couldn't count the number of deadbeats she'd met who looked entirely the opposite.

It was time to call. It didn't take long for a receptionist to patch her through to Michael. In their last two conversations he'd been tentative and nervous. If anything, he was even worse now. He stammered a bit as he said he was happy she'd arrived in Hong Kong.

"How do you want to handle this? Do you want me to come by the office?" she asked.

"That would be a good idea."

"I know where you are. I can be there in about twenty minutes."

"That's fine," he said.

She hung a left when she exited the hotel and then continued on uphill. In Toronto it would have been a ten-minute walk, but pedestrian traffic in Hong Kong was a different animal. The sidewalks were crowded, and people were bunched at every corner. Ava had no choice but to go with the flow, stopping and starting like a car on a freeway during rush hour.

Des Voeux Road in Central was a great address if you were near the Bank of China or the DBS Bank. Millennium wasn't. It was in a smaller office building, with only one elevator serving ten floors. Ava took one look at the crowd already waiting in the lobby and climbed the stairs to the sixth floor.

The hallway had linoleum on the floor, cheap acoustic ceiling panels, and walls that were beige or green, depending on the light. Ava walked through a large plain wooden door that was flanked on either side by the company name, stamped in brass and mounted on a plastic plaque. She had seen the office entrance in their video and it had looked more impressive then.

Michael sat in the tiny reception area, a cellphone stuck to his ear. He turned to look up at her, his face visibly distressed. *In two weeks he's aged five years*, Ava thought. He was beautifully dressed in a grey designer suit, a crisp white dress shirt, and a tightly knotted red tie. She looked at him and saw her father from her earliest memories: the same pointed chin, long, thin nose, and large, almost round eyes.

"We won't do that," he said to whoever was on the other end of the line.

Ava leaned against the wall, studying Michael. He was barely in control of his emotions.

"You need to talk to Simon; you need to talk to him or our lawyers. They both tell me we have no further liability, so I don't know how you can make those claims," he said, and gave her a weak smile.

She thought about backing out the door and leaving Michael to his call, but he suddenly stopped talking and looked at the phone. "Those sons of bitches hung up," he said to her.

"What's the issue?" she asked.

"They're squeezing the hell out of us. They want us to put up another eighty million or walk away from the money we've already put into the project. We can't do either."

"How far along is the project? I know you're behind schedule, but by how much?"

He grimaced. "The land hasn't been touched, not a spade in the ground. It's been more than twelve months. I'm beginning to think they have some zoning or government permit issues, although everyone denies it."

"I didn't realize it was quite that bad," Ava said slowly.

"Well, it is, and now they want more money."

"Why?"

"They claim one of the other investors pulled out and now we have to make up the difference. They say construction won't start until all the money is in place."

"Do they have a legal right to ask for the money?"

"No, no."

"And you've told them that?"

"They don't care. They keep asking for the money anyway, and not nicely," he said. "They say Simon verbally agreed to put in extra money if they needed it, right after the deal was signed."

"Did he?"

"He says no."

"What does your lawyer say?"

"He says we don't have to."

"What does he think about your right to get your original investment returned?"

"There's an addendum to the contract that says we're entitled to make that request if the project hasn't started within twelve months of the original signing date."

"I didn't see that in the papers you sent."

"Sorry, I was in a hurry."

"The twelve months is up now."

"Yes, it's been fourteen months."

"And you've made the request?"

"Repeatedly."

"And what do they say?"

"They say no, and when we persist, they tell us to sue."

"And we've talked about how difficult that would be."

"Even our lawyer agrees with that."

Ava looked down at her brother, who seemed lost in his own thoughts. "It seems to me, Michael, that the Macanese probably want you to abandon your investment. Asking for the extra money is just them leveraging you."

"We can't walk away from that money, or even just let it sit," he said absently. "The bank is already all over us for missing deadlines. We are in breach of some covenants and I'm afraid they're going to call in the loan."

"I understand."

Michael finally seemed to see her. "I'm sorry," he said, standing up. "I'm sorry to be so rude. Thank you for coming, Ava."

He was about a foot taller than her, lean and fit. He looked down at her, an awkward smile on his face. He started to extend his hand, then pulled it back and leaned over to kiss her on both cheeks. "Thank you for coming," he said again.

3

THEY SAT SIDE BY SIDE IN THE BOARDROOM, THE CON-
tract and its addendum between them. They went over it
line by line, parsing it until they were cross-eyed.

She saw Michael sneaking sideways glances at her; she
was doing exactly the same. It was as if they were each trying to accept the reality of the other's presence.

Ava finally said, "They're fucking you over. The contract
is very clear about the nature of your investment, and the
addendum is equally clear that you can request the return of
your money after twelve months if the project hasn't started."

"I know. Like I said, they don't care."

"How did you meet these guys?"

Michael looked uncomfortable. "Through Simon. Or
actually, through a friend of Simon's."

"His name?"

"David Chi."

"What do you know about him?"

"Not much. I'd met him socially a few times with Simon."

"So Chi brought the deal to Simon and Simon brought it
to you. Is that how it worked?"

"Yes."

"Did Chi get paid for this?"

"Not by us."

"By the other side?"

"I'm beginning to think so."

"How about this Ma Shing — how much due diligence did you do?"

She saw a bead of sweat on his forehead; his lips looked dry. "Not nearly enough," he said.

"What does that mean?"

"I left it mainly to Simon, although our lawyers did confirm that the land was owned by and registered to Ma Shing."

"So what kind of due diligence did Simon do?"

His discomfort increased. "Ava, I'm beginning to think that he didn't do any, that he just believed everything David Chi told him."

"Geez."

He said in a rush, "We've been friends for more than twenty years and I trust him like a brother. Besides, he has as much to lose as I do, and I just assumed he was looking after our interests... That's the way we run the business, you see. We each have our own turf and we don't meddle in each other's areas. Business development falls under Simon's watch."

"You don't have to defend him to me."

"I feel as if I do, because I want you to understand our relationship."

"The same kind of relationship Simon obviously had with David Chi."

"I imagine."

"So you trust Simon, Simon trusts Chi, and Chi trusts — or is paid to trust — Ma Shing. And you end up getting screwed."

"Not yet."

She looked at the contract in front of them. She suspected it wasn't going to have any bearing on how this deal played out. "I'd like to talk to Chi."

"Simon is trying to contact him."

"Trying?"

"Chi has been difficult to reach. Simon says he thinks he's gone to Malaysia."

"Hong Kong cellphones work in Malaysia."

"I know, Ava, I know," Michael said, a look of despair on his face.

"I also want to talk to Simon," she said.

"I just spoke to him to say you were in Hong Kong. The plan is to have dinner tonight in Sai Kung. His father owns a restaurant there."

Ava didn't like the idea of wasting an afternoon. "Where is he now?"

"In Shenzhen, visiting a franchisee."

She pulled her notebook from her Chanel purse. She asked, "What do you know about Ma Shing?"

"It's owned by a guy called Kao Lok."

"What's he like?"

Michael shrugged. "I don't really know — I met him only twice. The first time was when we toured the proposed construction site and then spent a couple of hours with the architects and engineers, going over plans. The second time was when we signed the contract at his lawyer's office in Macau. He didn't say much at either of those meetings.

He has a business manager by the name of Wu. Wu did most of the talking, he and Simon and Chi."

"What was Wu like?"

"Loud and crude, and I assume he doesn't have much of an education, because his Cantonese is really working-class. Actually, the few times that Kao Lok opened his mouth I noticed the same thing. Neither of them were that much different from other builders we've dealt with."

"Did you do a background check on them?"

"David Chi said they'd been in construction in Macau for more than ten years."

"Did you visit any of their finished jobs?"

"No."

"Did you talk to anyone they had ever done business with?"

"No, I left that to Chi and Simon."

"Geez."

"I know."

"And your bank let you get away with this?"

"All the bank cared about was that the land was actually owned by them."

"Is the bank holding your portion of the land as collateral?"

Michael tilted his head back and then rubbed his eyes with the tips of his fingers. "What a fucking mess," he said.

"Tell me about the bank," she said, wondering why he seemed even more pained.

"We don't own any of the land. For our investment we got thirty percent of the finished building but Ma Shing retained all ownership rights to the land."

"No land?" Ava said, hardly believing they'd sink twenty million into a property deal that did not involve land.

"No."

"So on what basis did the bank make the loan?"

"They liked our business plan, and obviously we pledged our shares in Millennium...and signed personal guarantees."

And the bank knows that Marcus Lee won't walk away from his oldest son, Ava thought. She made some notes as she gathered herself. "So here's what we have," she said slowly. "You have a deal on paper that looks okay, except for the fact that you don't know who you're doing business with. Now the deal is in limbo, maybe dead, and not only can you not get your money back but Lok and Wu are pressing you to put in more or the money you've already invested will disappear. Now it's possible that these guys are legitimate and they aren't blowing smoke about losing an investor. If that's the case, then we need to look at what that means for you. Maybe we need to go and find someone else to come in on the deal. Maybe we can find more money and renegotiate our position, take a bigger share of the building, get a piece of the land."

"Is that doable — the last bit, I mean?"

"If they're for real, why not? But Michael, we need to get in front of these people. I want to talk to them. It's too late to do due diligence on the money that's in there, but we won't find anyone else willing to sign on unless this is clean."

"What do you want me to do?"

"Call them, set up a meeting."

"Okay."

"And I want Simon there as well. If they're saying he made a verbal commitment then he needs to be there in person to refute it."

"I understand."

"Can we get Chi to attend?"

"We have to find him first."

"Do the best you can."

Ava checked her watch. It was almost lunchtime and she was hungry. "Can you do dim sum?" she asked.

He shook his head. "I have a meeting at the bank in an hour. It's supposedly to review the cash-flow projections for the noodle chain for the coming year, but I know they really want to grill me on Macau."

"Do you want me to go with you?"

"Not this time — it might make them anxious. I'm trying to project a business-as-usual attitude."

"That's sensible," she said.

Michael stood and looked down at her.

"I'm sorry if I was a bit aggressive," she said.

"No, don't be. We should have known better. Hopefully it's salvageable."

"The concept is sound," she said with a shrug.

"Where are you staying?"

"The Mandarin Oriental in Central."

"How about I pick you up at six for dinner?"

"Perfect."

He walked her to the elevator, his face pinched and distracted again. "Are you thinking about the bank meeting?" she said.

"Yes."

"Then think positive. They don't want to lose money. They want you to succeed almost as much as you do yourself. They won't pull the plug until every last possible option has been exercised."

The elevator door opened. "That's what I keep telling myself," he said.

Then start acting like it, she thought.

4

SHE STEPPED OUT OF THE BUILDING INTO A GORGEOUS day with hardly a cloud in the sky, a light breeze blowing in from the sea, and the temperature balmy. Hong Kong had, Ava believed, one of the worst climates in the world. The summers were long, hot, and unbearably sticky, and all of the hotels, shops, restaurants, and public places responded by jacking up their air conditioning to the max. Moving between indoors and outdoors, between those two extremes, had given Ava some of the worst colds of her life. The winters were long, dull, wet, and cold enough to put a permanent chill in your bones. The weeks that bridged those two seasons were the best time to be in Hong Kong, and Ava had lucked out on this trip.

She walked down the hill to her hotel, occasionally turning to face the sun. The previous two weeks had been spent in northern Europe, in a persistent damp drizzle. She was a fool for the sun.

She wanted to go for a run in Victoria Park, but she knew that at lunchtime she wouldn't be able to manoeuvre along the packed jogging path, so she decided to eat first and run later. Dim sum on her own didn't appeal to her. On the way to the hotel she stopped at a noodle shop and had a plate of lo mein with beef and XO sauce. She ate only half of it, just enough to take the edge off her appetite.

It was two o'clock when she stepped out of the MTR station at Causeway Bay and crossed the street into the park. The crowd had ebbed and she was able to run unimpeded. Normally she ran the inner jogging path, which was about seven hundred metres in circumference, but there were so few people in the park that the outer route was manageable. It measured just over a kilometre and she was able to work up a real sweat after eight laps.

As she ran, her mind turned over Michael's problem. She knew that nothing would be accomplished until she had met with Ma Shing. On the surface it seemed straightforward. The contract and the addendum were clear, so unless there was something she hadn't seen, it was going to come down to what kind of people Lok and Wu were. If they were serious businesspeople then a deal could get cut. If they weren't, she'd have to figure out a way to get the money back that didn't involve lawyers.

She had two worries. First, it was possible that Simon To had made a verbal commitment. Chinese businessmen took a handshake as seriously as, if not more seriously, than a contract. If To had been stupid enough to verbally commit to putting up more money, she would have to talk her way around that from a severely weakened position. Second, she didn't know if Ma Shing actually had the funds to repay Michael and Simon. If they had put the money into the land purchase and they weren't liquid, that could be a problem.

She rode the MTR back to her hotel in Central, sweating

like mad in the subterranean climate of the Hong Kong underground. She jumped into the shower as soon as she got into the room, and then put on a clean T-shirt and her training pants. She guessed they'd be eating outside at Sai Kung, so there was no reason for her to dress up.

She turned on her computer and checked her inbox. Her father had written: Sorry to have missed you before you left. Thank you for going to Hong Kong so promptly. Keep me posted if you can. Love, Daddy. Ava sighed. She made it a policy not to communicate with clients when she was on a job. They had a habit of taking every morsel of progress and exaggerating its impact. She preferred them to have minimal expectations, and one way to maintain that was to keep them in the dark. Her father might not be a client exactly, but she decided she would have to treat him like one. I have arrived safely. I'll let you know when I have something definite, she wrote back.

Maria had emailed as well, and reading her message brought a smile to Ava's face. I miss you already, but I haven't showered since you left and I can still smell you on my skin. Hurry home. Ava wrote: I'm in Hong Kong and things are fine. It looks like I'll be here for a few days. Please wash. Love you.

She logged out of her email and did another search for Ma Shing, and then one for Kao Lok in both English and Chinese, and came up with absolutely nothing. She sighed and told herself she'd find out more when they met. She hoped Michael would be able to engineer a meeting in Hong Kong, but she suspected it was going to be in Macau.

It had been a while since she'd had any dealings in Portugal's former colony, but judging from Michael's situation, it was evidently still a rough-and-ready place. Ava had been there once with Uncle, in 1999, just a few years after Portugal had returned the territory to the Chinese. They had a potential client, a furniture manufacturer, who had shipped two container loads of goods to Dalian and then been stiffed on payment.

It was winter, and he'd arranged to meet them in the old town, in the area where the wild-animal restaurants were located. Those restaurants did a booming business in the winter. In addition to the usual reason to visit them — to strengthen the male libido — many older Chinese people believed that eating snake or raccoon or bat or bear or any number of other wild animals thickened the blood and staved off cold-weather illnesses. In deference to Uncle, the furniture manufacturer took them to a very expensive snake restaurant. There was a glass cage in the front window where hundreds of snakes were displayed until they became someone's meal. Four snakes were extracted and fed to them in various forms, starting with soup and ending with grilled meat.

When the dinner was over, they agreed to take on the case. Then they found themselves with several hours to kill before catching the hydrofoil back to Hong Kong. So she and Uncle walked over to the Hotel Lisboa, where he said an old friend of his worked.

The Lisboa was also a casino, and at the time probably the premier casino in Macau. It was owned by Stanley Ho's Sociedade de Turismo e Diversões de Macau, as were the other four or five casinos in Macau at the time. Ho had been granted a monopoly in 1962 and still held it when they were there. Later the People's Republic of China opened the doors for competition, but at the time every property belonged to Ho.

Ava detested casinos in general, and the moment she walked into the Lisboa she put Macau's casinos at the top of her hate list. The place reeked of cigarette smoke and the carpets were stained and damp from people spilling drinks and spitting on them. There were lineups at the tables as people jostled to bet, fighting for a chance to give their money away. "Wait here while I look for my friend," Uncle said, leaving her at a blackjack table.

A *gweilo* with an American accent was seated at the table. Two old Chinese women crushed against his back, staring over his shoulders. Ava knew blackjack, but she hadn't seen a table like this one before. Behind the regular spot where a player placed his bet were two circles. As she watched, the *gweilo* placed his bet in front and then the two women reached around him to put money on the circles, betting on his cards.

He was dealt a ten and a five. The dealer had a jack. Ava listened to the women chatter in Cantonese; they wanted the man to stand on his fifteen. From what she knew, he should hit, which is what he did. When he motioned for another card, both of the women hissed at him. He obviously didn't understand the Cantonese word for "asshole." He bust with a nine, and one of the women flicked the back of his head with her middle finger. He turned and looked at them.

"They didn't want you to hit," Ava said. "When Chinese gamble, they like straightforward one-time win-or-lose bets. They don't want to have to think about what to do."

"Then they shouldn't play blackjack," he said.

"I'll tell them," she said, but she didn't.

The *gweilo* lost steadily over the next five minutes, the women getting more and more agitated. Finally his cards turned and he won five or six hands in a row, including two in which he took a third card. The hissing stopped. After the first win, Ava saw the dealer short-pay the *gweilo*. Before she could speak up, the dealer beat her to it, shrugging and saying, "Tell him I don't speak English."

Ava relayed the message.

"What the hell is she doing?" he asked.

"Why are you paying less than he won?" she asked the dealer.

"I'm taking my tip."

Ava told him what the dealer had said and then watched as the man's face turned red. "I decide when and how much to tip. Tell her to stop doing that."

Ava told the dealer what the man had said. The dealer, looking bored, said to Ava, "Those are Macau rules."

"I don't believe this place," he said. "It stinks, it's dirty, the dealers are so fucking rude. In Las Vegas this place would be scheduled for demolition."

Uncle rescued her. His friend was in his office on the other side of the casino. They walked across the floor, his hand looped through her arm as they passed a long line of baccarat tables. They were all nearly full, with lines of bettors behind the players. What was odd was the people who weren't playing but who sat with briefcases on their laps. They were tightly focused on the play in front of them, hardly ever looking up. Two who did glance their way saw Uncle and bowed their heads.

"Who are those men?" she asked.

"Moneylenders."

"In the briefcases?"

"Cash."

"What, they just open the briefcases and hand money to players?"

"The ones who are sitting next to a player have done that already. They are watching their money, ready to give more if it's needed."

"Is it legal?"

"This is Macau. Everything is more or less legal."

On the return trip to Hong Kong Uncle said, "I have never liked Macau. It was always a good place for business, but all the Portuguese left behind were Ho's casinos, one wall of a cathedral, and some lousy cuisine. For four hundred years of occupation, that's not much of a legacy."

"How about the language, the culture?" she asked.

"Less than one percent of the people can speak any Portuguese, and as for the culture, after African chicken there isn't much."

After several more trips she had begun to share Uncle's view. Compared to the other European territory attached to China — Hong Kong — Macau was an exercise in mediocrity. What the Chinese would do with it was anyone's guess; all she knew was that it couldn't get any worse.

Ava typed "Macau" into several search engines and tracked its changes since the handover, since it had become a Special Administrative Region of the People's Republic. The population hadn't grown that much: it was now about 500,000 people, 95 percent Chinese. And despite reclaiming some land, Macau was still the most densely populated place on earth, with close to twenty thousand people squeezed into every square kilometre of a territory that had almost no arable land, pastures, or woods. Despite the tight quarters, the Macanese had the highest life expectancy in the world — over eighty-four years on average.

Its economy was driven by tourism to its casinos, and the number of visitors had increased from just under nine million a year in the late nineties to close to thirty million today. Ava did some rough math. Las Vegas covered 219 square kilometres and had forty million tourists a year. Macau squeezed thirty million into 28 square kilometres. Almost eight times the density, and at least twice the intensity, given the Chinese mania for gambling.

Macau consisted of four regions: the Macau Peninsula, the most northern part of the province, which was connected directly to the Chinese mainland; Taipa, an island to the south accessible via three bridges, and a major residential area; Coloane, an island still farther south that was less developed; and Cotai, the strip of reclaimed land between Coloane and Taipa. That was where the Venetian had been built and where Michael's shopping centre was supposed to be going up.

In terms of location for gamblers Macau couldn't be much better. It was only 60 kilometres across the South China Sea from Hong Kong. Guangzhou was 145 kilometres away. The Zhuhai Special Economic Zone was right next door, feeding carloads — and, more often, busloads — of gamblers through the Portas do Cerco and over the Lotus Bridge. That was about a hundred million people right on Macau's doorstep.

Stanley Ho, Uncle maintained, was the least far-sighted businessman he had ever met. To have a monopoly on the only casino action in or near China and Hong Kong was like a dream, and for forty years it was Ho's reality. In Uncle's opinion, Ho should have used those forty years to make himself completely irreplaceable. But he hadn't. The problem, according to Uncle, was not the money he took out; it was what he didn't put back. His casinos were small and shoddy. The hotels were second-rate. The service was deplorable. Did he think that Macanese and Chinese government officials never went to Las Vegas? That they wouldn't make comparisons? That they wouldn't realize what Macau could become if they opened it up? So open it they did, in 2004, and in rushed the big boys from Vegas — Wynn, Sands, MGM, the Venetian — and in flowed some serious Australian and Chinese money to build hotels and casinos that matched their American rivals. Ho kept his little casinos and finally invested some money in them. All too little, too late, Uncle said. Even Ho's daughter, Pansy, had joined forces with outside investors to compete against her father.

Ava hadn't been to Macau since the big build-up started in 2004. Hopefully they would have their meeting with Lok in Hong Kong, and she'd be able to avoid it one more time.

At five to six she went down to the lobby wearing her training pants and a matching nylon jacket. Michael was already at the hotel entrance, his silver Mercedes coupe idling, a woman sitting next to him in the front. He got out of the car when he saw Ava, his eyes taking in her clothes. "Do I need to dress for Sai Kung?" she asked.

"No, no, of course not," he said.

Ava saw the woman in the car staring at her. She turned and smiled as Ava climbed in the back seat. "I'm Amanda

Yee, Michael's girlfriend," she said.

Everything about her looked expensive and, Ava had to admit, quite classy. She was young, in her mid-twenties, slim and fine-featured, her hair, long and loose, falling over the shoulders of a light blue jacket. When she tucked her hair behind her ears, Ava saw diamond earrings that had to be more than a carat each, and a diamond pendant around her neck that was around three carats. Her eyes were lively, friendly, and whatever misgivings Ava had felt when she first saw her began to dissipate.

"And I'm Ava."

"Oh, I know you are," Amanda said. "You're all I've heard about for weeks. And I have to say the family resemblance is remarkable. All of the Lees are too good-looking for their own good."

It was a forty-minute ride to Sai Kung, and Ava hardly said a word the entire time. Amanda talked and talked. She had been away from Hong Kong for two years, at graduate school in the U.S., she told Ava, and had been back for only nine months. She had met Michael two months after her return, at a charity event at Happy Valley Racetrack — her father owned several horses — and it was love at first sight. They'd been living together for five months and they were planning on marrying. She was an only child and her father had been a bit jealous at first, but he was coming around. It helped that Michael had his own, successful business. As for her, she was working at her father's import–export business, but her father was locked into the old ways and she could hardly wait for the chance to have more authority.

She stroked Michael's cheek as she nattered on, and several times she turned towards the back to look at Ava with eyes that were kind and gentle. Ava had lots of experience with self-absorbed Hong Kong princesses. There was something about Amanda, though, that prevented her from pinning on that label too quickly.

Ava couldn't help noticing that, as bubbly as Amanda was, Michael remained quiet. She figured the meeting at the bank hadn't gone that well. "Did you get hold of Ma Shing?" she asked during a small gap in Amanda's monologue.

"Left two messages and asked them to get back to me. Nothing yet."

Sai Kung Town was on the southern coast of the New Territories, just east of Kowloon. It had been a fishing village but was now more famous for its seafood restaurants, which sold species from all over Southeast Asia. The restaurants faced Clear Water Bay as they surrounded the harbour of the old town, their storefronts distinguished by tiers of huge tanks full of live fish.

Michael had to circle Man Nin Street three times before he found a parking spot a couple of hundred metres away.

Amanda was wearing four-inch stilettos, and even then she was barely taller than Ava. "There are Simon and Jessie," she said, waving at a couple seated at a table outside a restaurant that had six sets of tanks tiered four deep.

So much for a business meeting, Ava thought.

Jessie waved back and stood to greet them. She was short, a bit stubby without being fat, and had a mass of frizzy black hair that circled her face, making it look fuller than it probably was. She had a huge grin on her face, and the word *jolly* crept into Ava's mind. And then she felt a bit guilty because *jolly* was the word her mother used to describe every fat Chinese woman she had ever met.

Simon, on the other hand, barely glanced their way, more interested, it seemed, in the San Miguel beer in his hand. He looked stockier in person, but most striking was his hair, cropped short to his head and now dyed blond.

"Hey," Michael yelled.

His partner pulled himself to his feet. He couldn't have been more than five foot six, and Ava guessed his weight was close to two hundred pounds. The two couples exchanged hugs and then Michael introduced Ava. "This is my sister," he said.

He said it so casually that it startled her, and she almost added "half-sister." She caught herself and extended her hand. "Nice to meet both of you."

Jessie was drinking white wine and the bottle was nestled in an ice bucket. When she asked what everyone wanted to drink, Ava and Amanda opted for the wine. Michael joined his partner and ordered beer.

"I hope you don't mind, but we've already chosen dinner," Jessie said.

Ava had taken a quick look at the tanks as they'd walked past. It was hard to think of anything she wouldn't like. "That's perfect," she said.

"How was your day in Shenzhen?" Michael asked Simon.

"Not bad. The franchisee is thinking of opening a third shop and wanted to negotiate a reduction of his royalty fee. I told him that we couldn't do that until he had five."

"Sounds good."

"More important, how was your day?"

"So-so," Michael said.

Simon's face was strained. Beside him Jessie was chatting away with Amanda, neither of them noticing the tension in the men. Jessie and Simon were married, it turned out, and had one child. Ava listened to them and marvelled at the things that could occupy their minds despite their partners' travails. Then she realized that the women probably didn't know what was going on. Any last hopes she had about talking business over dinner disappeared.

"Did you reach Chi?" Michael asked.

"No. I left him a couple of voicemails, and unless he's in the middle of the fucking jungle and didn't get them, I guess he doesn't want to talk to me," Simon said, glancing at Ava.

She wasn't sure she liked the doubt, the suspicion, maybe even a little hostility, that she saw in his eyes. What exactly had Michael told him about her?

As if on cue, Jessie turned to Ava and said, "What is it you do? Simon was a bit vague about it, although I have to say the little I heard sounded really interesting."

"I'm an accountant."

"Oh, come on," Michael said with a laugh.

"Actually, I'm a forensic accountant."

"The only forensics I know are on *CSI*," Jessie said.

"My life is hardly so exciting."

"But what is it you actually do?"

"Well, when money goes missing, it's my job to find it. After I've found it I try to get it returned to its rightful owner."

"And how do you do that?"

"Persuasion."

"You make it sound so simple."

"It sometimes is."

Simon looked agitated and began to ask a question, but he was interrupted by a waiter carrying a huge platter. He placed it in the middle of the table while another waiter brought a bottle of soy sauce and a small plate of wasabi and ginger slices. "Lobster and geoduck sashimi," Jessie said.

Ava looked at the thin, translucent white slices of lobster meat and felt her appetite soar. *God, the Chinese know how to prepare seafood*, she thought.

The five of them ate slowly, savouring every bit. The bottle of wine was emptied and replaced. Two more beers were brought to the table, the chilled bottles glistening. No sooner was the sashimi finished than the platter was replaced by a plate of grilled sliced squid with a touch of teriyaki sauce and a bowl of Manila clams drenched in black bean sauce.

Every so often a short, round bald man wearing an apron peeked out from behind the restaurant door. Simon's father, Ava guessed. She gave him a vigorous thumbs-up. He beamed.

Next came a spiny Asian lobster, at least five pounds, steamed with garlic, ginger, and onions and cut into manageable portions; two blue crabs, deep-fried and served whole with a chili sauce; and bok choy drizzled with hoisin sauce. They were also served a plate of large whole prawns, the steam still rising from them, the garlic scent tickling Ava's nose. Jessie and Amanda ate the tails, leaving Ava and the two men to suck the meat from the heads.

Ava was expecting a steamed fish to finish the meal, maybe a sea bream or grouper. Instead the little man came out of the restaurant with a platter holding the largest deep-fried pomfret she had ever seen. She had eaten the fish in Thailand but rarely in Hong Kong or China. It had to be close to four pounds, its skin a golden brown, the flesh on either side cut into cubes they could pluck with chopsticks.

"This is one of the finest seafood meals I've ever had," Ava said to the man as he put the platter on their table.

He smiled at her, and then at Jessie and Simon.

"My father-in-law runs the best seafood restaurant in Sai Kung," Jessie said. "This is nothing special — this is the way he always cooks. So make sure you come back, and make sure you tell your friends."

"I will, I will," Ava said, pleased by the way Jessie had praised him and promoted his business.

They all reached for the pomfret, but before Michael could take his piece his cellphone rang. He looked annoyed as he pulled it out of his shirt pocket, and then anxious when he looked at the incoming number. "Excuse me, I have to take this," he said, standing and then moving off about twenty metres.

While the women ate, Simon focused his attention on Michael. Ava, watching the two of them out of the corner of her eye, saw Michael motion for Simon. Simon stood and left without saying a word.

Michael covered the mouthpiece of his phone as he talked to Simon, the smaller man nodding his head aggressively. Then Michael moved closer to the table and said, "Ava, can you come here for a minute?"

She thought the other women would find that to be a strange request, but they paid no heed when she walked over to join the men.

"It's our friends in Macau," Michael said. "They're available tomorrow."

"Where do they want to meet?"

"Macau."

"Tell them to come to Hong Kong."

"I tried. It's a no-go."

"Then tell them it has to be a neutral site, not their office or their lawyer's office."

"Okay."

"Make sure you tell them I'm coming. No surprises," she said.

The two partners exchanged glances, and Ava's previous sense that Simon hadn't been thrilled to see her was confirmed.

"I've already told them. They were reluctant, but I said that you're our financial adviser and we need a fresh set of ears and some different approaches to handle this matter. We can't just keep going around in circles," Michael said, as much to Simon as to her.

Simon shrugged. Michael returned to the phone and told the caller they'd come to Macau, but only if the meeting place was neutral. She could hear the caller arguing, and then Michael said, "If the place isn't to our liking, we're not coming." There was a long silence. Then Michael covered the mouthpiece again. "The Treasure Palace restaurant in the City of Dreams at one o'clock?" he said.

"That's fine," Ava said.

"You're on," he said to the caller.

Ava said to Simon, "I don't mean to be rude, but you don't seem overly pleased that I'm involved in this."

He took a deep breath. "I thought we could handle it without outside assistance."

"But we haven't been able to," Michael said, after ending the call.

"If you two want to talk alone and if the end result is that I fly home, I won't have any objections," she said.

"No, I want you there," her brother said.

"What the fuck?" Simon said.

"I want her there."

"Okay, okay."

They walked back to the table, Simon a few paces ahead of them, his tension visible to Ava's eye. This was immediately confirmed when he looked at his wife and said, "We have to leave. We have a meeting tomorrow in Macau and I need to get some rest."

Jessie pointed to the pomfret. "We aren't finished."

"I'll tell my father and I'll settle the bill," he said, and then turned and headed towards the kitchen.

The two women stared at Michael. "He's had a long day," he said.

Jessie stood. "He's been having a lot of them lately."

"It's a stressful time for the business," Michael said.

Ava sat at the table, her appetite lost. Amanda Yee picked at the fish, but her eyes were on the kitchen door, where Simon had reappeared with his father by his side. Ava watched the two men hug, and then the older man waved at the table.

Jessie gave a quick hug to Michael and Amanda and then extended her hand to Ava. "I guess we really are leaving now."

"Nice to meet you," Ava said.

"And you. Hopefully the next time it won't be so rushed," she said as her husband reached the table.

He took his wife by the hand and nodded at them. "I'll see you in the morning," he said.

Michael sat down, his eyes on the retreating couple. "I guess we should be heading back soon ourselves," he said quietly.

"Yes," Ava said, beginning to feel that she had wasted her time and money by flying to Hong Kong.

The car ride back was filled with Amanda's steady prattle. Michael drove as if every metre required his complete attention, while Ava's thoughts drifted to their meeting in Macau.

When they got back to the Mandarin, Michael got out of the car with Ava. "I'll walk you in," he said, taking a large brown envelope from the glove compartment.

"No bother."

"Please."

Inside the lobby he reached for her hand. "I want to apologize for Simon."

"No need."

"Yes, there is need. This is not like him, not like him at all. He's been a wonderful friend and a great business partner. This has thrown him for a loop. He blames himself for all of it and is struggling with the fact that his other best friend, David Chi, helped create the situation."

"I know," she said.

"I'm convinced Chi screwed us over."

Well, he understands that at least, she thought. "Probably," she said.

"And Simon has trouble accepting that."

"At the end of day, the business and you will win out."

"I hope so."

"One thing, Michael. What do Amanda and Jessie know about all this?"

"They know about the project, of course, but not that it's gone off the rails so badly. It's better that way. They couldn't handle the stress."

They couldn't do much worse than you and Simon, she thought, but simply said, "Whatever." It must have sounded dismissive, because she saw his face collapse. In that moment he looked exactly like her father the last time she had seen him. "Michael, relax. We'll work this out."

"We have to."

"Well, if we don't, at least that was one hell of a meal, and it was on the house," she said.

"You're joking?"

"Yes, I am."

His laugh was forced. "So, tomorrow?"

"We'll need to catch the jetfoil at eleven thirty."

"Then we'll pick you up at eleven."

"That's fine," she said.

He offered the envelope to her. "I brought along the financials of our company. I thought you might go over them before the meeting. We are viable, you know. I want you to understand that if we can get through this we have a bright enough future."

"That wasn't necessary."

"I figured the more you know, the better."

"Yes, that is normally true."

"And, Ava, as for Simon, he'll get past this."

"Michael, I don't care about Simon," she said. "I care about you."

SHE SLEPT BADLY, A DREAM SHE COULDN'T GET AWAY from waking her and then grabbing her again the moment she closed her eyes. She was with Uncle in some Chinese city that was all dust, smoke, and exhaust fumes, and they were being chased down, running for their lives. He was moving slowly, limping when he wasn't hopping on one leg. She felt the urge to run and had to hold back, though her energy was bursting. He kept telling her to leave, that he'd make it on his own. Every time she was at that point she'd wake, get up to pee and drink a glass of water, and then crawl back into bed hoping that the dream was over, only to have it return. Same city, different location, more thugs.

Dreams were common for her, but not dreams about Uncle. Usually it was her father who dominated her nighttime subconscious, in a recurring dream that had her desperately trying to connect with him and never succeeding. She wondered if keeping her presence in Hong Kong a secret had triggered Uncle's intrusion into her sleep.

At seven she finally gave up and hauled herself out of bed. It was already light outside, the sun glinting through a light layer of clouds. She knew Victoria Park would be a zoo, but she needed to clear her head. She put on her running gear, stuck money for the MTR into her pocket, and headed downstairs.

The park was awful, both the inner and outer tracks so crowded that she could barely walk at a brisk pace, let alone run. So she gave in and walked around the park's perimeter, taking in the multitude of tai chi practitioners, the old men with their birdcages, the badminton players, and at the southern end a throng who had come to exercise to the music of ABBA under the direction of one male and one female instructor, who loomed above them on a stage.

It was just past nine when she left the park and walked back to the MTR station. Hong Kong rush hour was in full bloom and an unbroken stream of people jostled on the station stairs in both directions. Ava knew what it would be like on the train, and the idea of being hemmed in so tightly that she wouldn't be able to move her arms held no appeal for her. She figured it would take her about thirty minutes to run back to the hotel, and without further thought she headed down Gloucester Road.

Before the Mandarin Oriental became her hotel of choice, she had often stayed at the Grand Hyatt, near the old Star Ferry terminal. It was only a ten-minute jaunt from there to the park, and the route took her along Causeway Bay, past the Hong Kong Yacht Club, the noon cannon, and the typhoon shelter, which was perpetually filled with sampans that in turn were filled with floating families. She retraced those steps, enjoying the morning air.

When she got back to the hotel, she took a shower and got dressed for business. She turned on her cellphone and listened to messages from Uncle and her father. Uncle wanted her to phone him. Her father was concerned about how things were going.

She swore quietly as she closed the phone. She didn't want to talk to Uncle just yet. She wanted to get the meeting behind her. Besides, she knew that if she did phone him the fact that she was in Hong Kong would emerge. She just couldn't lie to him and found it almost impossible to say no to him. When she told this to Derek one time, he had just smiled and said she had the same effect on him.

She thought about calling her father before going to meet Michael, and then pushed the idea aside. She had nothing to tell him. She turned on her computer to take a quick look at where the meeting was scheduled, the City of Dreams. Five minutes later she was still reading, and her reluctance to go to Macau had almost vanished.

The first thing that had caught her attention were the names Ho and Packer, except the names were Lawrence Ho, not Stanley, and James Packer, not Kerry. James was the son of the late Australian tycoon; he was in his early forties and already ranked as one of the wealthiest men in Australia. Lawrence was still in his early thirties — one of Stanley Ho's seventeen children from various wives — and had enough money, or access to it, to partner with Packer on the City of Dreams development. Ava knew of Ho through friends in Toronto. A Canadian citizen, he had been partly raised in the city and attended the University of Toronto. He had returned to Hong Kong to pursue his business interests but still came to Canada on a regular basis.

The development had opened in 2009 and was the largest

in Macau. There were four soaring towers sheathed in steel and glass, one home to a Hard Rock Hotel, one to a Crown Towers Hotel, and two towers for the Grand Hyatt, all of them connected to a central podium about three storeys high that looked like a massive glimmering flying saucer. The numbers associated with the complex were impressive: more than 2,200 hotel rooms, more than 200 stores, and, at 420,000 square feet, more than double the gaming space of the MGM Grand, the largest casino in Las Vegas.

This sure isn't the Macau I remember, Ava thought as she closed her computer and packed her notebook into her bag. She headed downstairs to meet Michael.

He was already in the hotel lobby, talking on his cellphone. He waved her over. He seemed as nervous as he had been the day before, and that worried her. Looking unsure wasn't a good negotiating tactic.

"We'll take a taxi to the Macau jetfoil terminal," he said, closing the phone. "Parking is brutal around there."

"Where's Simon?"

"Waiting for us at the terminal. He's already bought our tickets."

It was only a five-minute cab ride, but they had to wait in line at the terminal for another five minutes before they could disembark. Simon was at the gate, briefcase in hand, dressed in a blue pinstripe suit, white shirt, and red Hermès tie. Except for the blond hair he actually looked like a conservative businessman. Michael looked dashing in a pair of grey slacks with a blue blazer, white shirt, and light blue Gucci tie. Ava wasn't accustomed to travelling in such well-dressed company, and said so.

Simon stared at her as if seeing her for the first time. He had evidently forgotten about his rudeness the night before, or else didn't want to acknowledge it. "You look good," he said. "Maybe that'll distract them."

She wasn't sure if he was being sarcastic. "Thanks, and I can promise it won't," she said.

He had bought them three seats in first class, which was almost empty. Most of the hydrofoil was filled with gamblers making a day trip to Macau. *And gamblers don't spend money on unnecessary frills*, Ava thought.

Once they had sat down, Simon pulled some papers from his briefcase. "You've seen the contract?" he asked.

"Yes, we went over it in detail yesterday," she said.

"And what do you think?"

"You seem to be within your rights to request the money back."

"But...?"

She could sense he was ready to argue with her. "But nothing. You seem to be within your rights."

"How do you want to handle the meeting?" Michael asked.

"It's your meeting, not mine," she said. "I'd prefer to be an observer until we see what it is they really want and can figure out what is actually going on. Who normally talks to them?"

"Initially we communicated through David Chi. It wasn't until we saw the site that we actually met them, and then, as I said, we had one more meeting after that to sign the agreement. For the first six months or so we kept routing messages through David, but then he began to distance himself. Simon and I have both had a few phone conversations with

Wu — progress reports, or, more accurately, non-progress reports. And then, of course, David disappeared entirely. So it's been basically me and Wu on the phone. This will be our first face-to-face since we signed."

"Is Kao Lok going to be there?"

"So I was told."

The sea was choppy, the jetfoil bouncing up and down as it roared over sixty-five kilometres of water towards Macau. She'd never been in one that didn't bounce — it was only a matter of degree, and on this day the degree was severe. Ava was thankful it was only a one-hour trip.

"Only one of you should speak," she said. "It's important that there be only one voice. My experience is that if both of you try to talk, there could be contradictions, however unintentional or slight, and you don't want to give them any opening to create confusion or doubt. So, one voice."

"Simon, do you want to do it?" Michael asked.

He shook his head. "No, you."

Michael looked uncertain. Ava hoped he was a better actor when the lights came on. She said, "Now, when you're speaking to them, speak directly to Kao Lok. It is his business, and this is your business. Treat him as your equal. Even if Wu asks questions, direct your comments to Kao."

"Wu has done all the talking so far."

"That doesn't matter. You talk to Kao."

"Okay. How do you want me to approach things?"

"Above all, we really need to understand what's gone wrong here. Why hasn't the project proceeded? What happened to the other investors? What are the chances of bringing more people on board? Are they agreeable to the idea of our bringing others in? Keep asking questions."

"I've been trying to do that on the phone, Ava, and all Wu ever says is that if we want the mall to be built then we have to put up the money they say we committed to."

"So ask Kao. Maybe he'll be more receptive to an actual conversation."

"And if he's not?"

"Then we move on to Plan B, which is to say that we could be prepared to put in more money in exchange for a bigger share of the deal, and specifically an interest in the actual land."

"And if they're not interested?"

Then you're involved with idiots, she thought. "If we get to that point you need to make it clear that your bank is the one calling the shots, and that it is their demand, not yours."

"That's not completely untrue," Michael said.

"Tell them that they haven't lived up to the terms of the contract — through no fault of theirs, you're sure — and even though you hate to walk away from such a promising investment, your bank isn't leaving you any option. You need the deal restructured, with some hard guarantees built in, or you need your money back. I'd say that you've already breached several covenants and that the bank is going to recall the loan unless they see significant progress. Make the bank the bad guy as much as you can."

"Simon, what do you think about this approach?" Michael said. His partner seemed distracted, his attention on the view through the window. His hand kept reaching for his head, rubbing the blond stubble. Then, almost violently, he separated his fingers and pulled them from the back of his head to the front, as if he were trying to plow furrows. "That fucking David Chi," he said.

"Are you all right?" she asked.

"I haven't been sleeping well."

"Are you going to be okay for the meeting?"

"It's all I've been thinking about since last night. Yeah, I'll be okay, unless Chi is there. If he is, I'm not sure I can restrain myself."

Ava threw a worried glance at Michael. He simply said, "Chi won't be there."

Simon grunted. "I don't think they care about whatever problems we have, or might have, with our bank."

"That doesn't matter," Ava said. "You need to create the impression that they'll have to deal with your bank if you can't get your money back. Not many businessmen want a bank up their ass. Banks have more money and all the time in the world, and they're completely cold-blooded."

"What if they don't buy it?"

"Spin it anyway, and then leave all your options open-ended. Don't threaten them. And for God's sake, don't mention the word *lawyer*."

"Just where do you think this will leave us?" Simon asked.

Ava hadn't been sure he was listening. "We aren't going to resolve anything today, so don't go into the meeting expecting that will happen. As I said, what we need to do is find out as much as we can about the status of the project and what it is they really want."

"So we can do what?"

"Figure out an exit strategy."

"Compromise?" Simon said, making it sound like a dirty word.

Ava said, "Well, it may come down to that. I mean, you can't just keep saying 'Give us our money back' and have them answering no and asking for more. Sooner or later there has to be some kind of negotiation, there has to be a middle ground somewhere. The only other option you have is to go legal, and depending on how determined they are, that could take years and cost you tons of money, and many more sleepless nights, with no guarantee at the end that you'll win."

Simon looked angry. Ava didn't know if it was with her, his partner, or the situation. She waited for him to speak. Instead he turned his head and looked out at the sea again.

The jetfoil arrived on time at twelve thirty, and by twelve forty-five they had cleared Macau Customs and Immigration and were in a cab headed for the City of Dreams, about ten kilometres away. The driver avoided the old city, taking the Friendship Bridge to the northern edge of Taipa and then looping southeast past rows of small hotels and shops. When he made a right turn onto the Cotai Strip, Ava gasped. Skyscrapers flanked both sides of the street, filling seemingly every inch of land.

"This is like the strip in Las Vegas," she said.

"On a lot less land," Michael said.

They drove up the Strip past the Fairmont Raffles, the Hilton Conrad, the Sheraton, and the Shangri-La to their right. Across the street from the Shangri-La was a Four Seasons, and directly next to it was the Venetian Macau, an exact replica of the Venetian in Vegas. Ava had never seen such a concentration of luxury hotels, and that was before they got to the City of Dreams, at the very end of the Strip, its four towers and silver pod the climax.

"My God, I never imagined anything of this magnitude. So many five-star hotels," she said.

"They just keep building them bigger and better," Michael said. "The Crown Towers is supposed to be six stars."

"And someone will build one with seven stars," Simon said.

"Where is your lot?" she asked.

"Right there," Michael said, pointing to a long, narrow finger of sand adjacent to the Venetian.

She imagined the foot traffic all those hotels were generating. "What a great location."

"That's why we put up the money," he said.

"What kind of business are the hotel restaurants and shops doing?"

"We hear the casinos are doing great, but as for the rest of it—"

"I hear that the City of Dreams hotels, and a lot of the others around here, are running at about seventy percent capacity, and that's if you count the complimentary stays," Simon said. "In that pod there's every designer store you can name and more than twenty restaurants, including some of the best in Asia, but I'm told they're hard pressed to do enough business to pay their rent."

"Then why build something so huge, so luxurious?" Ava said.

"You'd have to ask Lawrence Ho and James Packer," Michael said.

"They must have done a lot of market research," she said.

"I don't know who they hired to do that, but whoever it was didn't understand the customer base," Simon said. "This isn't Vegas, where people stay for a week. Ninety-nine percent of the gamblers here are Chinese who've walked across the border or taken a day bus or the jetfoil from

Hong Kong. The average stay in Macau is a day and a half. Those people don't need hotel rooms. Shit, they'll stay awake for thirty-six hours or sleep on the bus instead of wasting good gambling money on a room or some upscale dining experience."

"And your shopping centre?"

"It was down and dirty. Give them something cheap to buy, give them lots of basic, affordable food options. At least that was the plan."

"That's still the plan until someone tells us otherwise," she said.

They pulled up in front of the Boulevard shopping complex. Ava looked past it on either side. The entire sky seemed filled with glass and steel. *It would take a full day just to walk through these places*, she thought.

The Treasure Palace restaurant was on the first level of the Boulevard. As they walked to it, Ava looked around. Simon hadn't been wrong about the dearth of customers.

The restaurant wasn't that busy — maybe thirty or forty diners. They stood in the doorway, Michael scanning the room. "There they are, at the back," he said.

There were two of them. Ava had expected them to stand as they neared, but they stayed seated, staring silently at them. She was about ten metres away when she noticed that one of them was looking directly at her chest. She had large breasts for a Chinese woman and her shirt was a bit snug, but she couldn't remember the last time she had been so blatantly ogled. As they drew close, the ogler turned and whispered to his companion, who smiled, showing teeth that angled in several directions.

Ava realized she knew him. She'd been with Uncle in a

Kowloon restaurant and the man had come to the table to pay his respects. Other than the teeth, which were remarkable, he was nondescript: medium height, slight build, a thin, wormy moustache, black hair cropped close to his skull. He hadn't changed much in five years. Maybe a little heavier, no eyeglasses, but still the same teeth and still the same affection for Burberry tartan shirts. She remembered that his name was Lok.

She extended her hand when they reached the table. Kao Lok came halfway out of his seat and reached for her hand, barely touching it. She searched his eyes for recognition but they were blank. "I'm Lok. This is Wu," he said, pointing to the other man.

Wu didn't budge, his gaze still fixed on her chest. *Bad manners and a pig as well*, she thought.

The Hong Kong group sat and Lok poured tea for them. Ava thanked him with a gentle tap of her middle finger on the table. He gave an awkward smile. "I wasn't very happy when I found out you were bringing a financial adviser, but now that I've met her I'm pleased you did. Maybe when she's finished with you, she can give me advice," he said.

Simon and Michael both looked uncomfortable. Ava knew it was only going to get worse. *You stupid sons of bitches*, she thought.

"Did you bring our cheque?" Wu asked.

"Did you bring ours?" Simon shot back.

Wu bristled. Ava looked at him. He was a short, compact, ugly man with thick arms, a big chest, and a small nose that turned up so much the nostrils stared straight ahead. He had a large black mole on his cheek with long, curly black hairs springing from it. The hairs were supposed to be good luck.

There goes Plan A, Ava thought when she noticed two men standing against a wall about ten metres from their table. They were watching them — looking bored, but watching them all the same. *This really isn't going to go well*, she decided.

"You made a promise and we're holding you to it," Wu said.

Michael struggled to interrupt, to start the meeting on a more even keel, but he had barely got the first sentence out of his mouth before Simon spoke over him. "That's bullshit."

"You told David Chi that you were committed, and that if more money was needed you'd find it."

"We were in a fucking karaoke bar, half-drunk, having a casual conversation about the project, and he said something vague about cost overruns. That was all I was responding to, and all I said was that if it came to that, we'd consider putting up more money. More money on the assumption that the fucking shopping centre was almost finished. You fuckers haven't even dug a hole yet."

And there goes Plan B, Ava thought, before interrupting. "Gentlemen, could we please just back it up for a moment."

Wu sat back.

"I apologize for Simon," Michael said, finally trying to salvage the meeting. "We're under tremendous stress on our side. Because of the delays in the project — none of which, I'm sure, are deliberate — we've breached a number of covenants with our bank, and they're ready to call in the loan we used to finance our portion. You can imagine how difficult that is."

"Not our problem," Wu said.

"It is if the bank decides to try to foreclose on the property, or if it decides to pursue action against all of us."

"Not our problem."

Ava waited for Michael to continue. He sat silent. *Well, let's play this out*, she thought. "Gentlemen, I'm quite confused about the status of the project. Could you give me an update?" she said.

"One of the investors pulled out. We need more money. There's no point starting what we can't finish," Wu said.

"When I reviewed the contract, I didn't see any provision that required us to put in additional funds."

"I told you, he agreed to it," Wu said, pointing to Simon.

"I did no such fucking thing," Simon yelled.

Lok reached into his trousers pocket and Ava flinched, afraid of what he might pull out. It was a piece of paper. "Here is a signed affidavit from David Chi."

Simon grabbed it and, without reading, tore it to shreds. "He's a fucking liar and so are you," he yelled, throwing the pieces at Lok.

Ava was so focused on the paper she didn't notice Wu get out of his chair until it was too late. He came around the table, and as he was moving forward he threw a punch at Simon's head. It caught him on the upper cheek, just below the eye. Simon reeled back and then, almost in slow motion, slid to the floor. Wu stepped in, ready to deliver a kick, but Michael grabbed his arm and tried to pull him back. Wu turned, shook his arm free, and wound up to hit Michael. That was when Ava moved.

The crack could be heard several tables away. Wu's scream reverberated around the entire restaurant as he held his arm, the break in the ulna so complete that a piece of bone had pierced his skin.

She turned immediately towards Lok as the two men who'd been leaning against the wall headed for them. They wouldn't use guns in a place this public, she reasoned, but she wouldn't put it past them to have knives. She was thinking about how to handle them when Lok said, "You work with Uncle Chow, don't you."

"I do," she said, her eyes still locked on the two men advancing on her.

"Wait," Lok shouted at them.

They stopped no more than two metres away. She saw that familiar mixture of anger and lust she had seen in every man ready to beat, or try to beat, a woman. Half of her wanted them to come at her; the other half knew she was in Macau and that Macau was Lok's turf.

Lok stood. "I thought I recognized you when you walked in. I wasn't sure until you did that thing to Wu. You have a reputation: a pretty girl with a nasty temper and a vicious streak."

"I only do what is necessary to defend myself."

"And these two, how about them? Could you take them?" he asked, pointing to his men.

"Probably, but I'd rather not make a scene."

"What would you rather do?"

"Leave quietly with Simon and Michael."

"Is Uncle involved with those fools?"

"No, this isn't a part of our business. This is strictly personal on my part."

"Good. I'd be unhappy if I thought he was representing them."

Simon had now struggled to his feet, leaning against Michael, who looked as if he was in shock. Wu had his head on the table, and was holding his arm, gently groaning. Ava had to admire his tolerance for pain.

"Can we go?" she asked.

Lok actually thought about it, his face impassive. Ava kept her eyes on the two men. If they took another step towards her, she decided she would have to be proactive. "I don't want to hear from these two again," he finally said.

She knew it was pointless to argue. She also knew she couldn't concede completely. "Let's go," she said to Simon and Michael. "We need to leave."

Neither of them seemed to understand. Ava moved to Michael's side and looped her arm through his. "Let's walk," she said, giving him a tug.

She hadn't noticed anyone in the restaurant except for Wu, Lok, and his men. Now she felt every eye on them as they made their slow exit, the boys like beaten dogs, Ava's head held high, her walk measured, her chest thrust out, senses alert to anything that might be coming behind her.

She took them to a coffee shop near the Boulevard entrance, sat them down, and went to buy three bottles of water. By the time she returned their shock seemed to be ebbing, only to be replaced by the growing, sickening, and inevitable realization that their money was probably gone, and along with it their business and whatever personal wealth they had.

"Hell of a meeting, but not much of a lunch," Ava said as she sat.

"I don't know what to say," Michael mumbled.

"We're fucked," Simon said, touching his cheek, which was already discoloured.

Michael drained his bottle of water in four gulps. It seemed to refresh him. "You shouldn't have opened your mouth," he yelled at his partner. "We had a plan. We needed to follow it."

"It wouldn't have made any difference," Ava said sharply. "That meeting was going to end badly no matter what you did. Simon just sped things up."

"Thanks," Simon said.

"For nothing. The two of you are idiots."

Simon shrugged. "Who are they, Ava? You say you know Lok. How?"

"They're probably triad," she said.

"Holy fuck," Simon said. Michael closed his eyes.

"You certainly knew how to choose partners for your biggest joint venture."

"You said 'probably,'" said Simon.

"I need to confirm it. One phone call will do it."

"And this Uncle, who is he?"

"My boss — my partner in business, actually. And don't ask me if he's triad because I've never talked about it with him. And in case you're wondering, I am not triad."

Simon said, "Michael told me you had good connections. He wasn't kidding."

"They're obviously not that good or we wouldn't be out here drinking water."

"No, but we're not flat on our backs in the restaurant getting the crap beaten out of us either."

Ava smiled. She was beginning to warm to Simon. He had shown some nerve, he had a sense of humour, and he was holding up to the adversity better than Michael, who looked lost in whatever dark thoughts were filling his head. "I wouldn't have let them do that," she said.

"No, I guess not," Simon said. "Where did you learn that

shit? I've never seen anyone move so fast."

"I've been training for years. Anyone can do it."

Simon sipped from the bottle, his mood faltering again. "For years all we've done is build a business, and now look."

"What are we going to do?" Michael said suddenly, as if he had just woken from a dream.

"Go back to Hong Kong," Ava said.

"And do what?"

"I don't know exactly. I'll make my phone call and then we'll figure out if there's anything we actually can do."

"There has to be," Michael said.

"No, that isn't always true," Ava said. She didn't care when Michael looked pained at her reply. She wasn't in the business of false hopes and, brother or not, she wasn't about to start supporting pipe dreams.

6

AVA WAITED UNTIL THEY HAD LANDED IN HONG KONG and parted ways before she called Uncle. He answered on the second ring, and his brisk *wei* told her he'd been expecting her call.

"Uncle, it's Ava."

"I understand you are in Hong Kong."

"I am."

"Is everything all right?"

"As well as can be expected. I imagine you have heard from Kao Lok and that he told you we met."

"Of course."

She knew he would have. "I didn't know it was him. I mean, I recognized him when I saw him, but the name meant nothing to me. I went into the meeting totally unprepared to see him there."

"He is not very happy, especially about the way you damaged Wu."

"And I'm not happy either, especially about the way they're destroying my brother's business and reputation and putting my family at risk." She knew she had said a lot that needed explanation, and she didn't want to do it over the phone. "Uncle, I'm sorry I didn't tell you I was coming to Hong Kong. This was strictly personal, not business. Can we meet to talk?"

"I think we have to."

"Where should we meet?"

"You know Andy owns a noodle shop near the Kowloon Tong MTR station?"

"Yes, and I know where it is."

"Meet me there in an hour."

It was only after she hung up the phone that she felt the stress of the day descend on her. It was a mess. More of a mess than she could have anticipated. And aside from asking Uncle to intervene, she didn't have a clue about what to do. She rarely felt helpless. There was always a way, always some lever you could pull. Except this time she couldn't think of a single one except for Uncle. What ate at her was the thought of having to ask him. And what scared the hell out of her was the possibility that he might turn her down. She wasn't sure she could handle that humiliation.

She showered quickly and changed into her track pants and a black T-shirt, then headed to the Star Ferry.

It was late afternoon and the harbour rush hour was just starting. Normally Ava sat at the rear of the Kowloon-bound ferry so she could look back at the Hong Kong skyline. Today she sat in the middle of the boat, with no interest in anything but the meeting with Uncle.

She caught a taxi in Tsim Sha Tsui and got to Kowloon Tong five minutes early. Uncle's car was already at the curb, with Sonny, his driver and bodyguard, leaning against it talking to a policeman, who was making every effort to be polite. Sonny wore a black suit and white shirt, but unlike his boss he had a black tie knotted at the neck. He was a large man, bigger than Ava and Uncle combined. Well over six feet, he had a body that looked soft, but his physique was deceiving — he was more agile than any man Ava had ever met, and even more powerful. He also had no fear and, she thought, no conscience.

"Sonny," she said.

He glanced at her and smiled. "He's waiting for you," he said.

The noodle shop was just inside the station, a location that Andy would have to have killed someone to get if his wife's father hadn't already secured the space before the station was even built.

Ava walked in and almost ran over little Andy. He was only slightly taller than her and weighed maybe ten pounds more. He was a good man to have by your side, though, and Ava had used him several times, the last time in Las Vegas, when his expertise with a meat cleaver had proven useful. "Hey, boss," he said.

"Hi, Andy," she said.

Out of the corner of her eye she saw Andy's wife looking at them. Ava smiled at her and waved. The woman put her hands together as a sign of respect. Over the years she had met a lot of wives like Andy's. There were times when Ava felt she was leading the life they all wanted.

"Where's Uncle?" she asked.

"In the back, in the kitchen. I put a little table there so you two could talk in private."

"Did he ask you to do that?"

"Yes."

He stood when she entered the kitchen. He was wearing his black suit and a white shirt buttoned at the collar. "You are as beautiful as ever," he said.

"I'm sorry about this," she said.

He sat. "Do you want something to eat?"

"Not really."

"We should not offend Andy."

"Then order for both of us."

"Steamed snow pea tips? Rice noodles with shrimp and scallops?"

"Perfect."

Uncle spoke to the cook, who was working five woks at once. The cook nodded without turning around.

"I was surprised when Lok called me," he began.

"I'm sorry, let me explain," she said.

It took her ten minutes. Uncle knew her father, knew about his extended family situation. What he didn't know was that Michael Lee had reached out to her. She went through it as best she could, not exaggerating but making her feelings clear, particularly her fears that her father and mother and her two aunties — one with small children in Australia — whom she didn't know were somehow going to be swept up in the mess in Macau.

Before she finished, the cook had deposited the snow pea tips and the noodle dish on their table. Uncle picked at the peas, his focus on her. When she finished, he put down his chopsticks. "You should have called me earlier," he said.

"Uncle, it was family business. I didn't think it was fair to involve you." And the moment she said it she wished she could cut off her tongue.

He went silent, the chopsticks working again on the snow peas, picking scallops from their noodle bed. "You know I never married."

"Yes, Uncle."

"I left Wuhan when I was eighteen. The family I knew died during the Cultural Revolution."

"I know, Uncle."

"I have no children that I am aware of."

"Yes, Uncle."

"During the past few years I have asked you several times to take on jobs that involved friends."

"Yes, Uncle."

"Did you hesitate?"

"No."

"So why could you not come to me?"

There were tears in her eyes but she fought them back. "I should have."

"Now I am afraid it is too late."

Ava turned her attention to the snow pea tips, concentrating on their tiny heads. They ate quietly, the cook working like a madman behind them, Andy poking his head through the door occasionally to make sure they were still there.

When the last of the noodles were gone, Uncle said, "Lok has pulled this stunt a few times. He owns several pieces of land in Macau, on the peninsula in Coloane and on Cotai. He switches ownership among his companies, often starting new ones. He hires an architect to design an apartment building, maybe an office and retail complex — and now, I guess, a shopping centre — then he goes looking for investors, and he always seems to find them. Everyone knows how scarce land is in Macau, and Lok does not normally have a problem finding willing and eager partners. Needless to say, nothing ever gets built. They will put off the investors with excuses for a while, and when they cannot be stalled any longer, the intimidation starts. No one gets their money back. Most are smart enough to know they need to walk away, but more than one has gone to Macau for a final showdown and never come back."

"How long have you known him?"

"Twenty years, maybe longer. He used to run a string of moneylenders at Ho's casinos, and then he managed the massage parlours that double as whorehouses for one of the larger societies. He is a Red Pole."

"What is that?"

"We have been together so long that I forget what I have told you."

"About the triad?"

"Of course."

"Not much. All I know is that you were chairman."

"An honorary position," Uncle said, waving his hand. "It had no real power."

Ava turned her head away, not wanting him see the incredulity on her face. "What is a Red Pole?" she muttered.

"The sharp end of a gang's stick."

"I still don't understand."

Uncle closed his eyes as if he were conjuring memories. "In the days when I was active, every gang was headed by a Mountain Master or a Dragon Head, as we were sometimes called. Each had three people reporting directly to him: a Vanguard, who organized operations; an Incense Master, who was responsible for ceremonies; and a deputy

Mountain Master, who actually executed the plans. The deputy Mountain Master in turn had three people under him: the White Paper Fan, who provided financial and business advice; the Straw Sandal, who liaised among the different groups; and the Red Pole. The Red Pole was the enforcer. He was the muscle who ran the troops on the ground — the 49ers, who were the pledged members of the society, and the blue lanterns, who were like apprentices."

"49ers?"

"Every position had a number derived from the *I Ching*. The Mountain Master was 489. The Red Pole was 426. The number none of us wanted to hear was 25. It was the designation for a mole that the police or some rival triad gang had planted, or for a traitor to his own gang."

"So Lok is an enforcer?"

"Yes."

"How many men report to him?"

"Somewhere between fifteen and twenty."

"Uncle, can you talk to him?"

"Yes, though I am not sure what good it would do."

"Is there anyone else you can talk to, someone who has authority over him?"

He shook his head. "The old structures have broken down. Lok is his own man."

"But you said he reported to a deputy Mountain Master."

She saw him hesitate and wondered if she'd slighted him by being so insistent. "Not anymore. Things are different now than they used to be. The old ways of doing business have changed and the need to be interdependent has disappeared. The large societies have moved on from moneylenders, whorehouses, and extortion. There is too much money to be made counterfeiting purses and watches, and even more to be made pirating computer software. It takes a different mentality to run that kind of business, so they have cut themselves off from the grubby stuff, handing it over to small-timers like Lok to run as they see fit. He does not report to anyone; he has no allegiances to anyone other than to himself."

"So we have to talk to Lok."

"We do."

"Uncle, I don't want to be unreasonable. He can keep some of the money. Tell him it's my way of apologizing for Wu."

He shook his head. "No, men like Lok do not think like that. He probably thinks the money is his by now. It will be all or it will be nothing."

"You know best."

He stood and walked around the table to her. He put his hand on her shoulder and then leaned forward and kissed her on the forehead. "I will call him. Wait here," he said.

She had no real expectation that he would be successful; she was just appreciative that he'd try. She prepared herself for disappointment, determined not to show a flicker of it. All Uncle would see was how pleased she was that he'd made the phone call.

The few minutes turned into ten and then fifteen. Ava sat at the little table, occasionally picking at the remaining snow pea tips, and despite herself starting to feel encouraged by the duration of his absence. The longer the discussion, the better her chances, she thought. That was until she saw Uncle walk back into the kitchen.

She'd known him long enough to recognize the signs: the tightening of his mouth, the slightly averted eyes, shoulders that weren't completely square. "So it was no," she said, making it easier for him.

"It was no," he said as he resumed his seat.

"Thank you for trying."

"We exchanged harsh words. He was always ignorant and he had been drinking, and Wu has been agitating him, so I think he liked the idea of my asking him for a favour. And he liked even more the fact that he could tell me to go and fuck myself without having to worry about the consequences. I was not polite in return."

"Uncle, I'm sorry now that I even asked."

"No, I wanted to do it."

"Now what? What do I do?" she said, more to herself than to him.

"You do nothing," he said quickly. "You cannot reason with him; you cannot scare him; you have no means, legal or otherwise, to get to him. You have to tell your brother that his investment is gone. He should walk away."

"Just like that?"

"Exactly like that."

She sighed. "I think you're right."

"So, assuming I am right, what are your plans?"

"I'm having lunch with my brother and his partner tomorrow. I'll let them know how this ends, and then I'll get the first plane I can back to Toronto."

He reached over and took her hand in his. "I am sorry I could not help."

"And I'm sorry for not calling you earlier."

"Go home and rest. Spend some time with your mother and sister. This business of ours is hard on all of us."

She walked him to his car. As Sonny opened the door for

his boss, Uncle said, "Wuhan called. They are very happy about the speed with which you retrieved the money."

"Has it reached the Kowloon bank?"

"Yes, this morning."

"I've prepared a breakdown of who got what in Europe and how our share should be distributed. I'll email it to you later," she said, realizing she should have done that the day before.

The art forgery case had been concluded less than three days ago. To Ava it felt like light-years.

7

AVA WASN'T MUCH OF A GIRL FOR BARS, ESPECIALLY when she was alone, but the day had jangled her nerves and she needed to calm down.

She went to her room first, collected her notebook and laptop, and rode the elevator two levels up to the twenty-fifth floor. She wasn't overly superstitious, as were many Chinese people, but she still had more superstitions than any *gweilo*, and one of them was that she wouldn't stay on or visit the twenty-fourth floor of the hotel; in fact, she closed her eyes if the elevator stopped there. It was from that floor that Leslie Cheung had jumped to his death. Ava wasn't a huge fan of Cantonese pop but she'd liked Cheung, maybe partially because he was gay, and it haunted her that his sexual orientation had somehow contributed to his suicide.

The M Bar looked out on Victoria Harbour, its lotus-bud–shaped counter positioned so that everyone sitting there had a view. It was early and she had a choice of seats. She took one of the high-backed chairs on the right side. The bar served tapas, Hong Kong style, and she was tempted. There were two restaurants on the same floor: Man Wah, which some people considered the best Chinese restaurant in Hong Kong, and Pierre, a Michelin two-star French restaurant. She was hungry. The snow pea tips and a few scallops were all she had eaten that day. She decided to wait to have a real meal, and ordered just a glass of white burgundy.

She turned on her laptop and made the wireless connection. She sent Uncle the financial summary of the Wuhan case and was about to connect to the Millennium website when her cell rang. It was her father. She knew he was still in Toronto and realized it was six a.m. there. Michael must have called him.

"Daddy," she said.

"How are you?"

"I'm okay. Has Michael been talking to you?"

"Yes."

"How upset is he?"

"He doesn't know what to be upset about first."

"It is a mess," Ava said, seeing no reason to be anything but honest.

Her father sighed. She could imagine him sitting at the kitchen table with a cup of coffee and the morning newspaper, dressed in a pair of the Holt Renfrew silk pyjamas her mother made him wear. He had thick black hair that he still wore long, and in the morning it was always rumpled. She and Marian loved to see him like that, rather than in his normal Hong Kong–slick mode.

"Michael is worried that you think he's a fool."

That should be the least of his worries, she thought. "Well, they certainly did a foolish thing."

"Obviously. And Ava, you are sure about this Lok character, that he is triad?"

"He is, and he's pulled this real-estate scam before. If they had done any serious due diligence they would have found that out."

"It is Hong Kong," Marcus Lee said. "We still do business on handshakes, we trust friends and family. Michael trusted Simon, Simon trusted this David Chi, and that overrode common business sense."

"I know. A lot of my business comes from people whose friends have screwed them over."

"Yes, you would know, and now Michael knows. A bit late, of course."

She heard the resignation in his voice. "Daddy, I'm still working on a few ideas. I'm going to meet with Michael and Simon tomorrow, so let's not quit just yet."

"Ava, Michael is clinging by his fingertips to the hope that you can come up with something. I'm a bit more realistic. Don't try anything silly."

"What do you mean?"

"He told me about the man Wu. He's upset about having put you at risk."

"I know how to handle people like Wu."

"Obviously you do. What I don't know is how often you've had to do something like that, and how you came to have those skills."

"You paid for martial arts training for years," she said, sidestepping the rest of his question.

"Michael found it alarming."

"Michael hasn't had to do business with men like Wu and Lok before. I have, more often than I care to remember."

"You need to be careful."

"I always am."

His voice became indistinct and Ava wondered if there was a problem with the phone line. "Excuse me, your mother just came into the kitchen and I was speaking to her. Do you want to say hello?" he asked.

"No, tell her I'll call later when I have more time to talk."

"All right."

"Daddy, I have some work to do here. I'll meet with Michael tomorrow and we'll see what we can sort out."

"Do you really have some ideas?"

"I do," she said before ending the call. What she didn't want to tell him was that the only one she thought was viable was to put her own money into Michael's company so he could get off the hook at the bank.

She opened the envelope Michael had given her the night before and re-explored the financials. They were bare-bones; she was going to have to see more detailed numbers before putting together a final offer. There weren't going to be any more deals done on a handshake if she was involved.

If the numbers did hold up, though, it looked as if the company could be valued at between US$12 and $15 million, based on a price of eight to ten times earnings. She wanted at least a third of the company, so she figured she could put in $5 million for share purchases and then loan the rest of what they needed at a reasonable rate of interest. She would want their shares pledged to her as collateral, as well as personal guarantees. They'd have to sign noncompetes, and there would have to be financial controls in place that gave her comfort.

She didn't have all the cash on hand, but when she got her share of the Liechtenstein money she'd have more than enough. Investing it in her brother's company had been the furthest thing from her mind when she came to Hong Kong, and it wasn't ideal in terms of how she saw her own financial position. The thing was, she didn't know what other options were available. If she did nothing then Michael's business would be destroyed by the bank, her father's business would come under attack, and the whole underpinning of the family's security — the extended family's security — was going to be threatened.

Ava had enough money to look after her mother, but that wasn't the point. Her mother's life was tied to her relationship with Marcus Lee. However strange outsiders found it, her mother had a husband and a structured family life. If Marcus became unable to sustain it and she was forced to rely on her daughters for support, the loss of face, the humiliation would be catastrophic. Ava loved her mother too much to let that happen, and she loved her father too much to watch him go through hardship that was not of his making. The way she saw it, it came down to a choice between family and money. She had only one family. And there were lots of ways to make money.

She sat in the M Bar for another hour writing in her notebook, trying to detail as much as she could the proposal she'd put to Michael and Simon at lunch the next day. It was difficult to find a balance. She needed to be fair, but it was her money and there had to be checks in place to make sure it wasn't squandered.

Just after seven she closed the book, thought about food, and left the bar. Man Wah or Pierre? She had often eaten at Man Wah. Their dim sum were superb, but they wouldn't be serving dim sum at this time. Dinner would be good, she knew — some shark fin soup, a steamed sea bass. She had never tried Pierre, though, and realized she felt like meat.

The restaurant shared the same view of Victoria Harbour as the M Bar. Night was descending and the Hong Kong skyline had begun to light up. She tipped the maître d' one hundred Hong Kong dollars and asked for a table near the window. If there was a more magnificent view than the Hong Kong harbour at night, she hadn't seen it.

The menu was skewed towards tasting options. Ava preferred to pick and choose, regardless of the cost.

She had carried a glass of burgundy with her from the bar and told the waiter to keep filling her glass with the same wine. He stood next to the table, pen in hand. "I'll let you know when I'm ready to order," she told him.

"They seem to be in such a rush," a voice said behind her.

Ava turned and saw a middle-aged couple sitting at the next table. The accent was American, the clothes were as well.

"In Chinese restaurants efficiency is valued," Ava said. "This restaurant may serve French food but the servers are all Chinese. They can't escape their culture."

"Why, thank you," the woman said.

"You're welcome," Ava said, turning back to the menu.

Although she loved foie gras, there was a limit to how much meat her system could absorb. It took her five minutes to decide what to have for dinner. The waiter stood against the wall now, trying to ignore her. She snapped her fingers. Her mother would have been upset. One of her life lessons was to never upset a waiter, particularly a Chinese one, as their penchant for spitting in customers' food was legendary. Ava had long ago decided not to worry about what waiters did with her food before it got to the table.

She ordered a black truffle, mushroom, and spinach tartlet, bouillabaisse mousseline, and a roast saddle of lamb Lozère with oregano, white beetroot purée, and tabbouleh.

The woman at the next table said, "Good choice. I had the lamb last night and it was wonderful."

Ava looked at them again. They were older than she had first thought, and the man was drooping, his chin falling onto his chest as he tried to keep his eyes open. "Do you mind if I join you?" Ava asked.

"Please," the woman said, introducing herself as Ellen, and her husband as, Larry.

They were from Shaker Heights, Cleveland, and this was their first trip to Asia. They were travelling with another couple who seemed obsessed with shopping, having bought a new suitcase already though they had been in Hong Kong for only two days. They were scheduled to go to Singapore, Bangkok, and Kuala Lumpur. The woman was nervous. Hong Kong was more than she could have imagined, and for the rest of it, well…

For once Ava enjoyed the distraction. The husband was out of it, barely able to stay awake long enough to eat, but the woman was smart and curious, and Ava found herself lecturing. She had been to all of the places on their tour and waded into the pros and cons. The woman had a little pad in her purse that she pulled out to take notes as Ava rambled on. Kuala Lumpur was okay; it was too bad they had scheduled Singapore, as Bangkok was worth more time. And how, how could they not go to China?

"Larry wants us to go to Macau tomorrow," she said, flicking a finger at her husband.

"Do you like Las Vegas?" Ava asked.

"No, I hate the place."

"Macau is a perverse Vegas."

"Oh."

"So what do suggest?"

"Go to Lantau Island, see the Buddha, see the part of Hong Kong that isn't all concrete and commercialism."

Their food kept arriving as they talked, Larry waking long enough to taste everything and then nodding off again. Ava ate as if she hadn't seen food in days. It was all wonderful, the lamb medium-rare and so tender she barely had to chew.

The women passed on dessert and ordered cognac. Larry was now sleeping soundly. As they sipped, Ellen asked Ava if she was married.

"I'm a lesbian," Ava said.

"That wouldn't go down so well in Shaker Heights," Ellen said.

"I'm from Toronto. Not so bad there, but in Hong Kong it makes you a pariah."

"Funny world."

"Not to me."

The bill arrived and Ava reached for it, but Ellen was there first. "No, you have to let me pay. You have been charming and so very helpful. I suspect that when I'm back in Ohio and I'm at a dinner or party and someone asks me what I remember best about Asia, I might very well tell them it was this meal."

"That's kind. Thank you."

Ava departed first, leaving Ellen to wake Larry and get him to their room. She found herself missing Maria in a way she had never done before.

8

SHE WOKE AT JUST PAST EIGHT WITH AN URGENT NEED to pee. She couldn't remember the last time she had slept so soundly, so devoid of dreams.

She thought about running but didn't have the patience for Victoria Park, and if she couldn't run in the park she didn't want to run at all. So she made a Starbucks VIA instant coffee, read the *South China Morning Post*, and then headed downstairs to the business centre with her notebook.

Despite — or maybe because of — her business experiences, Ava's proposals tended to get too detailed, too concerned about what could go wrong. So what should have been simple became horribly complicated, until even she could hardly understand what she meant. She persevered, starting from scratch four times, until it finally began to take the form and clarity she intended. It was important to her that Michael and Simon not see this as charity in any way. This was business. She was offering to buy in to their business and lend them money under terms and conditions that were serious, professional, demanding, and equitable.

In truth, if they objected to them she knew she was capable of walking away.

She finished at around eleven thirty, made three copies of her offer, and then headed for the shower. Uncle called just as she was walking back into the bedroom wrapped in a towel. Her first thought was that something positive had happened with Lok.

"Uncle," she said.

"I received your breakdown of the money in the Kowloon bank. I sent the Wongs' share on to them immediately. They phoned me this morning to say how grateful they are," he said.

Her deflation was immediate. "That's fine."

"May Ling was particularly anxious that you know that."

"Know what?"

"How grateful she is."

"Uncle, we've talked about this. I have no interest in what May Ling thinks."

She heard him sigh. He had said more than once that he thought she could be a powerful ally for Ava. "I hope that will pass," he said.

"She betrayed my trust," Ava said.

"That is true, but she has acknowledged that and explained herself. What more can she do?"

"I don't care what she does."

"When I spoke with her," Uncle said, "she asked if you would at least take her phone call. I told her I was not in a position to answer that question."

"She is the wealthiest woman in Hubei province. What does she want with me?"

"I told you before, she believes that you and she are connected."

"I don't want to talk about it any more," she finally said.

He sighed again. "Just do not close the door entirely."

"You taught me never to do that."

"That is all I can expect," he said.

"Now, Uncle, you must excuse me. I have to get ready to meet with Michael and his partner."

"You are not going to try to talk to Lok again, are you?"

"No, I know you're correct in your assessment. I just need to go over some other business with them."

"I am sorry there is not more I can do."

"*Momentai.*"

"When will you leave Hong Kong?"

"Tomorrow, I think."

"Please call me before you do."

It was eleven thirty. She reached for business clothes: a powder blue button-up shirt with French cuffs and a modified Italian collar, a black pencil skirt. She brushed her hair, fixed it with the ivory chignon pin, and then put on a light touch of black mascara and scarlet lipstick.

At twelve she was in Man Wah at a table next to the window. She ordered jasmine tea and waited.

At twelve ten she began to look towards the door for some sign of Michael or Simon.

By twelve fifteen she found herself getting annoyed.

At twelve twenty she became agitated.

By twelve thirty she was furious, and reaching for her cell to call her brother. That's when her phone rang and she saw Michael's name on the screen.

"Where are you? I said our meeting was at noon," she said.

"I'm in my apartment, the Mid-levels," he said, his voice wavering. "Ava, we fucked up. Simon and I, we really fucked up."

"What's happened?"

"Can you come here?"

"Where are you?"

"We're on Queen's Road," he said.

"Give me the number."

As he did she heard crying in the background. It sounded like Amanda.

She took a taxi, her imagination working overtime as the cab dragged its way through heavy traffic. The Mid-levels was on the Hong Kong side of Victoria Harbour. The streets to that area ran from the harbour through Central and up the mountain towards Victoria Peak, or "the Peak," as it was commonly referred to. The higher the real estate, the greater the cost. The Mid-levels, as the name implied, was halfway between the harbour and the Peak. The neighbourhood was mainly residential, nearly entirely apartment buildings, and home to the comfortably retired, senior managers, and a younger crowd that aspired to eventually buy higher.

Ava had no idea what to expect when she reached the apartment, other than that she was sure it somehow involved Lok and Wu.

They lived in an older apartment building, only twenty storeys high, with red-brick walls and small windows, but still posh enough to have a doorman. She told him who she was there to see. "They called down," he said as he opened the door for her.

Their unit was on the eighteenth floor. As Ava stood in the elevator her anger turned into anxiety. *If those guys are going to keep doing stupid things they'll have to do it on their own*, she thought.

When Amanda opened the door, her face streaked with black where the mascara had run, her eyes puffy, her nose running. She threw herself at Ava, wrapping her arms around her neck.

"What's going on?" Ava asked.

"He's in the bedroom," she sobbed.

"Then let's go to the bedroom," Ava said, untangling herself from Amanda's embrace.

Amanda grabbed her hand and pulled her across the room, which was furnished in black leather with large glass tables. The walls were bare and the tables had nothing on them. *A man's apartment*, Ava thought.

Michael lay on the bed. He was wearing the same slacks and shirt she'd seen the day before, except now the pants were grimy and torn at one knee and the shirt was stained with blood. He was holding an ice pack to his face, and when he heard them enter the bedroom, he removed it. His lip was cut in two places. One ear was red and mangled. There was dried blood under his nose.

"They've got Simon," he said.

Ava sat on the bed so she could have a better look at the damage they'd done. It was mainly superficial, except for a cigarette burn on the back of his hand that would leave a permanent scar. Nothing was broken. She opened his shirt to look for bruising but didn't see any, which calmed her concerns about injuries to his internal organs. Overall it was the kind of abuse that sent a message, meant to scare more than to hurt.

Michael seemed to be in a state of shock, his body twitching of its own accord. She knew his reaction was out of proportion to the physical beating he had taken, but he

was someone who had probably never encountered physical violence and didn't have the psychological means to put
it into perspective.

"I think it would be better if you moved around a bit,
assuming you can," she said.

He sat up.

"I'd like Amanda to take you to the bathroom. Have a
warm shower and change into some clean clothes. Then
we'll sit and talk, okay?"

He nodded.

"And, Amanda, wash your face too. He's going to be all
right. It looks worse than it is."

Ava sat at their kitchen table and waited. The refrigerator
door was plastered with photos fixed with magnets. Michael
and Amanda at Tokyo Disneyland. Michael and Amanda
at the Happy Valley Racetrack. A picture of Michael with
three other young men, perhaps his brothers — her brothers. She moved closer to have a good look and the family
resemblance almost blew her away.

When Michael emerged from the bathroom, he had
already regained some of his natural colour. Amanda had
washed, and without makeup she was actually prettier than
with it, Ava thought.

"Do you have coffee?" Ava asked.

"I brewed some an hour ago," Amanda said.

"Perfect."

"I'll have one too," Michael said.

As Amanda fussed with the cups, Ava reached out to
Michael, her hand caressing his cheek. He flinched and she
knew he still felt unsteady.

"How did this happen?" she asked.

He drew a deep breath. "We were so fucking stupid."

"That's obvious, but it isn't helpful. You need to tell me what happened."

"He phoned me last night around seven o'clock."

"Lok?"

"Yes, Lok. He phoned me to say that he and Wu had been talking and that they felt badly about the way the meeting had gone. He said they thought there might be room for compromise, and that if we were willing to sit down with them, then they'd sit down with us."

"Did he mention what compromise he had in mind?"

"No."

"Did you ask?"

"Yes, and he said it was something they'd rather discuss in person, but that we shouldn't come if Simon was going to keep being a hothead. Then he made a big point about my being able to keep Simon under control. I said that if they were really going to put a compromise on the table, Simon wouldn't be any bother. And then I added that if they were that worried about Simon I'd leave him in Hong Kong and just bring you to the meeting."

"And he wasn't agreeable to that?"

"Not in any way. He said they didn't want you at the meeting. No outsiders, just the principals."

"And that didn't make you suspicious?"

"I wasn't exactly thinking straight. I was still distraught about how things had gone down and this seemed to be a way out, so I guess I just wanted to believe everything I was hearing."

Amanda put cups of coffee in front of them and joined them at the table, her grief giving way to interest.

"Where did they want to meet?" Ava asked.

"Macau, of course."

"And you were still not suspicious?"

"Lok said they'd meet with us anywhere in Macau we wanted. They had no preference."

"And what did you say?"

"I told him I had to talk to Simon."

"And you did, and Simon leapt at the chance to make things right, didn't he."

"Yep."

Ava sipped her coffee. "So off you went."

"I called Lok back and told him we'd meet him at Morton's Steakhouse in the Venetian at ten o'clock. He pushed me about Simon again, insisting that I keep him under control. He said that if I did that he'd be able to get Wu to go along with something that was fair for both sides."

"Did he ask you if you'd called me?"

"No."

Lok's smart, Ava thought. He pushed just enough of the right buttons in the lightest possible way. Dangle the carrot, don't overpromise, don't make a big issue over her, and make it sound as if Michael and Simon actually had some control over the situation.

"How was Simon when you saw him?"

"Excited. He talked all the way to Macau. I kept reminding him that he had to behave himself. He said he'd kowtow and eat shit if he had to, and I know he meant it. Until the lunch meeting I don't think he'd really accepted that we might lose all our money, and when he did it was like his life was over. He kept saying this was a second chance and he wasn't going to blow it. And truthfully, Ava, I think he was really pleased that it was just me and him going over, a sort of reaffirmation of our partnership."

"And neither of you considered for a second that this was a set-up?"

Michael closed his eyes, his teeth grinding. Amanda shot a glance at Ava that said, *How could they be so dumb?*

"We heard what we wanted to hear, and we were going to Morton's. What could happen at Morton's?" he said.

"So you get to Macau . . ."

"Yes, and they're waiting for us outside the station. We start to walk towards the taxi stand when Wu — who has a big cast on his arm — and another guy come up to us. The guy has a coat on, a gun sticking out of it. Wu tells us to follow him," Michael said. "We should have run at that point, I guess, or screamed, or done something, but neither of us has ever had a gun in our face. We were so shocked, so scared that we just went along. They took us to a white van that was parked near the station. There was a driver I didn't recognize. They opened the rear door and made us get in. The guy with the gun jumped in after us. Wu took the gun and held it while the guy tied our hands behind our backs and blindfolded us. Then I think Wu went to sit in the passenger seat while the other guy sat in the back with us."

"Did anyone say anything to you?"

"Not a word."

"How long did you drive?"

"Fifteen, maybe twenty minutes, maybe more. I'm not sure; I was completely disoriented."

"So, no idea of direction."

"No."

"Did you stop at a border crossing?"

"No."

"Do you remember anything at all about the trip, anything out of the ordinary?"

"When we got to where we were going, the van stopped and I heard the driver yell at someone to open the gate. That's it."

"And then they took you inside a building?"

"Yes, we climbed five or six steps. I heard a door open and then I heard Lok ask Wu if anyone at the station had paid any undue attention to us."

"So Lok was there."

"Oh yes, he was there," Michael said, his voice cracking.

"Have some coffee," Ava said.

She finished her own. Amanda pointed to her cup, asking if she wanted another. "Sure," Ava said.

Michael barely touched his. She saw that his hand was beginning to shake. "Do you mind if we take a break?" he said.

Ava shook her head. "No, we need to get this out of the way. Drink some coffee." She waited for him to take a couple of careful sips. "Now you're in a building with Lok and Wu and they start to beat on you, right?"

"They put me on my knees and left me there for maybe ten minutes. I couldn't see anything, I couldn't hear anything. Then out of nowhere someone punched me on the ear. I fell over, then they picked me up and left me again."

"Where was Simon?"

"I don't know. They separated us when we went inside."

"Did you ever see him?"

"No."

"Okay, no Simon, just you on your knees getting punched. Did they say anything?"

"Not while that was going on."

"How many times did they hit you?"

"Maybe ten times, I don't know," Michael said.

"I'm sorry to have to ask these questions," Ava said, patting the back of the hand that wasn't burned. "I'm almost done."

"Maybe ten times — three or four times on my ear, less on my nose, my mouth, my chin."

"And nothing was ever said?"

"No. I sensed that someone was always near me though. I tried to stand once and they hit me immediately. After that I just stayed on my knees. That was the worst thing — not knowing when I was going to get hit, not knowing what else they might do to me."

"How did they end it?"

"Someone just grabbed me by the arm and hauled me to my feet. They walked me into what I think was another room and made me sit on a wooden chair. I could hear mumbling, whispering, but I couldn't make out the words. That's when someone grabbed my hand and put the cigarette out on it. I screamed, and I pissed a bit in my pants, and there was a lot of laughter."

Ava saw tears well in his eyes and she felt them in hers too. Amanda sniffled and then began to cry.

"Is that when they finally spoke to you?"

"How did you know?"

"Who spoke?" she said.

"Lok."

"What did he say?"

"He said they were going to hold Simon until we paid the money we owed them. He said they were giving me forty-eight hours to come up with the money, and if I didn't they would kill him. He said that if I went to the police, they'd find out and kill Simon anyway."

"Did you ask to see Simon?"

"No, I wasn't thinking."

"What did you say?"

"I said I would do what I could, and then someone punched me. It went quiet and I thought I was going to get hit or burned again, but Lok just said they were going to take me back to Hong Kong, and that I was to call him on his cell when I had the money."

"How did they get you back? Not on the jetfoil."

"No, they drove me. They put me in the trunk of a car and then we drove for close to three hours."

"They brought you in through Guangzhou."

"I have no idea."

"Where did they drop you off?"

"Here, about a hundred metres from the building. They pulled me out of the trunk, untied my hands, and told me to count to thirty before taking off the blindfold. And then someone — I think it was Wu but I was so out of it I can't be sure — said that they knew where I lived and that if I didn't come up with the money, Simon was dead and they knew where to find me."

The kitchen went silent. Amanda put her arms around Michael. Ava got up and walked to the living-room window. It was early afternoon on a beautiful Hong Kong day. She looked down and watched people going about their normal routines, and then she went back into the kitchen.

"Before you say anything, we can't call the police," she started. "They will know if you do, and they will most certainly kill Simon."

"Are you sure?" Michael asked.

"Listen to her," Amanda said.

"We also can't discuss this with the family — I mean, families. Not a word to Daddy, not a word to your brothers. And, Amanda, keep your family out of it as well."

She nodded.

"Now what about Jessie? Have you heard from her?"

"No, but I imagine I will," Amanda said.

"Simon is a Macau regular," Michael said. "He has pulled all-nighters there before."

"That'll get us through today, but not much longer," Ava said. "Amanda, I think we need to visit Jessie. She needs to know what's going on, and she needs to know that she has to keep quiet."

"Tell me what you want me to do."

"I have to figure out what I'm going to do first."

9

UNCLE DIDN'T ANSWER HIS APARTMENT PHONE, AND his long-time housekeeper, Lourdes, said she didn't know where he was. Ava called his cell and it went to voicemail. "I need to talk. It's urgent," she said, and then called Sonny.

"I need Uncle," she said when he picked up.

"He's in a meeting."

"Where are you?"

"Hong Kong side. He's at the Korean barbecue restaurant just up the street from your hotel."

"Please ask him not to leave until I get there."

She looked at her brother and Amanda. He was spent, exhausted. "You need to sleep. Take some pills if you have to, but get some sleep."

Amanda seemed better; the tears had dried up and she had a look of determination in her eyes. Ava couldn't help noticing how tiny she was, maybe pushing five feet without her stilettos, and she couldn't have weighed a hundred pounds. Without any makeup she looked even more like a teenager. Still, there was something to her, a strength. "Look after him. I'll call when I know something," Ava said.

"Don't worry," Amanda said.

Ava walked to the restaurant, her sense of urgency balanced by the need for time to think. The first thing she had to do was get over her anger at the stupidity of the two men she'd actually considered going into business with. How could they have imagined, for even a second, that Lok was being sincere? How could they think that in the few hours between the rancour of the lunch and early evening his attitude could be so completely transformed? How could they believe that Wu would so quickly forgive his broken arm?

Part of it is my fault, she thought. If she had called Michael after her meeting with Uncle and relayed the results of his conversation with Lok, he would have known for certain that there was no chance of reconciliation. She had played things too close to her chest, as was her habit, controlling the flow of information, playing God in her own little way. *Shit*, she thought. *Now what?*

There was no car outside the Korean barbecue place, just Sonny leaning against the wall, his eyes flitting in all directions, his vigilance a habit he couldn't shake despite the fact that it was no longer so necessary. He saw Ava the moment she came into view, then stood straight and turned to face her. When she first met him, he had worn nothing but jeans and tight T-shirts that showed off a rock-hard body decorated with tattoos. The years with Uncle had mellowed him.

"Uncle says you should go right in," he said.

He was sitting at a table in the back with two men she recognized from previous lunches. They were old comrades, now retired, and they met regularly to discuss the state of the world. None of the men stood as she approached, instead offering small smiles and nodding heads. "*Lang lei*," one of them said.

Ava sat and Uncle poured her a cup of jasmine tea. There was no need for introductions. She sat quietly at the table as the men continued their conversation. They had long since finished eating, the last empty platters still on the table, the barbecue grill coated with remnants of meat and sauce. Finally one of them called for the bill, only to be told by Uncle that it was his turn to pay. Then everyone stood and there was a round of handshakes. The men made arrangements to meet the next week at a Shandong restaurant on the Kowloon side.

Uncle didn't sit down until his friends had left the restaurant. Then he looked at Ava and said, "What has happened?"

She calmly repeated Michael's story. When she was done, he shook his head in resignation. "How stupid can they be?"

"They run noodle shops and 7-Elevens," she said.

"Over lunch I told Uncle Fong that Lok was causing a friend of mine some trouble. He knows Lok from before; he says he can be crazy. It was useful when he was a 49er, a fighter. He is smart, of course, and moved up in his society, but the craziness made him unfit to be anything but a Red Pole. Uncle Fong said a man like Lok should never have the autonomy he has."

Ava had listened more than once to the old men complaining about the deterioration within the Three Harmonies Society — the unity between Heaven, Earth, and Man — and how the thirty-six traditional oaths had no meaning anymore. When the triads fought these days, it was normally against each other. They were more of a threat to themselves than the police. Ava didn't feel like listening to another monologue on the good old days, even from Uncle. "What can I do?" she asked.

He poured more tea. "Nothing," he said.

"That's not possible."

"It is practical, and you are a practical girl."

"If we pay a ransom?"

"They will kill him, if he is not dead already."

"You seem so sure."

"Your brother's partner will die whether you pay the ransom or not. That is how these people operate. You asked for my advice, there it is."

"How about the threats to my brother?"

"They want to scare him into paying, probably nothing more than that."

"They told Michael not to go to the police, that they would know if he did. How much truth is there to that?"

"Lok has been in Macau a long time, and as far as I know he has never spent an hour in jail, never had a single charge laid against him. This is a man who ran moneylenders, whorehouses, did some drug dealing, and when he got bored he would hire out himself and his men for contract killing — all rather visible and sometimes violent activities. What does that tell you about his relationship with the Macau police?"

"I thought there had been a crackdown there, that the police had cleaned things up."

"They negotiated a truce, that is all. The government was worried about the bad publicity the territory was getting from crimes no one could ignore, crimes that made the front pages of all the newspapers — like the lawyer getting gunned down at the front door of the Grand Hyatt, the drive-by shootings, the gangs shooting at each other in broad daylight in the old town and killing two children who were walking home from school. So they sat down with the gangs and worked out a treaty to accommodate the new, Vegas-style Macau. The moneylenders disappeared from the casinos, the guns were put away, and everything else was prettied up, but it kept on going. And the gangs of course found new ways to generate income, such as Lok's revolving land deals, and you know that a percentage of every dollar finds its way to some police retirement fund."

"You make them sound like business partners."

"They are."

"But this is a kidnapping, Uncle, not some victimless crime."

"How many kidnappings are there in Macau every year? Ten, twenty, thirty, I do not know. But I do know that it has been the time-honoured way to collect debts in Macau. In the old days the moneylenders would book a client into a hotel room with a guard and leave him there until his family squared the account, and I still hear about business squabbles getting resolved that way. The police would say thank you for informing them about the kidnapping, file a report somewhere, and then call Lok to tell him and have a laugh about the idiot who did not understand how Macau works."

Ava felt her face flush. Uncle wasn't often so categorical, and his use of the word *idiot* stung. "So I do nothing," she said quietly.

"Nothing," he said.

She finally sipped some tea. It had gone cold. She tipped it into one of the empty bowls and held out her cup for

Uncle to pour some warm tea.

"They're holding him somewhere in Macau, of that I'm sure. Could you find out for me what properties Lok has, where he lives?"

Uncle sighed. "I could, but I do not want to."

"If you don't, I'll find someone who will."

"Ava, please —"

"No, Uncle, I have to do at least that much. I have to find out what I can. It may come to nothing — just as you wish — or it may not."

He seemed to sink into his chair, becoming as small as a child. Ava could see his mind turning things over and knew that he couldn't deny her.

"There are two things you need to do right away," he finally said. "You need to confirm that the partner is still alive. Have your brother call them and tell them he needs proof. If they will not do that, he is already dead. If he is alive, you need to buy more time. Your brother should tell them that he is willing to pay the ransom but he needs time to get the money together. Ask for a week. If they will not budge even a little, then it means they probably have no interest in the money anyway."

"I can't see them accepting a week."

"Your brother has to negotiate. Anything more than the two days he has been given is a plus. And if this were a normal kidnapping and ransom, I would tell him to negotiate the money as well. In this case I would not do that. It would be a waste of time and just aggravate them."

"Okay, we'll do that as soon as I leave here."

"And I will make some calls," he said. "I do not want to, but I will."

"Thank you."

They walked from the restaurant together, his arm through hers. He was doing that more often these days, and she wasn't sure why.

"Where does your brother live?"

"Mid-levels," she said, pointing up towards the Peak.

"Shall we give you a ride?"

"No, I'd rather walk. The day is so beautiful, and I need to organize my thoughts."

THE DOORMAN LET HER ENTER THE BUILDING WITHOUT hesitation, and Ava made a mental note to have Amanda instruct him not to let anyone in without her or Michael's specific approval. She checked her watch. Her brother had been resting for about an hour and a half. It would have to do.

After she rang the apartment buzzer, Ava saw Amanda's eye through the peephole. The door opened and there was the Amanda from the evening at Sai Kung — designer jeans, cashmere sweater, and lots of makeup.

"How is my brother?" Ava asked.

"Sleeping."

"You need to wake him."

"He just fell asleep."

"It doesn't matter, I need him to do something. When it's done, he can go back to sleep."

Ava went into the kitchen while Amanda went to wake Michael. There was an empty instant noodles bowl and a package of rice crackers on the table. Ava guessed Amanda wasn't much of a cook, but then neither was she.

It took five minutes to get him out of bed, into a robe, and out to the kitchen. His face was creased with sleep, his hair out of control, his eyes puffy. "Wash your face in the sink and grab a glass of water," Ava told him. "You need to make a phone call."

She watched and waited until he looked like he could manage some comprehension. "Michael, I want you to call Lok. Do you think you're up to it?"

"I don't know."

"It isn't complicated and you don't have to pretend anything."

Amanda stood behind him, her hands resting on his shoulders. "What does he have to say?"

"We need to confirm that Simon is all right."

"Is that all?"

"For now."

"How would Michael do that?"

"He could ask to speak to Simon, but I don't think they would let him. The best thing is to ask them to take a photo of Simon holding up the front page of today's *South China Morning Post*. Then ask them to email it to him."

"Why would they agree?" Amanda asked.

"Michael is going to start the conversation by telling them he's going to pay them what they're asking for."

He looked up at her. "Ava, how the hell are we going to do that?"

"One thing at a time," she said to both of them. "We need to do one thing at a time, not get ahead of ourselves. And right now that one thing is to find out if Simon is okay. Can you make the call?"

"Sure," he said.

"Good. Now I want you to talk to Lok, no one else."

"His is the only number I have."

"Don't try to chit-chat. You don't need to be anything but direct. Tell him you're prepared to get the money together but you need to be one hundred percent sure that Simon is fine."

"What if he refuses?"

"No confirmation, no money."

"They'll kill Simon," Michael said, panic returning to his voice.

"If they refuse he's probably dead already," Ava said, wishing he hadn't made her state the obvious.

Michael shivered. Ava knew he was tired and still a bit in shock. "The money — how do we manage the money?" he asked.

"One thing at a time," Ava repeated.

"What if Lok asks me about it?"

"Tell him you're going to get it but you're not prepared to go into detail until you know about Simon."

"What if he insists?"

Ava found herself losing patience. "Geez, Michael, insist right back. You're negotiating, not capitulating."

"If Lok is truly interested in getting the money he'll do what you want," Amanda interrupted.

"Okay," he said.

"Get Michael's cell," Ava said to Amanda.

As she walked towards the bedroom Ava said to her brother, "She's a good girl." He nodded.

When Amanda returned, Ava took the phone from her. "Where's the number?"

"It's programmed into my phone," Michael said.

Ava found it and hit the call button and the speaker phone button. "Remember, keep it simple. Don't get side-tracked. We only want one thing."

The phone rang four times before it was answered. It wasn't Lok on the other end. "This is Michael Lee. I want to speak to Kao Lok," he said. Nothing was said in reply, and Ava half expected the line to go dead. Instead she heard Lok's familiar voice.

"Lee, I'm glad you called."

"We're prepared to pay the ransom, but —"

"It isn't a ransom. It's the money you owe us."

"We're prepared to pay you the money we owe," Michael said, not missing a beat, "but we need to know that Simon is safe."

Lok hesitated, and Ava knew he was surprised. *He didn't believe Michael could come up with the money*, she thought, *and now he's reworking whatever plan he had*. "When will you pay?"

"I'm not going to talk about the money until I know he's safe."

"I gave you forty-eight hours, remember?"

"Unless I know Simon is well there will be no money. None."

"Can you get it all?"

"We're prepared to pay the money we owe."

"On time?"

"Lok, I'm not saying anything else until I know about Simon."

There was a long pause. Ava thought, *Simon is dead and Lok is trying to figure what he can get away with*. Then Lok said, "Okay, I understand your position. What is it you want?"

"A photo of Simon with the front page of today's *South China Morning Post*. I want you to use a digital camera and email it to me."

There was another pause and Ava waited for Lok to say no. Instead he said, "And then?"

"Then we'll talk some more," Michael said.

"You'll have the photo within the next two or three hours," Lok said.

"Fine," Michael said, and before he could add another word, Ava reached over and turned off the phone.

"Why did you do that?" he asked.

"We had what we wanted; there was nothing more to be said. We had to show him that we have some level of control, that this isn't all one-sided. Now he'll send the photo or he won't," she said. "And by the way, you were great."

Amanda put her arms around his neck, pulled him against her chest, and kissed the top of his head.

"Take him back to bed," Ava said.

Michael struggled to his feet, his eyes half closed. Given his emotional state, Ava was surprised he had done as well as he had. Amanda seemed composed as she walked her boyfriend to the bedroom with her left arm around his waist and her right hand clutching his right elbow. She talked as she walked, Michael nodding his head at whatever she was saying.

Women are running his life now, Ava thought, *or as much of his life as there is left to run*. But would Amanda stick with him if the business went under? The thought came to her out of nowhere, and she felt guilty for thinking it.

She closed her eyes. Michael and Simon had dug a hole so deep that she couldn't find the bottom. She began to mentally list the things that had to be done. Then she heard Amanda say, "Are you all right?"

"Just thinking," Ava said.

Amanda sat at the kitchen table across from Ava. It was the first time they'd actually been alone together. Amanda toyed with the package of rice crackers. Ava asked, "How are you managing with this?"

Amanda gave her an awkward little smile, and Ava figured she was looking at a hundred thousand Hong Kong dollars' worth of dental work. "Not so well."

"I understand."

"I'm scared. I'm scared for Michael, for Simon, for Jessie and their child."

"Me too."

"You don't seem to have any fear at all."

"It's an act."

"Michael told me what happened at the restaurant yesterday. That was no act."

"It was a reaction to a threat, that's all. I didn't have time to think about being scared."

"Well, I'm scared, and truthfully, Ava, I'm also a little angry."

"It isn't a good situation."

"No, it isn't, but more specifically I'm kind of angry with Michael."

"He and Simon made some mistakes. It happens," Ava said.

"Not the kind that result in a partner being held for ransom and death threats being thrown around like confetti," she said, her anger edging into her voice.

"I can't argue with you."

"But it has to do with more than that, actually. I'm upset that he never told me what kind of trouble the business was in. He treated me as if I couldn't understand and couldn't help, and he didn't turn to me until we were all blindsided and he didn't have any choice."

This is a different Amanda, Ava thought as she sifted through several clichés about his not wanting to worry her, then discarded them. "Would you have been able to help him?"

Amanda reacted as if she had been challenged. "I have a master's degree in international business from Brandeis."

"I didn't know."

She shrugged. "You act like you're not scared, I act like a Hong Kong princess. And although I moan about my father's business, I can hardly wait for him to retire so I can take over and really do something with it."

"I didn't mean to be derogatory."

"I'm not blaming you — I know the impression I create. It's just easier sometimes to get your own way when people don't take you seriously."

"That could be me talking," Ava said.

"I don't believe that."

"You'll have to trust me."

Amanda returned to the rice crackers, opening and closing the plastic wrap.

"Is there anything else you want to talk about?" Ava asked.

Amanda glanced at her and then just as quickly turned away.

"What is it?" Ava said.

"I'm also upset about you."

"Me?"

"Yes, you — but not just you. I mean, I've been living with Michael for five months and we've been talking about marriage for two months, and I didn't know he had a sister in Canada until two weeks ago."

"Two sisters in Canada, actually. The other one's name is Marian and she has two girls of her own."

"Yes, I know. He told me about Marian as well."

"And then there are two much younger siblings, a boy and a girl, in Australia."

Amanda's face fell. "I didn't know about them."

"It's a complicated family."

"I don't care about that, or how your father chooses to live his life. All I care about is that Michael hasn't been honest with me, first about you and Marian and now, evidently, about two children in Australia."

"I'm not going to make excuses for him. He had his reasons, and you should ask him what they were."

"And I'm going to. If we survive this drama."

"Is that it?"

"What?"

"No more worries?"

"No, but I have a question. Tell me, is it really true you hadn't met each other until two weeks ago?"

"It is."

"And then it was like for five minutes in a restaurant?"

"Yep."

"So tell me, because I don't really understand, why would you fly all the way to Hong Kong to help a man you don't really know? I asked Michael the same question when he told me you were coming, and he sort of mumbled something about your having some business expertise he needed, and that your father had suggested you to him."

"The truth is, I didn't come here for Michael," Ava said, deciding that at least one of the Lees should be straight with this woman. "At some time in the future I might have, because I think our father has decided it's time to try to bring the families — or at least the children — together, and he was encouraging Michael and me to start the process. But that's going to be a long, slow grind, and I wasn't really ready to jump right in.

"I actually came here to protect the rest of the family from Michael. I know that sounds harsh, and I don't mean it that way, but the fact is that he has put us at risk. You know about the whole family now: three wives, his brothers here, my sister and me in Canada, and the two little kids in Australia. None of the children chose their father and none of us chose the circumstances in which we were raised. Now, what you need to understand is that Michael's situation threatens them. If his business tanks, Amanda, Marcus will step in and sell everything he has to bail Michael out. Who knows what might be left? I'm here because I don't want it to come to that.

"Now, it is true that Marian, I, and the brothers can look after ourselves. But what about the two kids in Australia? What about my mother? What about the two aunties? The way I look at it, I came here to represent their interests — and, of course, my father's."

Amanda had listened quietly, her face blank, and Ava wondered if her criticism of Michael had gone too far. Then Amanda said, "And now we have to throw Simon, Jessie, and another child into that mix, don't we."

"I guess we do."

"Let me make you a coffee," Amanda said suddenly, getting up from the table.

Amanda's lips moved as she poured coffee into a cup. The younger woman put the two cups on the table and leaned forward. "I want to help."

"I'm not sure there is anything to help with."

"I know you need to confirm that Simon is okay, but from the conversation between Lok and Michael, it sounds like he is. And if he is, then I want to help, and I don't mean help in the sense of babysitting Michael."

Ava didn't know quite what to say other than "We'll see," and she was struggling with how to put that differently when her cellphone rang. For once she was happy to answer. It was Uncle.

"I have some, maybe most of the information you asked for," he said. "Can you come to Andy's?"

"I'm at my brother's apartment in the Mid-levels. It'll take me half an hour."

"See you then."

She closed her phone and looked up at Amanda. "I have to go."

Amanda leaned forward again. "I know you're not going to abandon Simon, and I want to help you get him back."

"I have no plans to do anything, but if you want to help, I'll tell you where you can start. Get into Michael's email and watch for the photo from Lok. The moment it comes through, call me on my cell. You might also call Jessie and make sure she's going to be home tonight. And keep it casual. One way or another we're going to have to talk to her."

"Thank you."

As Ava walked to the door, Amanda called after her, "Do you remember Jack Yee?"

Ava spun back. "Of course I do."

"He's my father," Amanda said.

Ava was too surprised to say anything. *I am so thick sometimes*, she thought. Jack Yee, Amanda Yee — why hadn't she made the connection? Why at least hadn't she asked Amanda if they were related?

Ava and Uncle had done two jobs for Jack, both of them successful, and one of which had turned ugly and exceptionally violent. Jack had been caught in the middle of the violence and Ava and Derek had saved him, none too gently. She wondered what he had told his daughter about that day in Yantai. There had been five men, and two had died.

"I called him last night and told him what happened at the lunch in Macau yesterday," Amanda said. "Of course, your name entered the conversation."

"Have you spoken to him since?"

"No."

"Don't," Ava said as she walked out the door.

11

THERE WAS NO SONNY IN FRONT OF THE KOWLOON Tong MTR, and Ava wondered if something had happened to delay Uncle. But when she went inside the restaurant, Andy saw her and waved her back to the kitchen.

The table was empty except for a pot of tea and two cups. Ava kissed Uncle on the forehead and said, "Thank you."

He reached into his jacket pocket and pulled out a sheet of lined paper. "Lok owns three plots of vacant land, the ones he keeps selling over and over again. He has an interest in several massage parlours that specialize in hand jobs and a nightclub that is mainly a whorehouse. I do not think he would take your brother's partner to either of those places. So there are two candidates.

"The first is a warehouse he has near the old town. According to my contact it is a busy place. He uses it as a distribution centre for wine he brings in from China and Portugal. It is also quite central, quite public, so though it is worth taking a look at, I think your best bet is his house. The house is on Coloane, in the most southwestern part of Macau, near Seac Pai Van Park. It was custom-built and is more of a compound than a residence. Some of his men, including Wu, stay there. It is quite isolated, I am told."

He slid the paper over to her. "There are the addresses, such as they are."

"Thank you."

"This does not make me happy, you understand."

"I know."

"Have you heard about the partner yet?"

"We're working on it. I'll know shortly, but I'm betting he's still alive."

"Lok is an animal. Wu makes all the noise and acts like the tough guy, but never forget that Lok is capable of just about anything."

She picked up the teapot and poured. Neither of them touched their cups. "Uncle, I was thinking of asking Carlo and Andy to do some work for me, but I wanted to clear it with you first."

"They are their own men."

"Still."

"If you have to ask them, I do not object."

"And money — I've never paid them directly. What is their rate?"

"That depends on what you want them to do. When I sent them to Las Vegas to help you, I paid them five thousand Hong Kong a day. If it is not dangerous work, you could pay three thousand."

"It isn't dangerous, but I'll pay five thousand anyway."

"They will be as loyal for three thousand."

"Now who's being practical?" she said.

Her phone rang. The caller ID read AMANDA YEE. "This is Ava."

She listened, nodded, and said, "I'll be about half an hour. We should head to Sha Tin as soon as I get there."

"Sha Tin?" Uncle said after she closed her phone.

"They sent us the photo we wanted. The partner is alive. He lives in Sha Tin, and the wife is there, evidently now going out of her mind with worry. We need to see her."

"Who is 'we'?"

"Amanda Yee, my brother's girlfriend, and me."

"Yee...any connection to Jack?" Uncle asked.

I should be so quick, Ava thought. "His daughter."

"Have they discussed you?"

"Evidently."

"Jack thinks you walk on water."

"That's the problem," she said.

As they left the kitchen he said, "Keep in touch. I do not want to hear things second-hand."

"I will."

Andy was standing by the cash register with his wife. They both gave a deep bow as Uncle passed. Ava saw him to the door and walked back. "Andy, can we have a word?"

"Sure," he said, not budging.

Ava looked at his wife.

"She knows everything," he said.

"Okay, I have a situation I need some help with. Could you get hold of Carlo and tell him I have a few days' work for the two of you, starting, say, tomorrow morning?"

"No problem."

"I'll need you both to go to Macau, so bring your ID cards or passports."

"No problem."

"Five thousand a day okay?"

"Perfect."

"Do you have binoculars?"

"No, but I know where to get a good pair."

"How about a camera with a long-range lens?"

"I have my own."

"Bring them with you. I'll meet at the Macau Ferry terminal at ten o'clock."

"Okay, boss. Good to be working with you again."

"Same here, Andy."

12

ON THE RIDE FROM KOWLOON BACK TO HONG KONG on the Star Ferry, she began to think about Derek. Three or four months earlier she wouldn't have hesitated to tell him to get his ass on a plane to Hong Kong. He was her personal security blanket. They had met at bak mai, the only two students of their Toronto instructor. He was the son of a wealthy Hong Kong businessman, and as far as she knew he hadn't worked a day in his life. His only source of income besides Daddy was the money she paid him for the support he had provided once or twice a year for the past few years.

The thing about Derek was that he never questioned, never hesitated. What had to get done got done. And if he had any fear, she'd never seen it. When they'd saved Jack Yee from what was going to be a horrendous beating, or worse, Derek had personally taken out three men, leaving Ava with just two, which he teased her about constantly. She loved Derek. The problem was that her best friend, Mimi, did too. And Mimi was pregnant.

Shit, why did I let them get together? she thought. It had been perfect the way it was before. They hadn't deliberately hooked up; in fact, she had done what she could to warn Mimi off Derek. Looking back, that was probably the wrong thing to do with someone who was always willing to burn her fingers when it came to men.

I can't do it, she decided as the ferry began to manoeuvre into the Hong Kong terminal. *If anything ever happened to him I'd be doubly devastated — no, with a baby involved, triply devastated.* She'd make do with Carlo and Andy for now. They showed very little initiative, which was a good thing, and they followed orders, which was also good. When she was working, Ava liked to be surrounded by low-maintenance men. These two qualified.

She took a cab to the apartment.

Michael opened the door, dressed, shaved, and with his hair slicked back. "Come to the computer," he said.

Amanda sat at the keyboard. "Hey, I was just getting caught up on my own emails. Let me close this window."

She hit a tab at the bottom and Simon To's photo appeared. He held the paper at chest level, the headline and the date clearly visible. His chin touched the top of the sheet. His face dog-sad but untouched, except for a bruise under his eye from the punch at lunch. *They didn't have to scare him*, Ava thought.

"Okay, great. Now, Michael, you need to make another phone call to Lok."

"What about this time?"

"You're going to thank him for the photo and you're going to tell him that you'll need a week to get the money collected."

A look of disbelief crossed his face. "He told us forty-eight hours."

"And now we negotiate."

"Are you sure about this?"

"You thank him for the photo and then you tell him you need a week. Tell him you've got ten contacts you've got to go to, that you can't just pull the money out of thin air. It has to be done bit by bit."

"He'll never agree to a week."

"Then you ask for six days."

Amanda turned away from the computer. "Michael, Ava is right. Lok has to be smart enough to know that forty-eight hours is impossible. He might not buy a week, but you can get more time."

"And when you do, tell him we need a photo of Simon sent to your email address every day at noon," Ava added.

"Do you want to listen in again?"

"No, you know the drill. Stick to the point. Keep insisting."

"Okay," he said, breathing deeply.

Ava turned to Amanda. "Did you call Jessie?"

"Yes, she's expecting us."

"The two of you are going to Sha Tin?" Michael asked.

"We are."

"Shall I come as well?"

"Not a chance," Ava said. "One look at your face and Jessie will freak out, and I'm not about to show her that photo of Simon either."

Amanda stood. "Jessie sounded concerned enough already."

"Call either of us on our cellphones after you've talked to Lok," Ava said, motioning to Amanda that it was time for them to go.

"I'm glad you left him alone to do it," Amanda said as

they left the apartment. "He was complaining that he felt like a child the way you handled it earlier."

"He was emotionally unstable then. He seems better now."

"Let's hope so," Amanda said as the elevator doors opened.

When they got to the lobby, Ava asked, "Taxi or MTR?"

"The MTR takes only thirty minutes and their apartment is right behind New Town Plaza in Sha Tin, no more than a ten-minute walk from the station."

They chatted as they walked to the Central MTR station. Amanda had called Jessie just after Ava left the apartment to meet with Uncle, and she had been more upset than she had let on to Michael. Jessie was convinced that Simon was either blowing his brains out gambling in Macau or had shacked up with another woman. Amanda had nothing to offer her but gentle assurances. Jessie had calmed down a little when Amanda said that Michael hadn't come home either, and that she was sure the boys were trying to close some business deal.

The train was packed and they couldn't get seats. Even standing, they were soon separated by a continual inflow of passengers fighting for every vacant inch. Ava couldn't comprehend how people could do this twice a day, every day.

The train had just pulled out of Central when Ava's cell rang. She couldn't get to it, her arms pinned to her sides. A moment later Amanda's cellphone was going off. Ava watched her struggle to get to her purse to remove it. It stopped ringing before she could.

At Sha Tin the train half emptied, the two women swept along with the throng. They both reached for their phones as soon as they had room to move. "It's Michael," Amanda said, listening to her voicemail. "Four days...Lok gave him four days."

Ava called him from the station platform. "Great work. Four days is good, but is that four days from today or from tomorrow?"

"We never actually discussed that."

"In that case we're going to assume it's from tomorrow. Was he okay about sending the photos every day?"

"Yeah."

"And how was he otherwise?"

"Actually quite co-operative. He didn't even go off on me when I told him I needed more time."

"He's got his head in the money now," Ava said. "He's not going to do anything that'll screw up his chances of getting paid."

Michael went quiet. Ava knew exactly what he was thinking, and before he could speak again she said, "I'm working on some options. The money is only one of them."

"How the hell can you get that kind of money? And even if you can, how are we going to pay you back?" he said.

"It's one option. You've bought us all some time, so let me use it."

Ava felt Amanda staring at her as she spoke to her brother. She ended the call and said, "Now, how do we get to Jessie's?"

They inched their way out of the station and then inched their way to New Town Plaza. At one time it had been the biggest mall in the New Territories, with more than fifty acres of shopping space in a nine-storey structure. Amanda led Ava through the maze to the back exit and right into a wall of apartment towers.

As they walked, Ava talked about how to handle Jessie. "We have to be upbeat, positive. The boys are involved in a business dispute in Macau, pure and simple. As a sign of good faith, Simon and Michael offered to have one of them stay there until the money that is owed is paid. Simon insisted it be him, so now Michael is back in Hong Kong organizing the money. He should have it transferred to Macau in a few days. It's a bit unusual, but that's the way business is often done over there. The really good news is that the deal seems to be back on track."

"Do you really think she'll buy that?" Amanda asked.

"That depends on how well you spin it."

"Me?"

"Hey, I'm a stranger. I don't have any credibility with this woman. Why should she believe anything I have to say? You're the one she knows and trusts — her husband's partner's girlfriend."

"I'm not a very good liar."

Ava stopped walking, reached for Amanda's arm, and turned her so she could see her face. "You are not lying, and you have to convince yourself of that before you can convince her. You're doing a little bit of shading, using gentler semantics, but the message is essentially true, is it not? He is being held in Macau. We are organizing the money. He will be home in a few days. What more is there to say? Just avoid loaded words like *ransom* or *hostage*."

"When you put it that way —"

"There is no other way to put it. And one more thing: lead with the bad news. Don't try to ease into it. It should just be 'Jessie, Simon is stuck in Macau for a few days over a business dispute, but we'll have him home by Friday.'"

"She'll want to talk to him."

"I know, but you'll have to be firm about the fact that he can't talk to anyone, not even Michael, until the deal is finalized. Again, try to keep it low-key, make it sound like the natural course of business in Macau. If you can, Amanda, try to raise the topic of communication before she can ask the question — be proactive. And, of course, you're going to have to tell her that she can't talk about this with anyone, not her mother or her siblings or any of their friends. Say that you're under the same restrictions, that the deal requires this level of confidentiality. She can always call you, night or day, right?"

"Right."

"If you're calm and in control, she'll absorb it."

"I believe you."

"Can you do it?"

"I think so."

"I think you can too."

The building wasn't quite what Ava had expected: gritty, mid-grade security in the lobby in a small office with a plastic shield, two elevators for thirty floors, and notices from debt collectors plastered on the walls. The notices were a standard Hong Kong debt collection technique, naming the debtor and the amount owed and making ugly references to his or her character as a way of shaming them in public, in front of friends and neighbours.

"Shabby," Ava said.

"They bought it when they were first married. Jessie's mother lives one floor below them, and she babysits. Simon wants to move but Jessie says this is too convenient to give up."

They waited forever for an elevator, and if Jessie hadn't lived on the twentieth floor, Ava would have walked.

She lived at the end of the corridor, a metal grille fronting the door. Amanda pushed the buzzer and the door opened. Jessie flew into Amanda's arms, knocking her backwards. Behind them Ava saw a short, round woman with a baby in her arms and a suspicious look on her face. The resemblance between her and Jessie was unmistakeable. Ava knew there was no way the conversation would take place without her.

"Hey, take it easy, Jessie. There's absolutely nothing to be worried about. Everything is fine, just fine," Amanda said.

It took an hour, two coffees for Ava, two pots of tea for the others, a plate of biscuits, and the same story repeated almost word for word four or five times before Jessie began to accept that things were fine, that they were being managed and there was no need to panic. As Amanda talked to Jessie, Ava tried to engage her mother with smiles of encouragement and direct eye contact. By the time they were ready to leave, the mother was weighing in too, telling Jessie not to be such a worrier.

As Amanda again emphasized to Jessie the need for discretion, Ava said to the mother, "This applies to you too, Auntie. You need to keep this secret. Simon and Michael stand to make a lot of money, and we don't want to mess it up."

They left the apartment in a flurry of hugs and kisses. As they walked to the elevator Ava could see that Amanda was very pleased with herself.

"You'll need to call her at least twice a day," Ava said. "Try to call at the same times so she comes to expect it.

You'll need to keep reinforcing everything you said in there, because Jessie won't be able to keep from getting anxious and you'll have to stop it from getting out of control. So twice a day — more, if you can do it."

"Okay."

They waited for the elevator, Amanda peering at Ava. "How did I do?"

Ava said, "I'm proud of you. How's that?"

"That's just absolutely fine."

Amanda talked for the entire MTR ride back to Central. Ava nodded, pretending to listen, her mind miles away as she tried to organize the day ahead.

"You'll come back to the apartment. We can go out for dinner," Amanda said as they pulled into the Central MTR station.

"No, I have too much to do. I'm going to the hotel. You spend the evening with Michael. And, Amanda, make sure to tell him I don't want him discussing any of this with our father, and I'd prefer it if you kept your father in the dark as well."

"I'll do that," Amanda said as they exited the train.

"Tell him as well that he needs to check his email tomorrow at noon for the photo. I'll phone him around twelve fifteen to confirm that he got it."

"All right."

"And that's it," Ava said.

They climbed the stairs from the MTR platform to the street. Ava turned to leave and saw that Amanda looked reluctant to go home. Ava said, "Amanda, I really do have things to do."

"Okay, I'm going, I'm going," she said, and still didn't move.

Then an idea Ava had had on the train revisited her. "Do you have plans for tomorrow?" she asked.

"Work in my father's office, that's all."

"Can you get the day off?"

"Sure."

"Then meet me at the Macau Ferry terminal at ten o'clock."

"Macau?"

"I'll explain in the morning."

"Do I tell Michael I'm going?"

"Better not. No need to worry him."

"Okay."

"And, Amanda, do you have a briefcase?"

"Of course."

"Bring it. Put some papers in it — it doesn't matter what they are."

"This is getting a little weird now, Ava."

"You don't have to do it."

"I'll be there, I'll be there."

"One last thing: dress down a bit, skip the stilettos, and look professional — middle-class if you can — and cut back on the makeup."

"What's wrong with my makeup?"

"It makes you look five years older. You have beautiful skin; you don't need that guck."

"God, what next, ditch my padded bra?"

"Actually, if you have one with even more padding, throw it on."

"Are you serious?"

"Not really," Ava said, kissing her on the cheek. "See you in the morning."

Ava walked back to the hotel, glad to be alone. The day had started with her drafting an offer sheet to help them save their business; it was going to end with her trying to figure out how to keep Simon To alive.

13

SHE WENT TO BED EARLY AND SLEPT WELL. SHE HAD placed a wake-up call for six, and by six forty-five she had had two coffees, read the *International Herald Tribune*, and was on the MTR to the Causeway Bay station and Victoria Park.

She got there just early enough to get in five quick laps before the morning crowd arrived to clog the jogging track. She took that as a good omen.

The night before she'd figured out how to structure the day; the only thing she hadn't done was organize a car rental. She stopped at the front desk on the return from her run and asked the concierge to make the arrangements.

She showered and put on a black T-shirt and her training pants and jacket. She normally didn't wear a hat, but she knew she could be out in the sun for most of the day, and took her Adidas baseball cap out of her bag. She didn't want to lug around her Chanel purse or her notebook, so she ripped out some pages and put them in her jacket pocket with two pens. Her passport, Hong Kong ID card, driver's licence, and a wad of U.S. hundred-dollar bills went into the other pocket.

She looked at herself in the mirror. *No beauty queen*, she thought.

Ava ate breakfast downstairs at Café Causette. She ordered plain black coffee and congee with abalone and read the *South China Morning Post*. She paid special attention to the front page. Hopefully it would be popping up on Michael's computer screen at noon.

At the terminal she first saw the two boys off to the side, standing close together, smoking as if their lives depended on it. Carlo was the bigger of the two at about five foot six and 140 pounds; Andy was an inch shorter and ten pounds lighter. The last time she had seen Carlo he had a moustache; now his upper lip was as bare as his shaved head. They were wearing T-shirts, and Ava kicked herself for not telling them to wear long-sleeved shirts. Both of Andy's arms were covered in tattoos; Carlo had only one arm decorated, but a dragon's tail wrapped itself around his collarbone and neck. Ava had never seen the actual dragon's head that she knew was situated somewhere on his chest.

They waved, greeting her less formally than at their last meeting, in Las Vegas. They were on their home turf and not so nervous. Andy had a carryall with him.

Amanda was at the gate that led to the ferry gangplank. She was wearing flat shoes, white linen slacks, and an unadorned navy blue silk blouse that still looked as if it had cost two thousand Hong Kong dollars. She held a Louis Vuitton briefcase that wasn't much bigger than a sheet of paper. *The girl couldn't look middle-class if she tried*, Ava thought.

With her baseball cap on, Ava got to within five metres of Amanda before she was recognized. "Hey," Amanda said, suddenly awkward as she took in Ava's clothes.

"Hey, yourself."

"Am I overdressed?"

"No, you're perfect," Ava said. "Now come and meet Carlo and Andy."

Amanda's reaction when she saw the boys wasn't much different from Ava's the first time a gun was waved in her face.

"This is Amanda. She's my brother's fiancée," Ava said, emphasizing the relationship particularly to Carlo, who fancied himself a ladies' man and was always prepared to give it a go, regardless of the likelihood of rejection. "And these are Carlo and Andy," she said to Amanda. "They've worked with me before, and I trust them with my life."

The boys smiled at the compliment. Amanda looked a little less uneasy but stayed close to Ava.

Ava bought tickets with an open return, and they hustled down the corridor to catch the ten-fifteen jetfoil. She told the boys to sit in a separate row, as she wanted to talk to Amanda. As always, they did what was asked and took no offence.

"So, how's Michael?" Ava began. Amanda seemed distracted, her attention still on the boys. "Hey, get over it," Ava said. "Everyone does silly things when they're young. They have tattoos but they're good guys; they don't bite."

"Sorry, it was just a bit of a shock. I mean, I wasn't expecting anyone else."

"Well, there they are, so get used to them. Besides, you won't be spending much time with them anyway," Ava said. "Now, about Michael?"

"He was suspicious as anything this morning."

"You didn't tell him you were going to Macau, did you?"

"No, of course not. I told him I had a meeting in Aberdeen, and I even called my office and gave them the same story in case he calls for me there. But I was still a bit jumpy. And I usually leave for work earlier and I don't normally wear this kind of shoes, and of course there's the makeup."

"Looks good, by the way. I mean, less makeup."

"Thanks. Michael actually said the same thing."

"How is his mood?"

"He seemed pleased enough when I told him about the meeting with Jessie last night. I know he was worried about her."

"Did you tell him about Marcus?"

"I did. No problem — he doesn't feel like telling him anything anyway."

"And he's going to check his computer at noon for the photo?"

"He said he would, and I told him to call you when it arrived."

"Did he ask you what I was doing today?"

"I said you were trying to organize the money and that you'd be calling him later."

"Good, that's just about right," Ava said.

Amanda tensed, and Ava knew something was bothering her. "What's the matter?" she asked.

"I didn't really know how much money was involved until last night. I mean, it never came up in any discussion. When Michael told me I almost fell over."

"Don't worry about it. I have it under control."

Amanda seemed to be gathering herself to ask more questions, but Ava cut her off. "Did you call Jessie this morning?"

"No, but I called her last night at ten o'clock and we chatted for about ten minutes. She was a bit anxious at first, but I repeated what I'd said earlier and it seemed to work. I told her I'd call her every day at one and every night at ten."

"Structure gives comfort," Ava said.

"So I'm realizing."

"Now today is going to be a bit unstructured, unfortunately, but I think you're up to it."

"What are we going to be doing?"

"Not we — you," Ava said. "I have some things to do with Andy. Carlo has a project of his own and you have your own job."

"Alone?" Amanda said.

"Relax, I don't want you to rob a bank or anything." She reached into her jacket pocket and pulled out a slip of paper on which she'd written the address of the house in Coloane and the address of the Macau land registry office. "This is where Kao Lok lives. I need you to go to the registry office and ask to see the actual registration documents. It isn't an uncommon request; real estate agents do it all the time. If they question you, just tell them you're thinking of making an offer on the property and you want to confirm some particulars.

"When you get the documents, there should be a reference to an architect, maybe an engineering firm, and for sure a construction company. The house was custom-built and that information should be on record. Write it down. If all three names are available, then contact the architect's office first, if it's in Macau, and arrange to go see them. If it isn't in Macau, go after the construction company.

"What I want are the floor plans for the house. Tell them you saw the house and loved it and that you want to build one just like it, but your husband wants to see more details. If you get to the architect first, tell him that your husband might want to make some changes, and ask him if he'd be prepared to work with you on the project. If it's the construction company, ask them if they could build a duplicate for you," Ava said. "And that's it. That's your job for today, to get me those floor plans."

"You make it sound so easy."

"I don't think it's that hard."

"What if they say no?"

"Amanda, there is no *no*. Tell them whatever the hell you have to tell them. Use all that natural charm you have and never accept the word *no*. If they seem reluctant, come at them from a different direction. Use your imagination, girl. And here," Ava said, pulling something from her other pocket, "is one thousand U.S. dollars. That should be the last resort, but if you have to, use them."

"I wasn't expecting anything like this," she said slowly.

"What did you think, that we're going to Macau for dim sum?"

"I'm not that thick."

Ava realized she was pushing a bit too hard. "I'm sorry, I didn't mean to be insulting."

"Will those people really give me this information?"

"Why not? The story is believable, and if you act as if you believe it and there's something in it for them, why wouldn't they give you some long-forgotten floor plans?"

"Yes, I can see that."

"Good. Now get your game face on while I go and talk to the boys."

Ava stood to leave, only to have Amanda reach up and

grasp her arm. "Ava, why do you need the floor plans, though?"

"Remember what I told you yesterday: one thing at a time. That's what we're doing, all of us here today — one thing at a time, not getting ahead of ourselves. So just go get me those floor plans."

It took less than five minutes to brief Carlo and Andy, and when she was done there were no questions.

When the jetfoil pulled into Macau, Ava held back her group until the swarm of gamblers desperate to give their money away had rushed towards the immigration desks. Andy got stopped at Customs, the officer looking into his carryall at the binoculars and camera, and then waving him through.

"We're leaving you here," Ava said to Carlo and Amanda. "We have to rent a car. You two take separate taxis. Keep in touch by cell."

Carlo nodded and left. Amanda hesitated.

"Scat — you'll do just fine," Ava said, and then turned and walked to the car rental kiosk with Andy in tow.

She wanted something bland and had booked a Toyota Corolla, its only frill a GPS. She typed in Lok's address. The system told her it was twenty-five minutes away, about as long a drive as you could make in Macau.

The system took her over the Friendship Bridge, bypassing the town, onto Avenue Dr. Sun Yat Sen and then onto the Taipa–Coloane Causeway. On her right, the casino complex on the Cotai strip dominated the skyline. She drove south and then cut west past rows of apartment buildings interspersed with strip malls. They skirted Coloane Village and found themselves in rocky, rugged forested country that Ava hadn't known even existed. Their route followed the shoreline, the sea crashing onto rocks about a hundred metres below. They passed signs for Seac Pai Van Park, and the GPS indicated they were getting close. Then they turned off the main road onto a broad dirt track and started down-hill. At the bottom the track veered to the right, and as Ava took the turn the house came into view.

It was, she figured, two hundred metres between her car and the gate to the house — nothing but empty space, a huge dirt courtyard. She stopped the car just short of the clearing. The house was completely isolated, set back against a rock outcropping, with a stand of trees to its right and a mountain face to its left. It was surrounded entirely by a brick wall that had to be five metres high, topped by thin strands of wire; the only visible entrance was the gate, which was made of decorative heavy-duty stainless steel crowned with rolls of razor wire. Her sight-line was unimpeded. If she went any farther the car would surely be seen.

She backed up until the house disappeared from view, and then climbed out. Andy joined her. "We need to find a place where we can get a good secure, uninterrupted look at that house," she said.

"There," Andy said, pointing at the horizon.

Ava looked and saw a statue soaring into the sky.

"That's A-Ma, the goddess of fishermen," he said. "She's standing on top of Coloane Peak. It's a public park. I think we could see the house clearly from the top of the peak, and we could stay there as long as we wanted without raising any questions."

"How do you know that stuff?" she asked.

"My father was a fisherman, and like I said, A-Ma is their goddess. When we were kids, he brought us here every year to pay homage, to pray for good catches and a safe return from the sea."

"How do we get up there?"

"Go back to the main road and head in the direction we were going before we turned off."

"Your father was actually a fisherman?" Ava asked as they got back into the car.

"Yeah. Then he drowned."

If anyone but Andy had told her that, she might not have believed them. "I'm sorry," she said.

They had driven less than a metre along the main road when the first sign appeared for Alto de Coloane Park. Ava turned left and then drove uphill for about two hundred metres. The road ended abruptly and she found herself in a large parking lot, occupied mainly by tourist buses. She pulled into an empty space.

Andy pointed to an exit and said, "We can get to the peak through there."

They began the climb to the A-Ma statue, the surrounding countryside opening up to them with every step. There was a crowd at the top, most of them looking out towards the sea. Ava's interest was in the opposite direction, inland, and she and Andy had that side of the statue to themselves.

She held out her hand and he gave her the binoculars. Ava began to scan in the general direction of the house. When she found it, she was almost able to see through individual windows. "These binoculars are incredible. Where did you get them?" she asked, her eyes not leaving her target.

"A friend who's a birdwatcher," Andy said. "Female birds, the kind that like to undress in apartments that don't have curtains."

"These would be perfect for that."

"So he says."

She zoomed out, trying to get a broader view of the house. There was a main building three storeys high and twenty metres across. It sat at least a hundred metres back from the gate, across a space that was entirely paved in concrete. The building surprised her. She would have expected something traditionally Chinese, but this was a grey stone-block structure. The red tile roof was its only attractive feature. It was built for function, not form, right down to the security cameras she could see bolted into the stone just below the eaves. To the left of the main structure was a one-storey wing with no windows and no visible doors. On the right was a garage, built for six cars. Three vehicles were parked out front: a BMW, a Nissan Pathfinder, and a white van.

"Andy, take a look at the wire that's strung along the top of the wall and tell me what you think it is," she said, giving him the binoculars.

He adjusted the focus, stared down at the house, adjusted it again, and then said, "Electric."

"You're sure?"

"Yeah, I can see the connections leading back to the house."

"Two strands?"

"In some places three, and they're unevenly strung."

"Now take a hard look at the gate. What do you think?"

"It rolls. I can see tracks embedded in the concrete. It

could be electric too," he said, and paused. "And that isn't just razor wire on top. I can see electric wire strung through it."

"Could we force our way through it?"

He stared down, his lips pressed together in concentration. "It would be tough," he finally said.

"Impossible?"

"No, tough. We'd have to blow it, or ram it with something huge, like a truck. Something with serious weight and power."

"Geez, I've seen prisons that weren't as secure."

"Except this place is built to keep people out," Andy said. "Who lives there?"

"Kao Lok."

"Then I'm not that surprised. Until two or three years ago the Macau gangs were constantly at war with each other and at the same time beating off the Hong Kong gangs trying to grab a piece of the action here. There were lots of attacks, ambushes, shootouts."

"Funny, he doesn't have any floodlights I can see."

"With all that other stuff why would he need them?"

All that other stuff indeed, Ava thought. She had figured it wasn't going to be easy, but this was more difficult even than she'd expected. "Andy, we'll take turns with the binoculars." She passed him a piece of paper and a pen. "You can start by writing down the licence plate numbers of those cars. Then I want you to keep track of everyone coming and going from the house. I need to get some idea of how many people are actually in there. Will the camera work from this range?"

"It should, but I'm not a hundred percent sure."

"Take photos anyway, and then note any physical details that are obvious, for backup."

"Okay, boss."

"I'm going downstairs for a coffee. I'll be back in about half an hour. Does this place close?"

"Six o'clock."

There was a small shop off to one side of the parking lot. Ava found a table, ordered a black coffee, and took out her cellphone to call Carlo, who was at Lok's warehouse in Macau. "How's it going?" she asked.

"In the past hour I've seen two trucks make deliveries and about five cars and another truck make pickups of cases of wine. It's a real business."

"How are you so sure?"

"Ava, the place is wide open. They've got three loading docks with the doors pulled up, so I can see inside. It's an open space with cases of wine stacked here and there. I can see one office door and the rest of it is open warehouse."

"Is there a second floor, a basement?"

"I don't think so."

"Go inside. Tell them you want to buy some wine for a restaurant you're opening. Ask to talk to the boss. I'll call you back in a while."

She thought about calling Amanda and then parked the idea. The girl was nervous enough without being harassed. Ava turned off her phone.

She sipped one coffee and then another, watching a steady stream of tourists come and go. The place was a real attraction, the countryside and the shoreline gorgeous. Ava's view of Macau as an urban jungle shifted ever

so slightly, and then she wondered how long it would take
before they ruined it all.

She left the café and climbed the stairs to A-Ma and
Andy. *Maybe the presence of the goddess will protect this
area from the developers*, she thought.

Andy hadn't moved from the spot she'd left him, the
binoculars glued to his eyes. She tapped him on the shoulder. "What do you have?" she asked.

"Two guys came out of the house, got into the van, and
left."

"Who opened the gate?"

"It started to open automatically and then two other guys
came out of the house to push it. It was slow, real slow. That
is one monster of a gate."

"I'll take over now," she said.

"I'll go downstairs for a drink, if you don't mind."

"Take your time," she said.

For half an hour she scanned every inch of the house,
looked in every window, examined and re-examined the
wire and the gate. She saw no movement in the house. The
wire was definitely electric, and Andy was right about how
craftily it had been strung. The gate was beginning to haunt
her. She couldn't see how they could get over it, and going
through it would be a test.

Just as boredom was setting in, the double doors at the
front of the house swung open. Two tall blonde women in
short, clingy dresses appeared in the doorway. Macau was
famous for its Russian hookers, and Ava guessed that's what
they were. A Chinese woman, also dressed for nightclub-
bing, followed. They walked into the courtyard, stopped,
and looked back.

Ava put down the binoculars, picked up the camera, and took a couple of quick shots. She picked up the binoculars again and saw Lok, Wu, and a third man come to the door. Wu's right arm was wrapped in a cast that covered his hand and went all the way to the elbow. The man Ava didn't recognize ran towards the cars. He got into the Nissan and drove over to the women. They waved to Lok and Wu and then climbed in. The car idled in front of the gate as it inched open almost ponderously. *Andy was right again*, Ava thought. *It is a monster.*

She counted slowly to twenty before the gate was fully open. The Nissan sped through. Wu went back into the house while Lok stayed on the doorstep, checking his watch. The gate didn't close. *He's expecting someone*, she thought.

Then she saw the white van appear from the dirt road she'd been on earlier. It rolled across the expanse in front of the house and through the gate. The gate began to close. The van parked by a garage door and two men jumped out and walked towards the house.

As they got closer, Lok took a couple of steps towards them and held out his hand. The man farthest from Ava, who was partially obscured by the other, held out his, and Ava saw a newspaper. She zoomed in as tightly as she could. It was the *South China Morning Post*.

Oh God, she thought, as she checked her watch. It was one fifteen. Lok was supposed to have sent a photo of Simon at noon and she was supposed to have called Michael. She reached for her cell and turned it on. "Michael, it's Ava."

"Shit, Ava, I've been trying to reach you or Amanda for more than half an hour."

"Sorry, my phone was off."

He was in a panic. "I didn't get a photo."

"I'm not surprised."

"What do you mean?"

"Nothing. Go on; have you called Lok?"

"Yeah. When it didn't get here by twelve, I didn't overre-act. I gave it another half hour before I called him."

"What did he say?"

"That he'd been tied up with something and would get it to me before two o'clock."

"Was he apologetic?"

"Are you kidding? Not in the least," he said. "Ava, I'm concerned something has happened to Simon already."

"Relax, Michael. It's entirely possible that Lok was tied up by someone, if not something, else and I'm reasonably sure you will get the photo before two."

"I wish I was as sure."

She could sense him starting to totter again, and won-dered if letting Amanda leave the apartment was such a good idea. "You'll get the photo. Just call me when you do. I won't turn off my cellphone again for the rest of the day."

"I keep thinking about him."

"I understand."

"And when I'm not thinking about him, I'm thinking about the money. Ava, just how the hell are you going to get it, and if you do, how are we ever going to pay it back?"

"Michael, that's the second time you've asked me that question, and my answer hasn't changed. I'm working on some things that may not involve money, or at least that much money. There may be room for negotiation after all, but honestly I don't want to talk about it, especially over the phone. So please, let me do my thing. We have a deadline;

I'm working to it. We can talk when I'm back in Hong Kong."

"You aren't in Hong Kong?" he said.

Geez, why did I say that? she thought. "I'm in China," she half lied. "I have some contacts here that may be helpful. I should be back tomorrow, and I'll call when I do."

He went silent. "Phone me when you get the photo," she said.

She spent the next twenty minutes with the glasses fixed on the house, and saw nothing. When Andy came to relieve her, she said, "I don't know how much more we're going to learn here. We'll give it another half hour or so and then decide if we stay or go."

Michael called as she turned to go back down to the café. "I got the photo. Simon looks okay."

"See, I told you."

"I'm not used to this kind of stress."

"Who is? Look, stay calm. I'll talk to you tomorrow," she called, looking back as she reached the bottom of the hill.

Ava checked her watch and decided to call Carlo. "It is a warehouse, and that's it," he said, sounding bored. "I even got into the office to meet the manager and was given a little tour."

"What are you doing now?"

"Waiting for you."

"We won't be that much longer, I think, and then we'll meet you in Macau. Find a one-hour photo place for me, will you, and phone me with the address. That's where we'll hook up."

She tried Amanda's cell and it went right to voicemail. "Amanda, this is Ava. It's going on two o'clock and Andy and I will be back in Macau probably around three. Hope things are going well. Call me when you can."

Ava downed another coffee and left the café.

Andy was still doing surveillance when she returned to the A-Ma statue. "Anything?" she asked.

"Yeah, there are two more guys I didn't see before. They're in the yard, washing the BMW."

Ava took the binoculars. She didn't recognize them either.

"So, that's five of them at least, plus Lok and Wu. There were two more with them the other day that I haven't seen, so we could be talking nine."

They took turns with the binoculars and the camera, but after the men went inside there wasn't any other activity to record and Ava began to get restless. "How hard is it to find a one-hour photo shop?" she said to Andy.

"What?"

"Never mind."

She waited another ten minutes and then called Carlo. "Haven't you found anything yet?"

"I just did, and it was harder than you think."

"Where is it?"

"Next to the Kingsway Hotel, in Porto Exterior."

"Name?"

"Super Photo."

"We'll be there in less than half an hour."

14

THEY ATE IN A PORTUGUESE RESTAURANT ALMOST directly across the street from the one-hour shop. Ava had dropped off the camera's memory card, offering to pay double if she could get two sets of prints in half an hour. Now she waited, in no mood for chit-chat and her appetite not functioning at its usual level. She picked at the bacalao, took a couple of bites of African chicken, and chewed a couple of slices of bread.

The boys made up for her lack of hunger. Carlo worked as a bookie during the Hong Kong racing season, and Andy loved to play the horses. As they ate, they dissected jockeys, trainers, and the relative merits of post positions at Happy Valley and Sha Tin racetracks. In Hong Kong, horse racing was a national sport. The season lasted only six months, with races on Wednesdays and Sundays, alternating between the two tracks, but when the season was in swing, it was all some people cared about. Every newspaper, every day, was filled with racing news. The television stations covered both the racing and the training sessions.

They worked through a whole loaf of bread and two servings of salted cod and demolished the chicken. She had always admired their ability to remain focused on the moment, whether it involved horse racing, food, or covering her back. They were arguing about whether the South African Douglas Whyte or the Australian Brett Prebble was going to be jockey of the year, at the same time dipping bread from a second loaf into the chicken sauce, when Ava checked her watch and saw that half an hour was up.

"I'll be back," she said.

The clerk saw her coming through the door, gave her a broad smile, and pointed to the envelope on the counter. "They were done ten minutes ago. I should get a bonus," he said.

She opened it. The photos were good, not great, but the faces were distinct enough. "How much do I owe you?"

"At the double rate, three hundred."

Ava paid him and went back across the street to the restaurant. Carlo and Andy had finished lunch and were smoking. She collected the bill from the table, settled it with the cashier, and then said to the boys, "Outside. I can't breathe in here."

She pulled the photos from the envelope and passed a set to Andy. "Not too bad from that distance," he said.

"These are of the three women I saw leaving in the Nissan. Two of them look Russian. I'm sure all three are hookers."

"Home delivery service," Carlo said.

"Whatever. The thing is, I need you to find at least one of them."

"And then what?"

"I want to talk to her."

"How will we arrange that?"

"I'll come to her or you can bring her to me, it doesn't matter."

Carlo frowned.

"What is it?" she asked.

"These girls normally aren't very talkative."

"What do you mean?"

"Whichever one I find first, if I tell her that you just want to talk to her —"

"I'll pay."

"She'll get suspicious as hell, pay or not."

"What do you suggest?"

"I'll just say I want a good fuck and that a friend recommended her to me." He looked across the street. "Take a room at the Kingsway and then phone me with the number. I'll take the girl there. Once she's in the room you can handle her."

Ava nodded. "You seem sure you can find one."

"If they're in Macau, I'll find at least one."

"He knows every mama-san over here," Andy said. "And there isn't a whore who operates without one."

"If I have a choice, I'd prefer the Chinese one."

"Okay, I'll target her first."

"Take Andy with you. I'll call you with the room number as soon as I have it. Now, do you need any money?"

Carlo looked offended. "Hey, I won't have to pay up front."

Ava went to the car and retrieved Andy's carryall, then climbed the ramp to the hotel entrance. The Kingsway was a three-star hotel, part of Stanley Ho's empire. It wasn't so fancy that a hooker going through the lobby would be bothered. Ava didn't think of that until she stood inside the hotel entrance, and wondered if that's why Carlo had suggested it.

She asked for a room on the eighth floor, wanting all the luck she could get. To her surprise one was available, a corner suite. She took it. Calling it a suite was a stretch. There was a sitting room and a separate bedroom, but they were small and, even though sparsely furnished, looked cramped. It was furnished in rattan: a couch and two easy chairs with floral cushions in the sitting room and a double bed and three-drawer dresser. The floors were covered in a pale green carpet that felt and smelled new. Ava walked to the window and looked out. The hotel was in old Macau, near the Porto Exterior, and from her window she had a great view of the old town and the new development around the port. She called Carlo. "The Kingsway, room 808," she said.

"I'll phone when I'm on the way."

She pulled the cover off the bed and fell onto the clean sheets. She thought about napping, and then Amanda popped into her head. Where was that girl?

She tried her cell again and this time Amanda answered. "Ava, I'm just leaving the construction company office and it's very noisy around here. I'll call you back in a minute."

The minute turned into two, and then five. Ava was just beginning to worry when Amanda's name popped up on her phone screen. "Sorry, he wouldn't let me go," Amanda said. "He's spent the past half hour trying to convince me to build another kind of house, and the hour before he drove me all over Macau looking at examples of his work."

"Congratulations — I assume you have the plans."

"Plans? I have plans for four different houses. He made me take all of them to show to my husband."

"Good girl. Any problems?"

"I had to spend a hundred dollars at the registry office."

"Other than that?"

"No. It amazes me; I've spent my whole life being truthful, and I had no idea that people could accept me for something other than who I am."

"Look, we'll talk when we meet," Ava said. "I've taken a room at the Kingsway Hotel, room 808. It's on Rua de Luís Gonzaga Gomes, in old Macau, near the port. Come on over."

"I'm getting in a taxi right now."

Ava lay back on the bed and closed her eyes. They had floor plans, but to what purpose? She thought about the house and inwardly groaned. The only thing the least bit encouraging was its isolation — no neighbours within sight or hopefully within hearing distance. Other than that, it was a son of bitch, a complete son of a bitch.

She dozed, waking with a start at the rapping on the door. She blinked, not sure where she was.

"Ava, it's Amanda."

Ava got up and opened the door. Amanda stood there, a cardboard tube stuck under her arm, construction dust in her hair and coating her shoes. "Here — the fruits of my lies and a hundred dollars," she said.

"Money well spent and lies well told," Ava said.

"Thanks, I think."

"You need to wash," Ava said, reaching for the tube.

"I know, and I'm parched and hungry."

"Those things are easy to fix."

Amanda walked past Ava. "Why did you take a room here?"

"We're waiting for a hooker."

15

THE HOUSE HAD SEVENTEEN ROOMS — NOT COUNTING four and a half bathrooms — each of them neatly designated by the builder, although Ava knew that meant nothing if Lok had decided a den could become a bedroom and a bedroom a den.

The front door led into a foyer. To its right were a dining room and kitchen and to its left a living room and the den. A stairway to the far left ran at an angle to the second floor, where an open mezzanine overlooked the lower level. *Lok probably hired someone to do feng shui,* she thought. There were five bedrooms on the second floor and two full bathrooms.

Also on the left, at one end of the den, was a door that led into the windowless wing Ava had seen from Coloane Peak. The wing had a corridor with four rooms and two full bathrooms on each side. It looked exactly like her old university dormitory, and it seemed to have just the one door, no other way in or out.

The top floor had no details. The diagram showed open space that could be accessed by a small set of stairs at the right side of the second-floor corridor. She checked the date on the drawings and saw they were eight years old. That floor could have been converted into anything.

Amanda sat at the coffee table drinking mango juice and wolfing down a plate of nasi goreng while Ava went over the plans.

The same contractor had built the walls. They were stone, a metre thick and six metres in height — higher than Ava had thought. He'd installed the gate as well, and it had a name: the Citadel Anti-ram Security Gate. Anti-ram. Ava wasn't happy to read that description.

She searched for information on the cameras, the electric wire, and whatever other security measures had been built into the place. There weren't any, which wasn't surprising. She leafed through the documents Amanda had gotten at the registry office to see if a name was recorded there. Again she came up empty. Given what she knew already, she had no doubt that Lok had built in some extras. Finding who had done them wasn't going to be easy, and getting them to share the information was going to be even harder.

Ava had felt Amanda staring at her as she looked at the plans, and she fought to keep her body language neutral.

"Is it what you needed, what you expected?" Amanda asked as Ava rolled up the drawings before putting them back in the tube.

"Exactly. You couldn't have done better."

"So now what?"

"We wait here for a while."

"Why?"

"Carlo and Andy are out looking for another piece of information. I expect to hear from them soon. If you want to go out for a walk or do some shopping, feel free. I'll call you when we're ready to go back to Hong Kong."

"I'll stay here, if you don't mind."

"I don't."

"And I'm tired. Would you mind if I lie down?"

Ava sat at the window, binoculars scanning the street, just killing time. She peeped periodically at Amanda, who seemed to be sleeping. She'd done well, but Ava was beginning to regret involving her. She was accustomed to working with men like Derek, Carlo, and Andy, people who knew her and with whom she didn't have to care how she acted. She didn't want to be constrained by concerns about how Amanda might react to any given situation. She didn't want to be constrained at all.

She saw Carlo before he phoned her. He was two blocks away, the Chinese girl by his side. Andy trailed them, looking around, always attentive. She saw him reach for his phone and smiled. He motioned for Andy and the girl to go ahead while he made his call. Ava focused on the hooker's face: puffy eyes, tired, bored. She'd probably been hauled out of bed by her mama-san. She was wearing jeans and a T-shirt from Hong Kong Disneyland.

"Where are you?" she asked when her phone rang.

"A few blocks from the hotel."

"I think you have the Chinese girl."

"Good guess."

"I bet she's wearing jeans this time of day, right?"

"Yep."

"And a tee?"

"Don't rag me, Ava."

"Disneyland?"

"We'll be there in five minutes," he said, laughing.

"If you have any problems with Security, call me."

"It's the Kingsway, not the Peninsula."

She waited a full five minutes and then went to the door to wait. She'd love for Amanda to sleep through her chat with the hooker. The elevator doors finally opened and the trio meandered towards the room. Ava swung the door open as they got close. The woman saw her, stopped, took two steps back, and said, "I don't do women."

"And I don't want to be done," Ava said.

Carlo grabbed her by the elbow and propelled her forward. "Relax, this isn't what you think."

When they entered the room, Ava opened the bathroom door and guided the woman into it. "Keep quiet — Amanda is sleeping," she said to the boys. "If she wakes, try not to alarm her. And keep her away from the bathroom."

Then she turned to the woman. "Don't be scared. I just need to talk to you."

"What the fuck is this?"

Ava closed the bathroom door, sat on the side of the bathtub, and pointed to the toilet. "Take a seat."

"What the fuck is this?"

"What's your name?"

"Fay."

"Fay, how much did you expect to earn this afternoon?"

"Two thousand Hong Kong."

"I'm going to give you five thousand, and you can keep your clothes on."

The woman looked at the door. "Don't think about it," Ava said. "You don't want to mess with me, and if you somehow made it out there, the boys would take care of you."

"What do you want?"

"Just some information."

"About what? I don't know anything that's worth five thousand."

"You'd be surprised."

"What the fuck is this about?"

"Kao Lok."

The woman raised her eyebrows. "That creep?"

"Yes. Now do you see how easy this is going to be?"

"Five thousand, right?"

"Yes."

"What do you want to know?"

Ava said, "Not so fast. You need to understand the rules first."

"Rules?"

"They're very simple. I'm going to ask you some questions and you're going to give me complete and honest answers. Where it gets tricky is that as far as the rest of the world knows — and that includes mama-san, your girlfriends, your boyfriends — this conversation never took place. No one, and I mean no one, is to hear even a whisper, because if they do, Fay, I'll send the boys next door to find you and punish you."

Fay leaned against the back of the toilet. Through the binoculars at Lok's house, Ava would have guessed she was in her mid-twenties. Up close, her face looked worn, small lines etched into the bags under her eyes, the skin along her jawline beginning to sag. *She's in her mid-thirties for sure,* Ava thought. *Maybe even early forties.*

"Do you mind if I smoke?" the woman asked.

"Actually, I do."

"Then let's get this over with. I know how to keep my mouth shut."

"I saw you leave Lok's this morning. How often have you been there?"

"I can't count."

"That many?"

"I'm a regular. Wu has a thing for me."

"For how long?"

"At least three years."

"Good. Now just wait a minute while I get something," Ava said, standing up.

The woman's eyes grew large, and Ava knew she'd frightened her. "It's a floor plan of Lok's house, that's all," she said.

"The castle, you mean."

"Castle?"

"That's what we call it."

"I'll be right back," Ava said.

Amanda was still sleeping. The two boys stood at the window, Carlo with the binoculars fixed on a smaller hotel across the street. Ava opened the cardboard tube and extracted the floor plans. The boys didn't even turn around as she headed back into the bathroom.

She spread the drawing across the bathroom sink and counter. "Come and look at this, please," she said.

When the woman was right next to her, Ava could smell the mixed remnants of perfume, sweat, and sex. "Couldn't you have showered?"

"I was told to move my ass, so that's what I did."

Ava sighed and passed a pen over the plans. "Okay, this drawing is eight years old. I need you to look at it and tell me if there have been any big changes. For example, there is a kitchen and dining room here on the right — is that still the case?"

"Yeah."

"How about the other side, with the den and living room?"

"It's one big room, that's all. Lots of couches and throw cushions and a huge high-definition television. That's where the guys hang out."

"And here," Ava said, moving the pen to the wing. "This is where some of the guys sleep?"

"Yeah."

"How many?"

"It's always changing. I've seen as few as three and I've seen the entire house filled with them."

"How many is 'filled'?"

"Fourteen, fifteen . . . I'm not sure."

"How many last night?"

"I think there were seven."

"Does that include Lok and Wu?"

"No, just the guys."

"And they all sleep in this wing?"

"Yeah, unless there's an overflow. Then they'll put some of them upstairs, but I know they don't like to do that. One time it happened when I was there and Wu didn't stop bitching about it."

"There are five bedrooms on the second floor. Where do Lok and Wu sleep?"

"Wu is here, the bedroom at the top of the stairs. Lok is at the other end."

"So, three empty bedrooms separating them?"

"No, there are two servants, a husband and wife. They sleep in the middle bedroom."

"Servants?"

"Yeah, they cook and clean. Nice old couple," Fay said, turning towards Ava. A raw odour hit Ava like a hammer.

"You didn't even brush your teeth," Ava said.

"I did, but we ate salty fish last night, and that smell stays with you for days."

"Then breathe away from me," Ava said. She pointed to the third floor. "What's there?"

"I don't know. Never been there, and I've never seen anyone go there."

"There are stairs."

"Yeah, but at the top there's a door, and I've never seen it open."

"When you're in Wu's room, have you ever heard any sounds coming from the floor above?"

"Like what?"

"Footsteps, furniture moving, a television or radio?"

"Never."

"What are the evenings like there? How does everyone spend their time?"

"What do you mean?"

"The other two girls were Russian, right?"

"Yeah."

"Both for Lok?"

"That's what he likes. Big girls, big tits, and always two."

"So how did the five of you spend your evening?"

"We didn't get there until eleven. We sat in the kitchen and had something to eat and drink, and then we went upstairs to fuck. That's it."

"Where were the other guys?"

"In the den, playing cards or mah-jong or whatever and watching TV, like every other time I've been there."

"Do they go to bed early?"

"Midnight is early for those guys."

"So what time do they go to sleep?"

"One, two, three, something like that. Every time I get up to pee it seems like the TV is on."

"How about in the morning — any early risers?"

"Yeah, the husband and wife, that's it."

"How early?"

"I don't know, maybe seven o'clock. I do know that I've gone down earlier to get something to drink and the entire place was empty."

"This is good, Fay," Ava said. "You're being helpful."

"Then can I have a smoke now?"

"No, but we're almost done."

The woman sighed, her breath leaking sideways. Ava almost gagged. "You can sit down, though," Ava said, motioning to the toilet. "Now I want to talk to you about security."

"Security? You've seen the place — how much more secure can it be?"

"Has it always been like that?"

"Since I've been going. The first time I was there I asked Wu about it, and he told me they had a place in Taipa that was attacked by another gang. They lost four men. That's when they moved to Coloane. Better safe than sorry, he said."

"I saw the walls, the wire, the gate. What other security do they have? Is there an alarm system in the house?"

"Yeah, the whole house is wired. There's a keypad at the front door and Wu has one in his room, and you can figure Lok has one in his too."

"Do you know the code?"

"As if."

"It doesn't hurt to ask," Ava said.

Fay gave her a *get real* stare.

"I saw cameras outside the house. Are they working?"

"Yeah, there's a monitor screen in the den and Wu has one in his room."

"What do the cameras record?"

"The courtyard, the front of the house."

"Fay, have the alarms ever gone off while you were in the house?"

"Yeah, a couple of times."

"What was the sound like?"

"A screech, a high-pitched screech."

"Loud enough to wake everyone in the house?"

The woman began to answer and then caught herself. "It's funny you should ask that, because one time when it woke me, I went to the top of the stairs with Wu. One of the girls who'd been with Lok had tried to go outside for some fresh air, so there wasn't any threat or anything. He went downstairs to get her back in the house, close the door, and reset the alarm. It wasn't until he was nearly done that the guys ran in from the wing, so I figure maybe the noise doesn't carry so well there."

"That's interesting."

"And when the alarm was reset, Wu phoned the police."

"He what?"

"He called the cops to tell them everything was okay. He told me the alarm was hooked directly into the police station and that the cops would already be on their way to the house. He said it cost them a fortune to set up that deal, but it was worth every dollar."

Ava couldn't hide the feeling of despair on her face.

"Guess you didn't want to hear that, right?" Fay said.

"No, I didn't."

"Sorry."

Ava took a deep breath, gathering herself. "But I needed to know, and thanks for remembering. So anything else about security you can think of?"

"No, that's about it."

"Then one last thing," Ava said. "When you were there last night, did you see a short man with dyed blond hair?"

"No."

"Did you notice anything out of the ordinary?"

"I don't understand what you're getting at."

Ava paused, unsure about how much she should say. "I think they've kidnapped one of our friends and are holding him hostage," she finally said. "And I think they're holding him in the house. If they are, I'd like to know where in the house. Would you have any idea?"

The woman shook her head. "No, I don't have a clue."

Ava gave her another few seconds, then said, "I'll get your money. You can go now."

"I need to pee first."

"Take your time," Ava said.

Amanda was awake, sitting at the coffee table and sipping another bottle of mango juice. Carlo and Andy had left the window and now sat side by side on the bed facing her, the three of them talking. Ava couldn't begin to imagine what they would have in common to discuss, until she heard the words *Happy Valley* and remembered that Jack Yee owned racehorses.

"We're finished here. I just have to pay the girl and we can leave," Ava said.

She took five U.S. hundred-dollar bills from her jacket pocket. Fay came out of the bathroom and stood at the hotel room door. Ava went to her and counted the money into her hand. "Thanks," Ava said.

"I won't say anything to anyone," Fay said.

Ava nodded and then went back into the room. "Okay, let's collect our stuff and get back to Hong Kong."

The elevator ride to the lobby was animated. Amanda was as much a horse-racing addict as the boys, and she seemed to know her stuff, because they kept asking insider questions and then looking appreciative as she answered them. Ava was pleased to see them distracted, since she was in no mood to chat.

When they got to the lobby, she excused herself and ducked into the business centre. It took her five minutes to find the Citadel Security Company. It was in Zhuhai, and she noted the email address and phone number.

The jetfoils back to Hong Kong ran every fifteen minutes, and at that time of day there were lots of open seats. "I have to make some phone calls, so I'm going to sit alone up at the front," she told them. "I'll come back when I'm done."

The call to Citadel was more difficult than it should have been. She had to argue her way past a receptionist who insisted on taking her number so someone could call her back, then finally got passed along to a man who seemed to have some idea of customer service.

"We're building a pharmaceutical factory in Zhuhai, and security is of pressing concern. We've seen pictures of your anti-ram gate and we think it could work for us. Could you give me some more information on it?"

Ava let him ramble, and when he was finished, she said, "Could you send me that information electronically, and whatever specifications you think I should be aware of?"

"What size gate are you thinking of? That does have a bearing," he said.

She checked her notes. "About six metres across, three metres high."

"That's big."

"We have large trucks coming and going all the time."

"I understand. We've built them that size before, so I'll dig up what I can for you."

"Thanks, I really appreciate it. And tell me, when you say 'anti-ram,' what does that really mean?"

"You could run any car, at any speed, into it and not make a dent."

"I assumed that, but how about a van or a Range Rover, say?"

"You couldn't generate enough impact."

"How about a truck?"

"What kind of truck?"

"Say a semi, fully loaded."

"The gate isn't built to withstand everything; it has its limits. It could repel a large truck, I think, but it would depend a lot on the velocity of the vehicle."

"So a truck could get through?"

"Possibly. Depending on what type, how heavy it was, and what speed it was going when it hit the gate."

"Thanks for this, and here's my email address. Please send me the specs," Ava said.

"Okay, I'll send something through in the next hour."

A lot of good it may do me, Ava thought as she made her second call.

"*Wei.*"

"Uncle, it's Ava."

"How are you?"

"Not terrific."

"Where are you?"

"On the jetfoil coming back to Hong Kong from Macau."

"So, not a good day in Macau?"

"No. Can you meet me for dinner?"

"Of course," he said. "Let's go to the Dynasty hotpot restaurant in Central. I will meet you in your hotel lobby at seven."

16

IT WAS PAST SIX O'CLOCK WHEN SHE GOT BACK TO THE hotel, just enough time to shower and check her emails. The guy at Citadel had already sent the specifications. She downloaded them onto a USB drive to print later at the business centre.

She got to the lobby early but Uncle was already sitting on one of the plush couches, his feet dangling above the ground.

"You look grim," he said, standing.

"It's bad."

He put his arm through hers. "We will talk at the restaurant."

Uncle had called ahead and booked his normal table. There was no host at the front of the restaurant. Uncle walked past the stand and led her directly to the table. Two pots — one spicy, the other milder — were already bubbling away, and a cart laden with trays of food sat alongside.

"I don't have much appetite," she said.

"Eat what you can," he said. "Now I am going to have a beer. Do you want some white wine?"

"Sure."

He waved at the owner, who ran over. "San Miguel and the house white wine. Make sure they are both cold." As they waited for their drinks he began to fill the pots with fish balls, oysters, thin slices of beef, mushrooms, strips of bean curd. He poured soy sauce into her bowl and added mixed green and red chilis.

Their drinks arrived, cold and glistening.

"Before you say anything, you need to know that I made some more phone calls today. I talked to Lok's old Mountain Master twice, asking him to intervene. He finally called me back about an hour ago."

She knew from his demeanour that it hadn't gone well. "Thanks for trying."

"Uncle Tong said you cannot reason with Lok. In his own crazy way he has convinced himself that your brother and his partner really do owe him money. He also told Uncle Tong that the partner started the violence in the restaurant, and that while Wu was trying to calm things, you attacked him from behind."

"That's bull."

"I know, but it shows his state of mind."

"Does Uncle Tong think he'll kill Simon?"

"Yes — pay or don't pay, the result will be the same. He said Lok is really amused that your brother is actually trying to negotiate and seems willing to pay."

Ava plucked a fish ball from the pot. "I have to get him out of there."

Uncle grimaced. "I knew you would say that."

"What choice do I have?"

"I spoke to Andy when he got back. He told me about the house."

Ava gazed into the spicy pot just as a large, plump oyster bobbed to the surface. She offered it to Uncle. "Thank you," he said as she put it on his plate.

"The house is difficult," she said.

"Andy thought it was nearly impossible."

"You can't get over the walls unless you parachute in. They're too high, and the way they've strung the electric wire makes it almost suicidal to try."

"He was as impressed with the gate."

"Well, again, we can't go over it, but maybe we can go through it."

"This is getting overcooked," he said, dipping into the pots with a strainer and putting the food on a separate plate.

"It's stainless steel and it's what the manufacturer calls 'anti-ram,'" Ava said. "But when I talked to them, they weren't so sure that a truck — a big one, obviously, and loaded with something heavy — couldn't force its way through."

"Not so sure? That is not exactly an endorsement."

"I have the gate's specifications. I need time to look at them and to talk to someone who can calculate the probability."

"Ava, I have to tell you that I hate to hear you talking like this. It is not like you to be so...uncertain."

She drained her wine. "I'll have another, please," she said.

Uncle finished his beer and held his bottle in the air. Within a minute, a fresh glass of wine and another bottle of beer were on the table.

"Actually, I'm even more concerned about something other than the gate."

"What is that?"

"The police."

"How so?"

"The alarm system is hooked directly to the police station. Lok evidently has had them on his payroll for years. The alarm goes off, the police show up. And fast. And believe me, the alarm will go off. So even if we can ram our way through the gate, I figure we've only got about ten minutes to neutralize Lok and Wu and somewhere between five and eight other men, find Simon, and get the hell out of there."

"Ava, that is not enough time."

She put a sliver of beef onto the bean curd, rolled them together and dipped them in her sauce. "The food here is always so good. My appetite is starting to return."

"I wish your common sense would."

"Is there any way, you think, that I could take the police out of the equation?"

"Can you find a way to bypass the alarm system?"

"No. The moment we enter the house, or maybe even the property, the alarm is going to sound and the cops will know we're there."

He looked at the food left on the cart. "I think I want some shrimp. Will you share?"

"Sure."

As he ordered, she could see he was distracted. She knew she was upsetting him, and she began to wonder again if his age was starting to erode his confidence. "You obviously have something in mind when it comes to the police," he said.

"I could buy them off."

"And just who would you talk to?" he said sharply.

She shrugged.

"Exactly — you do not know who his connection is. And let me tell you, it is more complex there than it used to be. They created the Macau Security Force in the late 1990s, combining different departments. There is still a Public Security Police Directorate, but you do not know who might make the decision. Even if you have a million Hong Kong dollars to spend, or two million, or three million, you need to find and speak to the right person. One miscommunication and Lok knows everything.

"Then let us suppose you find the right man and you make the offer. What is to stop him from going to Lok anyway? Actually, what is to stop him from cutting a deal with you, taking your money, or part of it, and then betraying you? You could walk into the house, find Lok waiting for you with his small army, and have the police waiting around the corner to finish you off."

"I know it isn't a perfect idea."

"Not perfect? Ava, I have not heard you say anything so silly to me in years."

The owner arrived with a plate of head-on shrimp. Uncle tipped all of them into the spicy pot. "Bring two more drinks," he said.

"I need a way to get to the police," she said.

"You are so stubborn."

"If I can isolate Lok, I'll find a way to get through the gate."

"Ava, listen to me," he said, reaching for her hand. "Lok is a man who, given what he does for a living, has limited *guanxi*. But what *guanxi* he has is tied to the police force. He is Macanese, and so are all of them. They share blood, they share years of mutual trust, and God knows

how complicated and intertwined their financial arrangements are. So trying to separate the police from Lok is, in
my mind, a plan with *disaster* written all over it."

She sat back, her attention on the spicy pot, waiting for
the first shrimp to pop to the surface. "I have three more
days," she said.

Fresh drinks arrived. Her second glass was still half full,
but Uncle downed the rest of his and picked up the third.
She'd never seen him drink so quickly. "That gives you
some time to think, and you need to do that. You need to
think this through better."

A thought that had been nagging her since Uncle mentioned Andy's comments on the house pushed its way
forward. "Uncle, if I do decide to visit Lok's place, can I
count on Carlo and Andy?"

He sighed. "Of course you can. Those two would follow
you anywhere."

"I would need more men than that, though."

He took a shrimp from the pot and put it on her plate.
"Then talk to the boys. Andy has a brother-in-law who is
very handy, and Carlo has some friends he trusts as much
as he trusts Andy. You have to be careful about whom you
choose and how you choose them. You do not want hired
guns who are strangers, because no matter how good they
are, there always comes a point when a decision has to be
made between them and you. The loyalty that the boys
have to you is absolute, you should know that. You cannot
expect anyone else to match that, but if they are as loyal to
Carlo and Andy as the boys are to you, that is enough."

"I'm not ready to talk to anyone yet. You're right, I need
to think this through a bit better."

"Good girl."

"But, Uncle, I'm telling you, I can't sit back and do nothing."

"I understand. Take some time; let that active imagination of yours see what it can come up with."

When they had finished dinner, he walked her back to the hotel, his steps a bit unsteady. She didn't like it when he drank too much, when he lost even a small amount of the self-control she so much admired. She was thinking that she should get in a taxi with him and ride back to Kowloon when she saw Sonny standing by the car in front of the hotel. She kissed Uncle on the cheek and passed him to Sonny.

Ava stopped at the business centre and printed the specifications for the gate. She glanced at them as she rode the elevator to the twenty-third floor, and saw that they were beyond her comprehension. *Maybe it's the wine*, she thought. *They'll be clearer in the morning.*

She undressed quickly, pulled on a clean T-shirt, turned on the television, took two cognacs from the mini-bar, and crawled into bed. A Hong Kong variety show was on, an endless parade of singers interspersed with comedy sketches that were broad, coarse. It was mindless entertainment, exactly what she needed, and she even had a laugh or two.

She downed the two cognacs quickly and was about to raid the mini-bar again when Eric Tsang, the chubby little actor from *Infernal Affairs*, came on the screen. He reminded her of Simon To. His hair had been dyed blond for the film and was now black again. She felt a tear on her cheek and wiped it away with a rough stroke of her hand.

17

HER FATHER HAD RETURNED TO HER DREAMS. THEY were alone, stuck in the middle of a city that neither of them recognized. They needed help — she wasn't sure why — and he asked Ava to try to call someone on her cell. She tried and tried and kept failing, every time hitting a wrong key, missing a number, dialling the wrong area code, while her father became increasingly frustrated and angry with her.

She woke with a start, happy to get away from him. It was nearly six o'clock, and she thought about rolling over and going back to sleep, except that her mind was already churning and she knew she wouldn't be able to drift off again.

She had turned off her cellphone the night before when she went to dinner with Uncle, and now she turned it on. Her brother had called twice; so had her father and her mother as well. She could only imagine the kind of conversations between Michael and her father that would have brought her mother into the picture.

It was early evening in Toronto, too early for dinner, so Ava called the house. "Ava, I'm so glad you called," Jennie Lee said.

"What's going on?"

"I should be asking that question."

"Why?"

"Daddy has been talking to Michael, and he's so worried that he wants to cut short his stay here and fly back to Hong Kong."

"What is Michael telling him?"

"Nothing, that's the problem. He just keeps saying not to worry, that things are getting worked out, except when Daddy asks what's getting worked out, Michael doesn't give him a straight answer."

"Mummy, tell Daddy there is no reason for him to come to Hong Kong. There's a business dispute and that's all. I'm working on it with Michael and I think we'll have it resolved in a day or two. Now listen to me. I don't want to discuss this with Daddy myself. Michael and I are working as a team, and I don't want him to think that I went behind his back to Daddy, and I'm sure that's why he hasn't gone to Daddy himself. So just tell Daddy that the two kids are on the same page and that he has to step back and let us work out this problem on our own."

"Is that true?"

"Mummy, stop it."

"Okay, I'll talk to Daddy."

"Love you."

"Love you too."

Ava made herself an instant coffee and then went to get the newspapers that were at the door. Her mother would handle Marcus, and Michael could wait.

She scanned the *Tribune* and the *Morning Post*, had another coffee, and then headed for the bathroom. *I'm stalling*, she thought. *I'm not ready to start thinking about Simon To again.*

Showered and dressed in a black Giordano T-shirt and Adidas track pants, she sat at the computer and logged into her email. She had cheery messages from Mimi and Maria, and she wondered how it could be so easy for them to be happy. She felt a touch of jealousy, and then guilt for feeling that way. It wasn't their fault they were happy.

As she worked at the computer, she kept glancing at the gate specifications next to her on the table. She was about to reach for them when her cellphone rang and Uncle's name appeared on the screen.

"I hope I did not wake you," he said.

"No, I've been up for a while, and in fact I've been waiting for a chance to call you."

"Me too, I have been waiting," he said. "Do you want to meet me for congee?"

"Sure."

"There is a place next to the McDonald's near Ocean Terminal, the one just off the Tsim Sha Tsui Star Ferry terminal. How soon can you be there?"

"Half an hour."

She took the specifications with her, intending to look at them on the ferry, but it was such a beautiful morning she spent the ten-minute trip looking at the sun rising over Kowloon on one side and illuminating the Hong Kong skyline on the other.

As usual, Uncle was already sipping tea when she walked into the restaurant. She kissed him on the forehead and then sat down across from him. "Let us order. I am very hungry this morning," he said.

Ava's mother made congee — rice porridge — nearly every morning. There were many ways to eat it — with salted duck eggs, bamboo shoots, pickled tofu — but Ava's mother liked to add just white pepper and a touch of soy sauce, and they always had a plate of *you tiao* — fried bread sticks — for dipping. And that is what Ava ordered, along with a coffee, which she knew would be instant. Uncle added an order of salted duck eggs.

"I spoke to the Wongs in Wuhan last night," he said when the waitress left.

"Why?"

"I could not sleep."

"So you called Wuhan? I didn't realize you had become such friends."

He looked across the table at her. "I could not sleep because I kept thinking about your problem in Macau, and about how I could help. There was a time, when I was chairman, when being chairman meant something, that I could have picked up the phone, made one call, and your problem would have disappeared. Those days are gone. But it occurred to me that maybe there was one person who could still make that kind of call."

"Wong Changxing?"

"No. I spoke to May Ling."

"Uncle, please —"

"No, Ava, you need to listen to me. You are a practical girl. Now be practical."

She knew he was right. "Okay, go on."

"Now, I did not know for sure if May could help or not until I explained the situation to her. So I told her everything."

"Everything?"

"Yes, absolutely everything. This is not a woman you keep secrets from when you are asking her for help. Besides, there is not much she has not seen or done…as you know. So I told her everything, including the fact that I thought you were determined to go ahead regardless of the danger. Her reaction was very calm. She said she thought she might be able to do something but she would need to make some phone calls. I told her to call me in the morning, and she said no, she would make the calls right away. She called me back in less than half an hour," Uncle said. "I told you, Ava, the woman has *guanxi.*"

"She has connections to the triad? How is that possible?"

"It is not possible. I have told you, no one can control that anymore."

"So who did she talk to?"

"Her friend the General. The one we met at the house in Wuhan. He spoke to a friend, another general — they are old classmates."

"I don't understand."

"Macau is a Special Administrative Region and has a certain autonomy, like Hong Kong, from China. But when it comes to matters of foreign affairs and defence, those are run by the Chinese. A senior general attached to the Guangzhou Military Region, which controls Macau, is the friend of a friend."

"What are you saying?"

"Your problem with the police — I think he can make it disappear."

"How?"

"The Security Force and the directorates are paramilitary, and when all is said and done, they know who they are accountable to, and they are smart enough to know who to be most afraid of. They will not say no to a very specific and, on the surface, very minor request from the General. At the end of the day he is the boss, and when the boss asks for a personal favour, they are going to say yes."

"What favour?"

"That they stand off, ignore any alarm that comes from Lok's house."

"The General told May Ling he could make that happen?"

"He did."

"Couldn't he do more? Couldn't he tell them to go in and get Simon?"

"You are always so quick," Uncle said with a little smile. "I asked the very same question, but it gets complicated. The General does not mind telling them to stand off for a few days, but he does not want to attach himself directly to what is basically a local police issue. There are rings within rings here, Ava. How many other gangs are the police tied into? If they move on Lok, what will happen to the trust they have built with the others? How much are the police kicking back to the army? The General wants to help May, but he is not about to piss off the Security Force and cut off his own cash flow."

"How long would they stand off?"

"Ask for as much time as you want."

"That might mean I have to tell them when I'm going in."

"Does that worry you?"

"People gossip. It wouldn't take very much for some cop to give Lok a heads-up."

Their food arrived and both of them went quiet. It wasn't until the waiter was out of hearing range that Uncle continued. "Discuss that with the General when you meet him."

"Meet him?"

"This cannot to be finalized over the phone. May is going to have to meet with him, and I just assumed you would want to be there."

"Uncle, I haven't agreed to this."

"No, but you will," he said. "Now look, our food is here and will quickly get cold. Let us eat."

They ate in silence. Ava concentrated on her congee, only looking away from it when she reached for more fried bread. Occasionally she caught Uncle glancing at her, a little smile playing across his face. The truth was, she wasn't the least bit unhappy. Her mind was racing again. If the alarm problem disappeared, the only other major obstacle was the gate.

"I want the help. What do I have to do to make it happen?" she asked as their bowls were cleared.

"Call May Ling."

"And what do I say to her?"

"'Thank you.'"

"Could you please call her for me on your phone?" she said.

For a man who had lived in the same Kowloon apartment for more than forty years, employed the same Filipina housekeeper for more than thirty, and owned the same television for more than twenty, Uncle was surprisingly up-to-date with his mobile — even though it was an Eye Phone rather than an iPhone and had cost him only fifty dollars at a Kowloon night-market stall.

"May, this is Uncle," he began. "Yes, she is here with me and I have explained about the generals." He looked at Ava.

"I am going to pass the phone to her now."

"Hello, May Ling," Ava said, taking the phone.

There was a long hesitation from Wuhan. When May Ling spoke, her voice had a tiny tremor in it. "Ava, is everything going to be okay between us now?"

"I think there is that chance," Ava said slowly.

She saw the glance Uncle shot at her and ignored him. She wasn't about to concede everything, not yet.

"This problem you have — General Feng can help."

"If he can, I won't be able to thank him enough, and I won't be able to thank you enough."

"Uncle said you have a tight time frame."

"Two days, maybe three."

"Then we need to meet with him as quickly as we can. I spoke to him this morning and he's at the garrison in Guangzhou, but he's prepared to meet with us in Zhuhai. I'm holding a reservation on the eleven o'clock flight to Hong Kong. How long would it take us to get to Zhuhai from there?"

She's booked a flight already. Am I that easy to predict? Ava thought. "It's right next door to Macau, so maybe no more than two or three hours from the time you land."

"If I schedule a meeting for four?"

"That should work."

"I'll call him now and phone you back to confirm. I can call your mobile, yes?"

"I'm going to be tied up this morning. I'd prefer if you could call Uncle. Please."

She handed the phone back to Uncle. "May, how are you arriving?" he asked. He listened and then said, "I will meet you at Chek Lap Kok and I will reserve a helicopter at the ferry terminal...I agree, the sooner we get the two of you to Zhuhai the better."

Ava stood as if to leave, triggering a look of concern on his face. *I have to use the restroom*, she mouthed.

When she returned, he was still on the phone, and she wondered what more he might have to say to May Ling. He saw the question in her eyes and covered the mouthpiece. "I am talking to Carlo," he said.

She waited until he had finished and then asked, "What was that about?"

"I told him you were going to need more help, and to contact his friends and have them on standby. I told Andy the same thing about his brother-in-law. I said you would call them later, once you had a schedule in mind."

"Thanks. How much do I pay them?"

"Five thousand each per day, with maybe some kind of bonus thrown in if things go well. You should pay Carlo and Andy a bit extra, for having brought the others on board."

"Will I have to supply them with anything?"

"Weapons?"

"Yes."

"They will have their own."

"How will we get them to Macau? We can't carry them on a ferry."

"Give Carlo that job; he will figure it out. But make sure he does it as early as possible. You want to know that everything you need is there before you leave Hong Kong."

"I'll need something for myself."

"What do you want?"

"A nine-millimetre pistol. A Kahr if you can get it."

"I'll look after it today."

Her attention wandered as she began to make a mental list of everything that needed to get done, and as she did, it seemed to her the time frame might be too tight. She didn't even have a plan yet, just some rough ideas, and she couldn't brief the men without a concrete strategy. Then there was the gate. She was going to need a truck and a driver, and she didn't have a clue about what to get or where or how to go about it. *Michael is going to have to ask for an extension*, she thought.

"Do you want to go to the airport with me to meet May?" Uncle asked.

"No, I don't have that kind of time. Besides, I don't intend to suck up to her. I'll meet her at the ferry terminal. You can call me when she gets in and confirm what time the helicopter will leave."

He shrugged, and Ava could tell he wasn't pleased with her remark about May Ling. "I'll be polite enough when I see her," she added.

"So now what are you going to do?"

"I hardly know where to start. I need to sit down and make some notes and get myself organized."

"Then go and do that. May's flight should be in at one. I will call from the airport and we will arrange to meet at the ferry terminal."

"Uncle, I can't thank you enough for all of this."

He pressed the palms of his hands together and raised them, the tips of his fingers resting against his lips. His eyes searched her face. "I wish so much that none of it was necessary."

"I don't know what else can be done."

"Ava, you do understand that Lok and Wu are not men who capitulate. Even if you surprise them, even if by chance you outnumber them, their initial reaction to any threat will be violent."

"I have assumed that."

"And Ava, if you are successful, and if you can do it without a bloodbath — have you given any thought about what you are going to do with the two of them?"

"No," she said softly.

"It is something that needs consideration. These are not men who forget."

18

IT WAS RUSH HOUR AND THE STAR FERRY WAS AS crowded as an MTR train. She couldn't find a seat and found herself wedged against an outside rail, barely able to turn her head to look at the skyline. Time was beginning to weigh on her, and she was annoyed that she hadn't been more precise with Michael in pinning down what the four days he had negotiated actually meant. Was Lok counting from the day of the call? If he was, they were already into the third. Talking to Michael moved to the top of her must-do list.

Then there was the gate, and the truck. She'd have to talk to the guy at Citadel again, try to pry more information out of him. Then it occurred to her — he was in Zhuhai. She could go to see him.

When she got to her room, she went directly to the desk, opened her notebook, and began writing. As she did, she realized just how ill-formed her earlier thought process had been. Removing the cops from the scene made all the difference in the world. What it came down to was her ability to organize a plan properly, to control it, to take as many elements of luck out of it as she could.

She called Michael at the apartment. He sounded tired, depressed. Without offering explanation she said, "I need you to talk to Lok today. Wait until you get the photo, then call him and tell him you need to start making arrangements for exchanging the money for Simon. Ask him if he has a place in mind. He'll try to tell you that he'll release Simon once he has the funds. Tell him that won't do. You want to make an actual physical exchange, and you insist that it happen in a public place."

"Ava, you have the money?" he asked, brightening.

"We'll talk about that later. Just concentrate on what I'm telling you now. I expect Lok will fudge it, say that he needs time to think about it, and that's fine. What I really want to do is fix the day, the time. Today is Wednesday. For us the ideal situation would be to do it on Saturday afternoon. So tell him you want to do it Saturday and see if you can get him to buy in to that. If you can't, then it has to be Friday. And Michael, it cannot — I repeat, cannot — be any sooner than Friday afternoon, because I don't think I'll have control of the money until then."

"I think Friday is what we agreed to anyway," he said.

"But get me one more day if you can."

"I'll do my best."

"Now, you don't fix the location until you fix the day. I think the lobby of one of the new hotels would be perfect, so suggest the Four Seasons or the Venetian, someplace with good internal security."

"All right. If he's getting his blood money, he shouldn't care."

"Good. Now, I'm at the hotel this morning and then I have to go to China this afternoon, but I'll be back tonight.

Call me on my cell the moment you have a day for me. Now let me talk to Amanda."

"She's not here; she went to work. She wanted to stay but I sort of pushed her out the door. Call her mobile."

Ava called her number. Amanda picked up right away. "I was hoping you'd call."

"How are you doing?"

"I'm okay. Michael is a bit droopy, and I was worried about you last night — you seemed down."

"Last night was last night. Do you have time to do something for me today?"

"I'll make the time."

"Where are you now?"

"I'm at the office."

"Later I'd like you to drop by the concierge desk at the Mandarin and pick up the floor plans. I'll have left them there. Take them to a print shop and get them blown up as big as you can. Then find a map of Coloane, as detailed as possible, and blow up the entire southern area. Concentrate on Coloane Peak and everything around it."

"Then what?"

"Bring them to me first thing tomorrow morning at the hotel."

"Will do."

Ava hung up and dialled Carlo's number. He sounded as tired as Michael, though she guessed it wasn't from stress. "Uncle said he talked to you," she said.

"My two friends are in already."

"They don't know what I'm paying."

"They don't need to."

"Everyone has weapons, right?"

"How much firepower do you think we're going to need?"

"As much as they have and can carry, and they're going to have to move quickly, so take that into account."

"All right."

"Carlo, Uncle said you could get everything we need to Macau ahead of time. Can you?"

"Yeah, sure. I have a cousin who's a day-boat fisherman. He's constantly back and forth between here and there. He can take the stuff over, no problem."

"I'd like to get it there tomorrow and then have him wait for us to arrive. That might take another day or two. Will he be okay with that? I mean, I'll pay him whatever he wants."

"It's better than fishing for a living."

Ava checked her notes. "You'll need to round up the weapons today, then, and get them to your cousin. Uncle said Andy and his brother-in-law are in as well, so you need to touch base with him. Organize it from his end. And Uncle's getting a gun for me and said he'd have it today. I'm going to be in China for most of the afternoon and early evening, so I need to leave it to you to collect it for me."

"No problem."

"Tomorrow we're going to have to meet — all of us, I mean — to go over the plan. I have to find a place and set a time. I'll call you when I know, and then you can give the other guys and Andy a heads-up. Just make sure everyone leaves the next two to three days completely open. And let them know I'm paying as of today. I'll guarantee at least four days' work at five thousand a day for the men, and ten thousand a day for you and Andy."

"That's too much."

She ignored him, her attention focused on the notebook, certain she had forgotten to tell him something. And there it was. "We'll need a ram for the front doors. They're wooden."

"I have a Cobra ram. It can open any wood door in about five seconds."

"Give that to your cousin as well, and throw in a large crowbar, a dozen sets of handcuffs, and a couple of rolls of duct tape."

"With the ram, we won't need the crowbar."

"Add one anyway."

The line went quiet, and Ava wondered if Carlo had hung up on her. "Hey, you still there?" she asked.

"I was just writing things down, and I don't write that fast," he said.

"Take your time."

"Okay, I'm done," he finally said. "I'll get on this stuff right away, and you won't hear from me unless I have a problem."

"That's the way I like it."

"And, Ava," he said carefully, "Andy was a bit nervous yesterday when we talked about this job. If you hadn't been involved, we might have backed out. You didn't seem too hot to trot either, to be honest. But you seem more upbeat today. Did something happen?"

"Yes. I went from thinking this might work to thinking this will definitely fucking work."

"I'll let Andy know."

"I appreciate that, and everything else." She closed the phone.

Ava stood up, walked to the window, and stretched. It was a glorious day. Victoria Harbour was as beautiful as she had ever seen it. She checked her watch and calculated whether she had time to squeeze in a quick run in the park. It would be cutting it close, but all she had left to do was call the Citadel Company in Zhuhai, and then it would be a matter of waiting and thinking. Then her phone rang.

"May just called me from the Wuhan airport," Uncle said. "She got an earlier flight, so she will be in by noon."

"That's good. Phone me when you pick her up and I'll head over to the Macau ferry terminal."

"I did reserve a helicopter. Go directly to that wing and we will meet you there."

So much for a run, she thought as she called Zhuhai. "I got the specifications, thank you, but I'm not exactly technical and I'm having some problems understanding them. Fortunately I'm going to be in Zhuhai this afternoon, and I'm wondering if I could drop in to go over them with you. Where is your office?"

"We're in the Hi-Tech Industrial Development Zone, but I'm afraid dropping in may not be possible. We have a very strict company policy about visitors."

"Our chairwoman is going to be with me — Wong May Ling, the wife of Wong Changxiang. I'm sure you've heard of them."

"Who hasn't heard of him? He is the man behind your project?"

"Yes."

"I'll talk to my boss. Let's see if he'll agree."

"You can also tell him that Madam Wong is in Zhuhai to meet with General Feng from the Guangzhou Military Region headquarters. Ask your boss if he needs a recommendation from the General, because if he does, we'll get it."

"You know what, I'll talk to my boss, but I think it will be okay for you to visit. Let's just plan on it, shall we?"

"Somewhere between three and four?"

"My name is Su, I am director of sales. You are Ms. Lee, right? I'll leave passes for you and Madam Wong at the security entrance."

Guanxi, Ava thought as she hung up.

19

AVA STOOD TO ONE SIDE OF THE ENTRANCE TO THE
helipad. There was hardly a customer in sight, a situation
that would change when it got to Friday and the gamblers
were anxious to make an early start.

She wore her best professional clothes: black linen slacks,
pink Brooks Brothers shirt with modified Italian collar,
crocodile stilettos; her hair was pulled back and secured
with her lucky ivory chignon pin. She wore as little makeup
as she could without looking washed out, just a touch of
red lipstick and some black mascara. When she had met
May Ling in Wuhan, the older woman had worn no jewellery, and Ava had mimicked her there. But not today — she
had her gold crucifix around her neck and her Cartier Tank
Française watch on her wrist. By Hong Kong princess stan-
dards, she looked almost like a pauper.

They appeared at the farthest end of the terminal,
walking slowly side by side. Ava tried to figure out who
was keeping up with whom. Uncle was in his black suit
and open-necked white shirt. May Ling shone in the
same pink and white Chanel skirt and jacket she'd worn

when Ava met her for the first time in Wuhan. Was that deliberate? In any event, she looked stunning, and she walked gracefully, erect but flowing, without an iota of self-consciousness. Ava had never seen anyone so elegant and so intimidating at the same time. As she worked her way towards the gate, Ava noticed the attention May was drawing. There wasn't a man she walked past who didn't stop, turn, and stare.

Ava stepped forward so that she would be visible. Uncle gave a little wave, May a tentative smile. *This is too awkward*, Ava thought. She walked towards them, more purposeful than graceful, but drawing her own share of attention.

May Ling held out her hand. Ava moved past it, slipped her hand around May's waist, and leaned forward to kiss her on the cheek. "Thanks for coming," she said.

May was flustered. Uncle beamed. "You know what everyone is thinking? 'What is that old man doing with the two most beautiful women in Hong Kong?'"

"The helicopter is leaving in five minutes. We'd better board," Ava said.

"How long is the flight?" asked May.

"About fifteen minutes."

"I called the General from the car. He's sent someone to meet us at the Macau terminal and drive us to Zhuhai," May said, calmer now.

"We have to go now," Ava said to Uncle.

He stepped between them and then kissed each of them on the cheek. "Good luck."

They were the only two passengers on the helicopter, and Ava thought that would give them a chance to talk. But as soon as the rotors kicked in, she knew she'd have to yell to be heard. May spent the flight looking out the window and occasionally glancing at Ava.

Ava remembered how anxious May had been in Wuhan, her eyes dull with worry, the skin around her mouth etched with lines. Now her face had taken on a younger, vibrant look. Her eyes were black orbs in a sea of pearl white, her skin taut, not a line, not a sag. She was in her forties at least, maybe even fifties, but if Ava had been paid to guess, she would have said late thirties.

There was one more obvious difference from Wuhan — her jewellery. May wore diamond stud earrings that had to be a carat each, a Movado watch with a large diamond at the twelve-o'clock mark, a ring with the largest diamond Ava had ever seen, and a delicate white nephrite jade bracelet. It was the bracelet that really caught Ava's attention. The jade had been carved into small round beads that were separated by slivers of what looked like platinum. Ava knew the bracelet was rare, and probably old. It was so Chinese — if you had the taste to want it and the money to acquire it.

Macau appeared on the horizon and Ava braced as the helicopter began to descend. As it did she felt a rush of anxiety. An awful lot — perhaps too much — depended on one woman's *guanxi*. She glanced at May Ling. Her face was completely impassive.

As they disembarked, Ava couldn't help saying, "You're wearing jewellery today."

"In Wuhan I don't have to impress anyone. When I travel, I have an image, there are expectations, and I don't like to disappoint," she said.

What looked like an army officer stood at the entrance to the helipad. He opened the door for them and then stepped back. "I'm Captain Kuo. General Feng sent me to meet you."

"A pleasure, Captain," May said.

"The car is outside. Please follow me."

"How about Customs and Immigration?"

"No need."

The two women slid into the back seat of the Lexus and the captain sat up front with the driver. "We're going to meet the General at a restaurant. He thought, given the time, that lunch would be appropriate."

"Wonderful," said May.

The car took what to Ava was now a familiar route over the Friendship Bridge to Taipa and the causeway to Coloane. But instead of turning west towards the park, they went east. The Barrier Gate, the entrance to China proper, was in the distance. There was a lineup of buses, trucks, and cars that Ava knew would take hours to clear the border. She was thinking that they would be late for lunch when the driver pulled the Lexus to the far right and drove along the shoulder until they reached a lane marked RESTRICTED, which led to a guard booth. Ava reached into her bag for her passport. The captain looked back at her and said, "No need." The car drove through, the driver waving at the guard.

The two women hardly talked during the drive. Ava was comfortable with silence, and it seemed to her that May was as well.

Ava hadn't been to Zhuhai. She knew it was the second of the Special Economic Zones set up by the Chinese government, hard on the heels of Shenzhen. But whereas Shenzhen had gone from being a town of twenty thousand to a city of ten million in twenty-five years — visually, culturally, and environmentally representing everything ugly about uncontrolled growth — Zhuhai had barely grown at all. Its population was just over one million, and it was more of a sleepy tourist destination than a boomtown.

They were somewhere near the centre of the city when Ava's phone rang.

"I spoke to Lok," Michael said.

"And?"

"We'll make the exchange Friday afternoon, and he's agreed to the Venetian."

"You couldn't get Saturday?"

"Ava, he blew up at me. He said the original deadline was Thursday. I had to argue with him for ten minutes to get him to agree to Friday."

"I wasn't being critical, Michael. Friday will just have to work."

"It wasn't easy."

"I believe you."

"And I got Simon's photo. Physically he looks fine, just completely depressed."

"That's natural enough."

"Ava, the money?"

"I'll get the money," she said sharply.

"And the exchange — I have no idea how something like that will work."

"Don't sweat it. We'll meet Friday morning and go over everything in detail. Did Lok say how he wanted the money?"

"No, actually he didn't."

"He will, if not today, then tomorrow. Knowing him, he'll ask for cash. Tell him that's difficult — we'd need about four suitcases — and ask if he'll go along with a certified cheque."

"What if he insists on cash?"

"Then we'll find a way to do it. At least carrying a bunch of suitcases into a hotel lobby won't look strange."

"God, this is so complicated."

"Michael, relax. Friday will be here before you know it and then this will be over."

May threw her a quizzical glance. "My brother," Ava said, as she put away her phone.

"He doesn't know what your plans are?" May asked.

"No. He's not much of a liar and he has to handle communication with Lok. I decided it would be better if he really believed we were going to pay."

"Sounds like he needs his hand held."

"Sometimes."

"Typical. I mean, typical for a man."

"This restaurant is very famous for its dim sum," the captain interrupted as they drove past signs saying they were headed towards the Pearl River.

When they pulled up in front, they saw that the lineup had spilled onto South Lovers' Lane. *Is there a North Lovers' Lane?* Ava wondered. *How about a West and an East?* The captain led them past the throng and towards an army of hostesses. "The ladies are joining General Feng," he said to the only woman in a cheongsam. And then he turned to May and said, "I'll be waiting in the car."

The restaurant was enormous, with a seating capacity of about two thousand. The hostess guided them through seating area after seating area to a section at the rear that had four private dining rooms. She knocked and waited. "Come in," a voice said.

General Feng sat at the table with another young officer. They both leapt to their feet to greet the women. "Madam Wong, a pleasure," he said. "This is Lieutenant Chao, my personal assistant."

"And this is Ava Lee, my associate," May said.

There was a brisk round of bowing and then they settled into their chairs, the General pouring the first round of tea. "General Zhao sends his regards," said May.

"We were classmates and have been good friends and colleagues for thirty years," Feng said.

There was a knock at the door and two servers came in, followed by a host in a tuxedo. "I hope you don't mind, I ordered two specialties of the house — a soup made from black chicken and steamed squilla. The squilla is a particular favourite of mine."

As the host ladled soup and portioned out the shrimp, Feng and May made small talk about Zhao. The host hovered as they tasted the soup. "It's wonderful," May said.

"Good, and now we'll order some dim sum. Any preferences?"

"Order whatever you want, General. I trust your judgement," May said.

When the staff had left, the room grew quiet as the soup and the squilla were shown due respect. May finished first; she had eaten only half of what she had been served. "General, our friend Zhao tells me you have a son studying in Shanghai," she said.

"Yes, my only child, a fine young man. He has decided that economics and business are for him."

"He is an undergraduate?"

"Yes."

"And how is he doing at school?"

"His marks are outstanding."

"I don't know if Zhao has told you or not, but our company is always on the lookout for bright young graduates with an interest in business."

"Well, that is my son's interest."

"And what are his plans after Shanghai?"

"He wants to go to business school in Australia, maybe Canada."

"Would he consider the United States?"

"Why not?"

"I ask because our company has a relationship with the Stanford School of Business: we put one student a year into their post-graduate program. We pay the tuition fees and all their other expenses for as long as they are there. Of course, they have to commit to working at our company for at least two years after graduating. We naturally put them into a management position right away — the fast track — and then it's up to them how far they progress. Not many of them ever leave our company."

"That sounds very interesting," Feng said.

"I wonder if you could mention this to your son."

"I'd be pleased to."

"You would be doing me a favour. Young men like him are our future."

"I'll be sure to do that, you can count on it."

"Here," May said, taking a business card from her purse. "Tell him to contact me directly. My personal number is there, and my email address."

The first wave of dim sum arrived — chicken feet, har gow, and fried octopus.

"Now, Zhao tells me that you ladies have a small problem you need some help with," Feng said as he held a slippery chicken foot an inch from his mouth.

"I'd like Ava to explain," May said.

Ava sipped tea, watching Feng suck the skin and meat from one foot and then another, a small pile of bones growing on his plate. When she thought he was done, she said, "There's a house in Coloane owned by a man named Kao Lok. We're in the middle of a commercial dispute with him." She paused. "Just how candid can I be?"

"Zhao told me the basics. I need to know the specifics."

Ava passed a slip of paper to Feng. He looked at it and then slid it to Chao. "That is the address of the house. It has an alarm system that's connected to the police force. I need the police to either ignore any alarm or disarm the alarm at their end for a few days."

"When?"

"Say, starting tomorrow until Saturday night."

Feng said to Chao, "A lot of the hotels, bigger businesses, and influential people on that side get the same service from the police. I find it offensive that they should get such preferential treatment."

"Yes, sir," Chao said.

"Is that all you want?" Feng said.

"Yes, General," said Ava. "But it's really important that this be kept confidential. We don't want the resident informed that this has happened."

"Call Chu," Feng said to his assistant, and then turned to May. "How do you find the food?"

"Excellent, really excellent."

Chao called from the table. He asked for Chu and then

waited for several minutes, his impatience becoming increasingly apparent. *These men are used to getting what they want when they want it*, Ava thought. Finally he said into the phone, "Just a moment, General Feng wants to speak to you."

Feng took the phone. "Excuse me, ladies, I need to go outside."

He was gone for no more than five minutes. When he returned, he gave the phone to Chao and said to May Ling, "The alarm will be disconnected at the police end today. You have until Sunday."

"Thank you."

"If there is any problem, you call me. And if you can't get me, call Chao. He'll find me."

"Thank you again."

"Any friend of Zhao is my friend."

May finally bit into her har gow. "Tell me about your wife, General. Zhao has so many nice things to say about her."

For the next twenty minutes Ava watched as two masters of small talk kept each other occupied. Chao just listened as well, once in a while stealing a glance at Ava, his attention on her chest.

Five minutes after the last of the food had been consumed, Feng looked at his watch. "You have to excuse me now, ladies. I have to head back to the garrison. Kuo is waiting outside to drive you back to Macau."

"Excuse me, General, but is it possible he could make a short stop on the way? There's a company in Zhuhai we'd like to visit," Ava said.

"Of course, we'll let him know."

They all stood and exchanged bows, but this time the General and May Ling also shook hands. Ava and May left the room first, walking side by side through the restaurant.

"That was wonderful. Thank you," Ava said.

May Ling smiled.

"That Stanford program is really progressive on your part."

"We don't have a Stanford program. Or at least, we didn't until now," May said. "I spoke to Feng last night. He has one child, the son, and he loves him madly. The son wants to go to Stanford, and even on a general's salary Feng can't afford that. We'll make it possible. I just hope the boy isn't an idiot."

"But then why — ?"

"Why come here?"

"Yes."

"That little bit of theatre was for the benefit of the General's assistant. Changxing and I have always been careful, and the more successful we are, the more careful we become. We take the time to learn the needs of our friends, and we try to meet them in a way that never compromises them or us. We can't be too circumspect these days, especially when the government in Beijing seems to launch an anti-corruption campaign every six months or so. None of us wants to end up on our knees with a gun to the back of our head."

Kuo was leaning on the car, speaking on the phone. He stood to attention when he saw them, putting the phone away. "I understand we're making a stop?"

"Yes, at the Citadel Security Company. It's in the new Hi-Tech Development Zone here in Zhuhai."

"Maybe a ten-minute drive, not a problem."

As they pulled away from the restaurant, May asked, "Why are we going there?"

Ava lowered her voice. "They built the gate at the house in Coloane. I have the specifications but I don't understand them all that well. They tell me that a truck might be able to crash through. I need more details."

"If any truck could, it would probably be the Volvo FH15, or better, the FH16," May said.

Ava turned to her. "How do you know that?"

"We've been in the distribution business for twenty years, and distribution is all about trucks. We've owned thousands of them, and I did most of the buying and selling, so I had to know something. The Volvo FH16 is a relatively new model and it's supposed to be the most powerful truck in the world. We own four of them. Seven hundred horsepower, tremendous torque, and it can carry an extremely heavy load. They are real brutes."

"How much weight can it carry?"

"Thirty tonnes easily."

"Su, the guy at Citadel, told me that I had to factor in power, weight, and speed. What speed could we generate with the Volvo?"

"What are the distances?"

"Well, from the highway there's a side road. You can't go much faster than about thirty kilometres an hour on it. It starts to straighten about a hundred metres from a clearing, and you could get the speed up to, say, forty or fifty. Once you hit the clearing you have a clear run of two hundred metres to the gate."

"I would imagine the Volvo could get up to a hundred kilometres an hour, maybe even more."

"Let me call Su," Ava said, reaching into her bag for her phone.

"Mr. Su, I'm with our chairwoman," Ava said. "I'm not sure we'll be able to make the meeting, but we had one of our people look at your specifications and put together some theoretical situations. He seems to think that a Volvo FH16 truck, loaded with thirty tonnes and impacting the gate at a hundred kilometres an hour, would take it down. We're curious as to your view."

"Ms. Lee, a tank couldn't cause more damage than a truck that size, carrying that weight, at that speed."

"You're sure?"

"I'm familiar with the Volvo FH series, and yes, I'm sure."

"Thank you. I'll contact you as soon as we finalize our plans," Ava said.

"Well?" May asked.

"Get one of those trucks to Macau."

"Are you always this bossy?"

"Please."

"I have to call Wuhan. I have no idea where they are right now."

"And we'll need a driver."

"I have one in mind; his name is Song."

Then Ava's caution kicked in. "We need someone who knows how to keep his mouth shut," she said. "And remember, there's going to be a tremendous impact when the truck hits that gate. He has to be prepared to face that danger."

"Song races sports cars, so collisions are nothing new for him. And he's a nephew of Wife Number One, so I'm not worried about his mouth."

"Okay."

"Now let me call my logistics manager and see if we can track down a truck."

"Ms. Lee, are we still going to Citadel?" the captain asked from the front seat.

Ava realized he'd been listening to their conversation. *He must think we're insane*, she thought. "No, you can take us directly to the ferry terminal."

They recrossed the border at the Gongbei Port of Entry, where the traffic lines were even longer than they had been at the Barrier Gate. The Lexus sped by, hardly stopping at the customs booth.

May was on the phone nearly the entire distance to the terminal, doing more listening and waiting than talking. Finally she said, "We'll have to tag-team the truck. I don't want Song getting here dead tired. Call me when they leave Wuhan, and make sure they check in with you or me if they have any problems at all." She covered the mouthpiece and said to Ava, "Where do you want to meet the truck?"

"The Macau wharf is fine."

May relayed the message.

"When will it arrive?" Ava asked.

"The truck is two hours from Wuhan. We have to pull it back into our yard, load it with thirty tonnes of whatever we have lying around, and then get it on the road. It's a twelve-hundred-kilometre drive, so we'll put two drivers on the truck. Barring any problems, it could be in Macau as early as noon tomorrow."

"Does Song know my name?"

"Why is that necessary?"

"Well, I assumed you were flying back to Wuhan tonight."

"No, I'm not. I'm staying over."

"I didn't see any luggage."

"Uncle has it. I've booked a suite at the Mandarin. He's taken it there for me."

"I see."

"I'll be going to Macau with you too."

AVA WALKED WITH MAY TO THE MANDARIN ORIENTAL Hotel, and then she backed away when she saw the fuss the staff was making over their new guest. They would have carried May to her room if she'd asked.

"I'm going to go now," Ava said. "I have a tremendous amount of preparation to do."

"We'll have dinner?"

"Sure," Ava said, putting aside more than one misgiving. "Let's make it around eight. Why don't you choose a restaurant? I'll call you around seven thirty."

As Ava rode the elevator to the twenty-third floor it seemed to her that her days were taking on the shape of elevator rides. She'd started down at the lobby the day before with the offer sheet in her hand, and returned with it rendered meaningless and Simon To's life at stake. This morning she'd started the day feeling down, full of doubt verging on desperation, and now she was up again: she had a chance, a real working chance to salvage this mess.

When she got to her room, she took off her shirt and slacks and put on a T-shirt and track pants. She grabbed her notebook and a bottle of water and sat down at the desk.

Phone calls — she had to make her phone calls first or she'd never be able to concentrate on planning anything. She made a quick list and then turned on her phone. Uncle and Amanda had left messages. Both were on her list, him at the top.

"I was waiting," he said.

"Sorry, we just got back."

"How did it go?"

"The alarm will be disconnected, effective today, through Sunday."

"I am not surprised."

"Uncle, she is very sharp, very shrewd."

"No more than you."

"No, she operates at a different level."

"All you need is the time, experience, and opportunity."

Ava let the compliment slide. "She got us a truck as well. It will be in Macau tomorrow."

"How confident are you about this working?"

"As much as I can be. The people who built the gate tell me it won't withstand what we can throw at it. I have to trust them."

"So, things are considerably brighter than they were this morning."

"Thanks to you."

"When do you plan to make your move?"

"Friday morning, as close to dawn as possible."

"That's quick."

"No option."

"I gave Sonny the message about your gun. He has been talking to Carlo and I think things have been arranged."

"Thanks again."

"Now what?"

"I have a lot of planning to do, and I want to get at it."

"Do you want to have dinner tonight?"

"May has asked me already. Do you want to join us?"

"No, I think it is better for the two of you to eat alone."

Amanda was breathless when she answered her phone. "What a crazy day," she began. "I ran all over Hong Kong looking for your map, and Michael kept calling me every hour, and I've just got off the MTR from Sha Tin."

"You went to see Jessie."

"I had to. When I spoke to her this morning, she was a basket case, and I was afraid she'd start calling Michael or go to the police or God knows what. So I hustled over to Sha Tin and spent a couple of hours trying to calm her. Her mother is terrific, you know. She believed everything we said the other night, but Jessie is not so gullible. She knows something is not right and kept hammering at me for details."

"How is she now?"

"I have no idea. I'm going to call in a little while."

"Look, call her right away. Tell her we've finalized our arrangements with the people in Macau and that the deal closes on Friday. In fact, tell her that Simon will be home for dinner Friday night."

"Ava, are you sure about this?"

Well, if he's not home by Friday he's not coming home at all, Ava thought. Either way, maybe they could spare Jessie an additional day and a half of anguish. "Tell her he'll be home Friday."

"Ava, you're going to Macau then, aren't you."

How much can I tell her? Ava thought. And then she realized there was probably not much that Amanda hadn't figured out already. "I am, and it isn't something I want you to discuss with anyone else — not Michael, not your father, not Jessie. I'm trusting you with this."

"Do you have to do it this way? I mean, I know how you went in and got my father, so I know you've done it before, but is it really necessary?"

Ava switched gears. "I take it you got my map?"

"And I got the floor plans blown up."

"Good. There's one more thing I need you to do today. Do you know what a balaclava is?"

"Of course."

"I need eight of them, black preferably. In fact, black most definitely."

"Where will I find those?"

"If I knew that, I wouldn't be asking you to do it."

"I'll see what I can do."

"I need them by early tomorrow. Try to drop them off at the hotel, with the map and the plans, around nine o'clock."

"We're not seeing you tonight?"

"No, I have a heavy night of work ahead of me."

"Okay. I'm going to call Jessie now."

"Good girl," Ava said, wondering if Amanda realized that neither of them had talked about Michael.

Carlo was next on her phone list. She debated whether it was too early to call, then finally did anyway. His voice was indistinct, the sounds of traffic and strange horns bellowing in the background. "I'm at the Aberdeen harbour with my cousin," he yelled. "Let me go indoors to call back."

As she waited she chose an empty page in her notebook and sketched the floor plans for Lok's house from memory. She finished as the phone rang.

"We're packing the boat, getting ready for it to leave tomorrow morning."

"What time?"

"He'll leave at dawn. That should get him into Macau Harbour before noon."

"He's sure the boat won't get searched on the other side?"

"We wrapped everything in double layers of plastic and then put them in his bait bin. If someone wants to inspect the bin they'll have to work their way through a metre of fish guts before they get to our goods."

"You managed to collect everything already?"

"Everything. And we have some firepower, Ava."

"Did you get my nine-millimetre?"

"Sonny dropped it off about an hour ago with the Cobray M11."

"I didn't ask for a Cobray."

"It's for him."

"Sonny isn't coming."

"Then someone had better tell him, because he sure as hell thinks he is."

Ava felt a flush of anger, then disappointment. Why hadn't Uncle told her he intended to send Sonny along? "I'll talk to him," she said.

"Better you than me."

She pushed the Sonny issue aside. "Can you reach Andy and all the other men tonight?"

"They're on standby."

"I want to meet at my hotel tomorrow morning — all of

us — at, say, ten. Tell the guys to dress conservatively. Long-sleeved shirts, no shorts. Wait in the lobby and I'll come and get you; I'm not sure where we're going to meet yet... And you can give them another heads-up: we're going over to Macau later tomorrow night, so whatever personal stuff needs to get done should get done now."

"Okay, boss."

"See you in the morning."

She thought about calling Uncle, but she couldn't imagine what she could say that wouldn't sound childish. Having Sonny alongside would in fact be a godsend; she should be grateful rather than peevish. So she phoned the man himself.

In the ten years she'd known him, she doubted they'd had more than two or three conversations that went past "How are you?" and "Do you know where Uncle is?" He was Uncle's creature, and had been for close to thirty years.

"Sonny, it's Ava."

"How are you?"

"I'm good, Sonny. I just finished talking to Carlo, and he told me you're coming to Macau with us."

"If you want me."

"Oh, I want you. I just wish Uncle had mentioned something to me."

"He doesn't know."

"Pardon?"

"I'm taking the next three days off — holidays. I'm free to do with them as I want."

"Sonny, you need to tell him."

"That's not how he and I work."

All of a sudden Ava felt like an outsider to a relationship

she'd always thought she understood. "I wouldn't know that."

"That's how it is."

"He could still worry."

"Ava, why do you think I'm going in the first place? He hasn't slept in two nights. Lourdes says he's been up, pacing the floors, making phone calls. He's worried sick about you."

"I can look after myself, Sonny."

"You've never taken on the triad before, at least not so directly. When he was in the car with me yesterday, after you and he met at the Korean barbecue house, he was going on and on about Lok and his crew. And then he started to talk about the old days, when he was chairman and his opinion on anything mattered. He hasn't talked about that in years. Did you know he served four terms?"

"No, I didn't."

"The societies elect a chairman every two years and the position is supposed to be for one term. He served four because they asked him to, not because he wanted it, and they asked him because he knew how to maintain harmony, to keep peace, balance among the societies. And when he finally stepped down and left the societies altogether to start the new business — the one he brought you into — I think he believed he had left a legacy. Except, of course, without him it turned to shit within six months."

"He doesn't talk to me about things like that, Sonny."

"But you know. I know you know."

"I know enough."

"Then know this: that fucking piece of crap Kao Lok has to pay for the disrespect he's shown Uncle. He told me what was said, and I couldn't believe it. There was a day when

Lok wasn't senior enough to wipe Uncle's ass. I'm going to make sure when I'm done with him that he'll be begging for the chance to do just that."

"Sonny!" Ava yelled. "You stop right there. This is not about the disrespect shown to Uncle, terrible as that is. My brother's business is at risk, my entire family's well-being is at risk, and my brother's partner's life is at risk while his wife and baby sit in Sha Tin wondering if he's ever coming home. That's why we're going to Macau."

"I know that, but—"

"But nothing. Those are the only reasons we're going to Macau," Ava said. "Now, I want you with me, but you have to accept that I'm the boss and you're going to have to do what you're told. And what I'm telling you now, so there is no misunderstanding later, is that Lok is mine. And mine alone."

The line went quiet.

"Can you accept that?" she said.

"Okay, Ava."

"'Okay, Ava' what? I agree or I pretend to agree?"

"I agree."

"We have a meeting tomorrow morning at ten o'clock at my hotel, all of us who are going. I would very much like you to be here. And Carlo and Andy look up to you. I would appreciate it if you could treat me with something close to the same respect you give Uncle."

"That isn't hard to do."

"Thank you."

"You know we love you, right?"

Where did that come from? she thought. "And I love both of you."

"I'll see you in the morning," he said.

She was about to remind him about long sleeves and no shorts before she caught herself. She'd be surprised if he showed up in anything other than a suit.

21

SHE STOOD OVER THE DESK, THE SKETCH OF THE FLOOR plan in front of her, and tried to imagine the perfect scenario.

They would go in at dawn, she had decided. They'd be wearing the balaclavas to give the men anonymity, some protection from the security cameras. There was also something more sinister about being attacked by masked men, and she wanted that psychological edge. And dawn was important. The courtyard wasn't floodlit, so the house would be in semi-darkness. They already had the element of surprise working for them, and she wasn't about to squander it by having her men stumbling about in pitch black in a physical space they had seen only in a drawing. She wanted to see and be seen.

As she thought through the process she began making notes on her sketch. By the time she was finished the page was covered with handwriting and she could barely recognize the original floor plan. She turned to a clean page in her notebook and began to summarize the points she needed to emphasize with the men in the morning. Anticipating what to expect would help them react well to whatever did happen.

She was reviewing that page for the third time when her room phone rang. She picked it up absentmindedly. "Ava, it's May Ling. It's past eight o'clock; I thought you were going to call me at seven thirty."

"May, I'm sorry, I just got wrapped up in this thing."

"Well, no real worry. I've booked a table at Man Wah in the hotel, and I'm sitting in the M Bar having a drink. Join me when you can."

"Give me five minutes and I'll be there." She threw on the same clothes she'd worn to Macau, brushed her hair, dabbed on some lipstick, and headed for the twenty-fifth floor.

The bar was crowded, with knots of suits standing outside waiting for a table. Ava saw May sitting on the stool closest to the window, wearing a black silk sheath cocktail dress that came just to the knee, black hose, and black stilettos. The dress had spaghetti straps and was cut in a straight line across the chest, exposing the top of an ample bosom. Around her neck was a companion piece to the white jade bracelet Ava had been admiring earlier in the day. Even from a distance it was exquisite. And so was May. It was the first time Ava had seen her without a jacket on, and she couldn't help noticing how delicate her frame was.

Ava waved from the door. May didn't see her but the bartender did and caught May's attention. May slid from the stool and walked to the door, glass in hand. It was a young crowd in the bar, and mainly men. That didn't stop them from openly admiring a woman who had to be at least ten years older than most of them.

May said, "This is my second martini. We should eat before I get tipsy."

The restaurant manager grinned when he saw them. "Welcome back, Ms. Lee, and it's a real honour to have you here, Madam Wong."

He led them to a table next to the window. "I think this is the best table in house," he said softly.

They had hardly sat down before a pot of jasmine tea was on the table and two menus and a wine list had been placed in front of them. "Whenever you're ready," the waiter said.

"You look absolutely stunning," Ava said to May. "I feel like a wallflower."

"You have a gorgeous body. Why don't you show it off more?"

"Remember what you said about image earlier today? Well, I'm an accountant and this is how my clients expect to see me dressed."

May picked up a menu. "I'm starving."

"I eat everything, so choose what you want."

"Are you okay with only seafood?"

"Sure. How about your drink? I'd like wine. Are you going to stick with martinis?"

"No, I'll switch to wine. You order that."

May lifted the menu from the table and flicked it in the direction of the waiter. He came running.

"We're going to have the double-boiled fish maw soup, a stewed whole abalone — make it the Yoshihama — and a steamed pink *garoupa*. Ava, can you handle live shrimp?"

Ava nodded.

"Then we'll have the live drunken shrimp and the rice with minced shrimp and sea urchin."

"And a bottle of Pinot Grigio," Ava added.

As the waiter hustled away, both of them looked out

onto the harbour, the skyline lit up like a magic kingdom. "I haven't travelled that much, but I can't imagine anything more beautiful than this," May said.

"I would have thought you'd seen everything worth seeing," said Ava.

"Hardly. The business keeps us grounded. We have capable people, of course, but Changxing is old-fashioned and has a hard time entrusting things to them. If he's not in Wuhan, all he does is worry about what's going on in Wuhan, so we stick close to home. I come to Hong Kong two or three times a year and I go to Shanghai often; I've been to Singapore, Tokyo, and Bangkok, and San Francisco once for three days. But other than that I'm provincial, rather unworldly."

"I've been to more places than I can count, and I don't think that makes me any less provincial than you. It's more a state of mind, isn't it? I mean, I met an American woman here the other night. She was on a tour of Asia with friends, and from the way it sounded, all the friends wanted to do was shop. I told her if that was going to be their Asian experience, they shouldn't have left Cleveland."

"Did she think you were rude?"

"No, I don't think so. She was bemoaning them herself. She was a woman with curiosity."

"Like you."

"It comes with the job, though I do admit it is a natural bent."

"Oh, and speaking of the job," May said, "I spoke to Wuhan an hour ago. The truck has left and should be in Macau early tomorrow afternoon."

"Thank you. Thank you for General Feng and thank you for the truck."

The waiter arrived with the wine. Ava went through the tasting ritual and for the thousandth or so consecutive time said the wine was just fine. He poured them each half a glass and retreated. When he did, May slid her hand across the table, her fingers touching Ava's. "I really need to apologize to you — properly, I mean."

"That's not necessary," Ava said, lifting her glass. "*Salut.*"

Glasses clinked. "*Salut,*" said May. "And, yes, it is necessary. I want you to understand that what happened in London wasn't planned. I want you to believe that when I sat on your bed that night in my house, I was being completely honest with you. It is true that Changxing had blood in his eyes, but I didn't. When I told you I was prepared to use legal routes to pursue the people who cheated us, I meant it. But when Changxing found out you were on their trail, that changed. I wish it hadn't."

"May, you don't have to —"

"I want to. I want you to understand. I love my husband more than my life, Ava. He is all I've ever had. When he found out about the fraud, the change in him was so profound it scared me. As I told you in Wuhan, it went beyond any normal loss of face. He was devastated, and so depressed that I worried he might do something silly. That was why I begged you to take the job. I needed to do everything I could to make things right for him. And then, of course, he found out, and everything changed. I just couldn't say no to him. I'm so sorry, Ava. I know I've caused you pain. So, please, accept my apology."

"I understand why you want to apologize, and I think an apology is justified," Ava said carefully. "What I don't understand is why it seems to mean so much to you."

May sipped her wine. "That is where things get a little more difficult, a little odd," she said.

Ava felt a chill run down her back. *No*, she thought, *please, not that.*

To Ava's relief, the double-boiled fish maw soup arrived at the table in a silver tureen. Ava watched as it was ladled into two bowls, lowered her head, and began to eat. May did the same. Then, halfway through, she put her spoon down. "You know I have no children," she said. "I also have no brothers or sisters. I have nothing to do with the other two wives, and the only friends I have are the wives of business and government associates who struggle to find things to do to fill their rather empty days, and who are friends with me for a reason."

"I have one sister, and I'm the younger child of a second wife," Ava said.

"I know," May said. "I made a point of learning some things about you."

Ava glanced up from her soup. May was looking out over the harbour. "When we had our problem and Changxing wanted to bring Uncle to Wuhan, I was opposed to it. Despite what Uncle does now, he still has a reputation, and I wasn't sure it was wise for us to associate ourselves with him. But then my husband said there was a young woman who for all intents and purposes ran the business, and she would be the one doing the work. That was the first time I heard your name. I made some phone calls, naturally, and I liked what I heard. In fact, I found it rather intriguing that a woman — a young one at that, and one with Canadian roots — could attain such a position of trust with a man like Uncle and could earn the respect of just about everyone I spoke to."

The steamed abalone arrived at the table, glistening gold, its aroma rising like perfumed mist. "Leave it, I'll serve," May said. She began to slice the meat into slivers. Then, passing a plate to Ava, she said, "Do you have any religion?"

"I'm Catholic."

"I'm Taoist. Do you know anything about Taoism?"

"Not really."

May bit into a slice of abalone. "This is divine... Well, as I was saying, I learned enough about you that I told my husband he could invite Uncle to Wuhan on the condition that you came with him. And, of course, you did. What I didn't expect was that when I saw you I'd feel such a tremble in my heart."

Ava's chill travelled up her neck. "I'm not sure we should continue with this conversation," she said softly.

May reached for her hand again. "Ava, I've been told that you are a lesbian. I don't know if it's true or not, and I don't care, because it has no bearing on what I'm trying to say. So please, don't think this is an older woman trying to win her way into that kind of affection."

They were interrupted when the waiter brought the *garoupa*, rice, and shrimp. "And we'll need another bottle of wine," Ava told the waiter as he put the platters on the table. May spooned portions of rice onto their plates and then separated meat from spine. Ava peeled several shrimp, their pink flesh twitching slightly, and passed some to May.

"I'm quite uncomfortable," Ava said.

"And I'm sorry for that. It's just that I wanted to be clear," May said, tilting her head back so the shrimp could slither down her throat.

"You've been clear enough."

"Well, let me go back to Wuhan and the day you and Uncle arrived. My husband was quite put out when Uncle insisted on having his own man meet him at the airport and drive him to the house. So between that, our problems, and having to go ahead with that ghastly birthday party, we weren't in the best mood. We stood at the top of the stairs, remember? That was rude on our part. But anyway, there we were at the top and I found myself looking down at you, and I felt as if I were looking down at myself twenty years ago.

"It was a bit of a shock to me. And it's not just the physical resemblance. When you looked at me, I felt a connection. The Taoists call it *qi* — life force — and I felt it pass between us. And I thought, 'I know this girl, and this girl knows me.'

"I didn't say anything to my husband, but I didn't really have to. For the next hour he kept repeating how strange it was to see you, how much it reminded him of meeting me for the first time. And then of course we had to endure that dreadful evening — the party, the karaoke, and then our meeting in the gallery. I knew, the moment my husband made the reference to revenge, that he had lost you. I also knew, almost right away, that regardless of what Uncle thought or wanted to do, he would defer to you. And I found that remarkable."

"You give me too much credit."

"No, I saw what I saw, and I knew what I knew," May said. "And then I came to your room and begged you to help my husband, and I cried. I can't begin to tell you how unlike me that was. You know my husband's nickname is 'Emperor Hubei'? Well, mine is 'the Stone Lady.'"

"I never felt that about you."

"I know. You seemed to see into me, just as I thought I could see into you. Taoists believe in kindred spirits, in soulmates. We have *yin* and *yang*; some people believe their symbol represents man and woman, but they don't necessarily mean that. We all lack something in our lives, and most of us never find that missing piece. When I saw you, I thought you could be my missing piece, that you could be the friend, the kindred spirit, I've never had." She paused and drank deeply from her glass of wine. "That's why I'm apologizing, that's why I'm so anxious to make things right between us. Unless things are made right, we'll never know what kind of friends we can be."

Ava sat back and looked across the table at May Ling. She was so formidable and yet so vulnerable, and her eyes, strong and warm, reflected both. "I think, May, that I would like to know that too," Ava said.

"Two strong women in a world run by men."

"Two strong women in a world that men think they run." Ava laughed as she said it.

May stood up and came around the table. Ava rose from her chair and held out her arms. They hugged, and then smiled. "I've had too much to drink," May said. "But I would never have gotten through that otherwise."

They left the restaurant with arms looped together. Ava wasn't sold on the kindred spirit idea, but she couldn't deny she felt a connection to May Ling. Maybe it was *qi*. She decided to let events unfold and let them lead to whatever destiny had in store for her and May. Then the practical part of her kicked in. *There are worse things*, she told herself, *than being friends with a woman who can command a general in the PLA.*

"What are the plans for tomorrow?" May asked.

"I have to brief the men in the morning. Actually, thanks for reminding me, because I need to book a meeting room downstairs."

"I have a three-room suite, and one room is set up like a boardroom. You can use that if you want."

"You really don't mind? These guys aren't boardroom kind of guys."

"What time will they be here?"

"Ten."

"Bring them up."

"Great."

"And so we go to Macau tomorrow?"

"Yes."

"And when do you invade the house?"

"Dawn on Friday."

"You aren't afraid?"

"I'm always afraid, but it's an emotion I can't succumb to because it will affect everyone around me. The men need to see me calm."

May Ling stopped at the elevator. "Do you really have to go in yourself?"

Ava shrugged. "I'd never ask anyone to do something I wasn't prepared to do myself. "

22

SHE SAW WU AND LOK STANDING ON THE SECOND-
floor mezzanine with guns aimed at the front door of
the house. She and the men were sitting ducks. She was
screaming, "Get down, get down!" when the hotel phone
woke her. She realized at once where she was but her senses
were still on edge.

She made a coffee and got the papers at the door. She
opened the *South China Morning Post* first, turning to the
day's forecast. Dry and sunny for the next two days, sun-
rise at six fifteen a.m. She leafed through the *Post* and the
Herald Tribune, her mind too distracted to concentrate on
the details of more financial fallout, this time in Europe.
With a fresh cup of coffee she went to the desk and opened
her notebook.

Ava read and reread her notes from the night before
and then made a list of things that had to be organized in
the next few hours. She started with the cars, and a phone
call downstairs to the concierge. She asked him to reserve
two SUVs for her in Macau, tinted glass if possible. She
put both on her credit card and listed Sonny Kwok as the

driver of the second vehicle.

Then she called the Kingsway Hotel and booked five rooms for that night, all on her credit card. One room was under her name, the others under the names of Carlo, Andy, Sonny, and May.

Finally, Ava took six hotel envelopes from the desk drawer and carried them to the bed. She removed a wad of U.S. hundred-dollar bills from her jacket pocket and took another stack from her purse. She apportioned the money, wrote names on the fronts of the envelopes, and put the envelopes into her bag.

It was eight o'clock when she finished. *By this time tomorrow*, she thought, *I'll have Simon To and all my men halfway back to Hong Kong.* She went to the bathroom and brushed her teeth hard. Then she showered, washing her hair with as much vigour as she had brushed her teeth. There was something about being clean that fuelled her optimism.

She dried her hair, pulled it back, and clasped it with the ivory chignon pin. She put on a clean, crisp white shirt, fastening the cuffs with green jade cufflinks, and black linen slacks. She finished off the look with a pair of black leather pumps, her gold crucifix, and her Cartier watch, then applied black mascara and a light touch of red lipstick. She was dressed for business in a way the boys expected. *More than presentable*, she thought, looking in the mirror. Then she packed her runners and tracksuit into her Shanghai Tang "Double Happiness" bag.

She went back to the desk and turned on her computer. Into her inbox tumbled two days' worth of emails from Maria, Mimi, other friends, and her father. Out of nowhere she felt a need to connect with them. The feeling caught her by surprise, because it wasn't in character for her to call home when she was working. All that did was make her feel more isolated, more alone, and she hated any negative vibes, any distractions, when she was on a job. She started to answer the emails and then stopped and picked up her cellphone instead.

"*Buenos días*, this is Maria. I'm sorry I can't take your call right now. Leave a message and I'll get back to you as soon as I can."

It was Wednesday evening in Toronto. Maria would be at salsa. "Maria, this is Ava. It's Thursday morning and I'm still in Hong Kong. I'm going to be out of touch for a day or two. Not to worry — I'll be home maybe by the weekend. Anyway, miss you and love you."

Mimi answered her phone on the second ring. "Ava, are you okay?"

"Yes, I'm fine."

"You never call when you travel."

"I miss home this trip. I just wanted to see how you're feeling."

"I'm great. I've never been happier."

"It's real, huh?"

"As real as it's ever been. Derek is such a doll."

"Have you told the parents about the baby?"

"We told mine two nights ago. My mother was thrilled for me, but my father was slightly pissed off that I'm not married yet. The fact that we're engaged doesn't impress him. But he likes Derek, he really does, and I think it will work out. I'm not sure about Derek's parents, though."

"Why?"

"He emailed them to tell them that we were engaged *and* that I was pregnant. I said that wasn't the way to do things, that he should have at least called, but he insisted that they email each other all the time and it was no big deal. He sent them a photo of us with his hand on my belly. The problem is, they haven't answered him yet, and we're into the second day. If he doesn't hear from them by morning, I'm going to make him call. Ava, you've met them, right?"

"A couple of times."

"They wouldn't resent the fact that he's marrying someone who isn't Chinese, would they?"

His father just might, Ava thought, remembering some intemperate remarks about *gweilo*s. With the mother, an aging Hong Kong princess, it would probably be more a case of jealousy. It was one thing to have as a daughter-in-law a flat-chested Chinese girl who understood the roles and rules in the family hierarchy, but it was quite another to have a six-foot-tall blonde, busty Canadian with a mind of her own. "I'm sure they're happy for you and that there's some other reason they haven't contacted Derek. His father travels a lot, you know, and his mother often goes with him," Ava said.

"When are you coming home?"

"Hopefully this weekend, and when I get there I'm going to plant my ass in Yorkville and not go anywhere for a while."

"Ava, I really like Maria, you know."

"Me too."

"What do you think you two guys are going to do?"

"You mean, like move in together?"

"Yeah, something like that."

"I don't know, Mimi, I really don't know. And right now isn't the time to think about it."

The hotel phone rang. Ava let it go to voicemail. "Look, I have to go. I'll email you when I make the travel arrangements for coming home. Give Derek my love."

She hesitated, trying to decide between the two phones. *Well, I'm on a roll*, she thought, and dialled her mother's home line.

"Marcus Lee."

"Daddy, it's Ava."

"How are you? I've been worried."

"I'm fine, and listen to me: things are moving along very well here. By this time tomorrow I expect I'll have resolved most of Michael's problems and I'll be on a plane back to Toronto. We'll be able to spend some fun time together before you have to go back to Hong Kong."

"I'm getting a different feeling from your brother," he said.

"I haven't told him everything. In truth, I haven't told him very much at all. He has a low threshold for stress, and I don't need him badgering me," she said, and then realized how critical that sounded. "Daddy, he's a great guy, and he may be a capable businessman, but he's not cut out for the kind of people he was trying to deal with."

"We all have our strengths and weaknesses," he said.

"Speaking of which, have you spent much time with Amanda Yee?"

"A little. She's a nice enough girl, comes across as a bit spoilt."

"She's a keeper. You make sure Michael marries her. She'll be a tremendous asset to him and the family."

"I don't hear you throw around compliments like that very often."

"Well, there you go. Now can I speak to Mummy?"

Marcus Lee laughed. "She's not here. She's gone to play mah-jong. This is closing in on the fourth consecutive week I've spent with her. That's the most time in one year since she left for Canada. I think I'm beginning to wear on her, and by the time I leave she'll be more than happy to put me on the plane so she can get back to her regular schedule."

"How is Marian?"

"I speak to her every day. She's getting over the cruise fiasco. I may fly up to Ottawa to see her and the girls before I leave."

"If I'm back I'll go with you. How about Mummy?"

"I think we'd do better to let things settle a bit more first."

"That's probably smart. Well, okay, I have to go — busy day today. Give Mummy a kiss for me. I'll email you when things get finished here."

He paused, and she knew she shouldn't have mentioned things getting finished. "Ava, are you really sure that this will get worked out? I'm already getting emails from my bank — nothing dramatic, but there are hints they're concerned about Michael and Simon."

"Thing will get worked out, and by tomorrow," she said.

"You aren't taking any foolish chances, I hope."

"I have everything under control."

"I really want to believe you," he said, doubt in his voice.

"Tomorrow. It will be over tomorrow," she said, and ended the call.

The message light on the room phone was blinking. She

entered the code and listened to Amanda saying she was downstairs in the lobby. Ava checked the time. It was nine thirty already. She put Toronto completely out of her mind, grabbed her bag, and left the room.

Amanda sat by herself on a lobby sofa, the cardboard tube leaning against her leg, a small box next to her. She was wearing designer jeans and a baby-blue cashmere sweater. Her hair, which looked freshly washed, sparkled under the lobby lights, and her skin was radiant and without makeup. She looked as if she were still in high school.

"Hey," Ava said.

Amanda jumped to her feet and reached for the cardboard tube. "Here are the copies, and I've got the balaclavas in the box, black balaclavas."

"Thanks. Now, would you have time for one more errand?"

"Sure. I booked the day off at the office."

"I need a megaphone, a power megaphone."

"And where would I . . . Oh, never mind, I'll figure it out."

"I'm going to be in May Ling Wong's suite on the twenty-second floor for the next few hours. Bring it there."

Amanda did a double take. "May Ling Wong? *The* May Ling Wong?"

"I know only one."

"From Hubei? That May Ling Wong?"

"Yes, that one."

"What is she doing here?"

"She's helping with our project."

"Ava, this is nuts. How is this possible?"

"It's a long story and we don't have a lot of time, so go and get the megaphone. I'll introduce you to her when you get back," she said, spotting Carlo at the hotel entrance. He was glancing around and looking decidedly uncomfortable. Ava checked her watch; it was only nine forty. "Here, I'll walk with you," she said to Amanda.

Carlo smiled when he saw them, and Ava was pleased to see Amanda smile back. The girl had manners. "You're early," Ava said.

"You said ten o'clock and not to be late. Everyone else is already outside, including Sonny."

"Wait here," she said to him, and then turned to Amanda. "Come up to the suite when you're done."

Ava went to the house phone and asked for May's room. "Everyone is here early. Can we come up?" she said.

"Of course."

"We'll be there in five minutes."

Ava went to the hotel tuck shop to buy some cellophane tape and then left the hotel. The six men stood off to one side; she could see Andy laughing at something Carlo was saying. Sonny was in a suit and the others all looked respectable, or at least as respectable as they could, in jeans and long-sleeved shirts that covered most of their tattoos. Ava walked over to them and an uneasy silence greeted her.

"Hi, I'm Ava," she repeated as she went from man to man, holding out her hand. "Thank you for coming." When she got to Sonny, the idea of a handshake seemd ludicrous. She got on her tiptoes and kissed him on both cheeks. "Let's go inside," she said.

She had Carlo gather the tube and the box from the lobby and then she led them to the elevators. She saw hotel security eyeing them, and wondered how far they would get if they weren't with her.

The door to May Ling's suite was open when they got there. Ava walked in, the boys following close behind. "This room over here," May called from an open doorway on the right. She was in a white Chanel suit with black trim and gold buttons.

They filed in, the men looking around as if they felt guilty for being there. There were eight chairs around the table and one at the far end. Carlo and his two men sat on one side, with Andy, his brother-in-law, and Sonny on the other. Ava moved to the head of the table. To the side she saw a table with a tea urn and bottles of water and soft drinks. "This is May," she said to the men. "She's working with us on this."

May was standing against a wall. One by one, they got up and bowed. While they did, Ava took the enlarged floor plan and the map of Coloane and taped them to a wall.

When they were seated again, Ava pointed to the map. "This is where we're going." Then she pointed to the floor plan. "This is the house. We enter it at dawn tomorrow, that's six fifteen. There are no neighbours and we don't expect any police response. It's just us, the house, and the guys in the house.

"I want to make one thing very clear before getting into detail. Our sole purpose is to rescue a guy, Simon To, they're holding for ransom. Here is his picture. Please pass it along," she said, giving it to Carlo. "Now, we aren't at war with Kao Lok and his men. If we can get Simon without a single shot being fired, that's perfect, so I don't want anyone taking it upon themselves to turn this into something else, something unnecessary. Now obviously, if they fire on us we're going to defend ourselves, and you should all know that I don't do that in half measures and wouldn't expect any less from you. So no shooting unless we have to, but if we have to, make it count."

She took out her notebook and turned to the pages she had worked on the night before. "Now let me get into specifics."

She spoke for more than an hour, giving them every detail, every possible negative scenario and how they were to react to it. The first time she had briefed Carlo and Andy on a job they had tried to wave her off, saying they didn't need to know everything, just to give them the basics. She had refused. The details, in her mind, showed that planning had been done, that thought had been brought to the process, and she felt that should impart confidence. She wanted confident men. And the wrinkles were just as important. Things would not go smoothly, she told them — they never did. And then she went over what could go wrong, to the extreme perhaps, and then addressed each possibility specifically, making it clear what the appropriate reaction was. "I don't want you guessing," she said. "If A happens, do B; if B happens, jump to C. Don't waste time thinking, just do."

When she was finished, she told them to go outside for a smoke break. "I'm sure you must have questions. When you come back, we'll try to answer them," she said.

Sonny stayed behind. "What do you think?" Ava asked.

"A good plan."

"You have any worries?"

"The mezzanine."

"I know, I actually had dreams about that last night."

"If Wu and Lok are up there when we come through the door, it isn't going to be any fun."

Ava sat across from him. "I know. The thing is, I think Wu is right-handed, and that's the arm I broke. If he wants to shoot, he'll have to use his left hand, and that's not an easy adjustment. As for Lok, he doesn't seem the type to even carry a gun, although that doesn't mean he won't have one. In any event, I know we can't just waltz in there. I think when we go through the door, we should head right up the stairs. Lok's room is on the far right, and I'm going to cut hard in that direction. You need to focus on Wu's room."

"How about you?" Sonny said. "What else worries you?"

Ava was about to say "everything" and then caught herself. Sonny deserved more than a glib answer. "The more I think about it, the more I analyze it, the more concerned I get about the left wing. On the surface it seems like the easiest part of it. I mean, if the men who are housed there react as slowly as I've been told they have in the past, then we should be able to neutralize them without any bloodshed.

"But it's all a matter of timing. If we're fast enough getting through the gate and through the door, and if we're lucky enough that they don't hear anything until we're actually at the door, then we should be able to seal off the wing without too much trouble. What scares me is that they might hear the gate crash, or the gate is hooked up to the alarm system and we're slow getting to the house and through the door. Then they have time to figure out what's going on, get armed, and be waiting for us. There could be as many as seven of them. And then what? Twelve men firing at each other in close quarters? It would be a mess."

Sonny walked over to the table and poured himself a cup of tea. May leaned against the wall, watching him. He looked up and smiled at Ava. "It would remind me of the old days."

Carlo and Andy came back into the suite with the other men and all of them took their seats again.

"Okay, questions," Ava said.

There was silence.

"Nothing?" Ava said.

"When do we go over?" Andy asked.

"I want you all on standby until we get confirmation that the boat has docked and is secure and we know the truck has arrived. We should know both those things early this afternoon. So plan on going over starting late this afternoon and into the early evening, but don't leave until you're given the green light. And when you do go, don't do it as one big group.

"Now, when you get there, head for the Kingsway Hotel. I've booked three rooms under the names of Carlo, Andy, and Sonny. Figure out among yourselves who stays with whom.

"I've rented two SUVs. I'll be driving one, Sonny the other. Sonny, you'll have to collect yours when you get to the Macau ferry terminal. We'll have the cars at the front of the hotel at five a.m. Meet us there, and bring your bags — we're not going back to the hotel after the job. We'll drive to the wharf, pick up the hardware, connect with the truck, and then convoy to Coloane. We should be there comfortably by six.

"Carlo, you need to call me, Andy, and Sonny as soon as you hear from your cousin. May will let me know about the truck, and I'll pass it along."

"The truck is on schedule to be in Macau by one," May said.

Ava heard a noise from the adjacent room. Amanda peeked in from around the corner. "Come in," Ava said.

She carried a megaphone in her hand, and Ava had to smile because it was almost half her size. "This is Amanda, everyone. She's been helping me."

"What is that for?" Carlo asked.

"That's for you," Ava said. "We don't know how loud the alarm is going to be, and I want to make sure you can communicate with the guys in the wing. This should help if the noise is too loud. Try it out — but wait until you leave here."

Amanda put the megaphone on the table in front of Carlo and then moved back against the wall next to May. They exchanged nods.

"Two more things before you go. There are balaclavas in the box over there; each of you take one."

"I hate wearing those things," Andy's brother-in-law muttered.

Ava stared at Andy, who nudged him. "We'll be wearing them," Andy said.

"You can get rid of them when you're in the house and it's secure. Until then, keep them on," Ava said.

"Last, I want to talk about money. I'm paying all of you for four days," she said, reaching for her bag. She extracted the envelopes and gave them to Carlo. "Pass those out for me, will you?"

She saw Sonny hesitate and said, "Sonny, it isn't fair for me to treat you any differently."

When the envelopes had been distributed, she said, "That's your full four-day advance. If the job is as successful as I think it's going to be, there will be a bonus for everyone as well. So that's it. We should be in touch with you in the next few hours."

The men shuffled towards the door. Ava trailed after

them and touched Carlo lightly on the elbow. "Just a minute," she said to him.

"What is it, boss?"

"What were the men saying when you went out for a smoke?"

"They have a good feeling about this, and having Sonny along is a big plus."

"They know Sonny?"

"If they don't know him, they've heard of him. He's a legend."

23

AMANDA HAD TAKEN THE MAP AND FLOOR PLANS from the wall and was rolling them up. May was still leaning against the wall, now with a phone to her ear. Ava grabbed a bottle of water and sat at the table. She'd never had a woman involved in her business before, even marginally, and now she had brought two of them into it. She had no way of telling them how the day would transpire. Derek had described it best, she thought, when he said that working with her was twenty-three hours and fifty minutes of waiting and boredom followed by ten minutes of action and terror.

"The driver is two hours from Macau," May said, ending her call.

"Great. If he gets in early enough we'll have a chance to drive over to the house. It would be useful for him to see the road," Ava said. "Now, have you two introduced yourselves?"

"Not yet."

"May Ling Wong, this is Amanda Yee. Amanda is my brother's fiancée."

"You hardly look old enough to have a boyfriend, let alone be engaged," May said.

"Thank you," Amanda said.

Ava said, "She has a master's degree in international business from Brandeis, and she's biding her time before taking over her father's modest company and turning it into a massive conglomerate. I think you two could do some good business together."

"She's exaggerating about my ambitions," Amanda said.

"Everyone has to start somewhere," May said. "Anyway, pleased to meet you."

"And you. I've heard of you, of course. All the Chinese girls at business school have heard of you."

"That's kind."

Amanda looked awkward and Ava wondered if she felt intimidated. "May has been instrumental in arranging the things that will help me get Simon back," she said.

Amanda took a seat. "This so weird," she said.

"I owed Ava some favours. This is my way of paying her back."

"That's not what I mean — No, it is partly what I mean, because how could I expect to have May Ling Wong helping me and Michael? I mean, the closest I ever thought I'd come to meeting you was looking at your photos in the *Hong Kong Tatler*. And now here you are."

"Here I am."

"And here you are with those men and that map and God knows what else Ava has been working on . . ." Amanda said, and then turned to Ava, her face taut. "Are all those men going with you?"

"They are."

"That's good... At least, I think that's good."

"Amanda, I'm going to need you to be really supportive over the next twenty-four hours," Ava said.

"Whatever you want — you know that."

"The most important thing is, you have to help me manage Michael and look after Jessie. In the next hour or so he should be getting his photo of Simon from Lok, and after he does he has to call Lok and finalize the arrangements for the exchange.

"I'm going to call him from here when we're finished and tell him that I have all the money he promised to deliver to Lok. He's to tell Lok that and to finalize the form of payment. I will tell Michael that whatever Lok wants, I will arrange to get it to him — to Michael — by noon tomorrow."

"And what does that have to do with me?" Amanda asked.

"I want you to be there when he makes the call to Lok. Don't let him waver. He has to sound confident and eager. Hammer that home."

"He's almost as worried about repaying the money as he is about Simon."

"I know. I'm going to tell him I've arranged a long-term, low-cost loan with interest postponed for the first year. If he says anything, just repeat that. Tell him I've called in some favours. Actually, tell him whatever you think will keep him calm. I can't have Lok having doubts about the money. He has to believe that Michael has it, and that Michael is going to bring it to Macau in one form or another on Friday afternoon."

"Okay, I understand."

"And then there's Jessie. We don't want her doing anything to upset our plans, and frankly, after talking to you last night, she worries me. So, if you don't mind, after Michael makes his call I think it would be a good idea for you to go to Sha Tin. Is there any way you can arrange to spend the night there?"

"Sure. I'm certain she'd like it."

"And you would be there tomorrow morning, wouldn't you."

"You'll call, right?"

"The first call is to Sha Tin."

Amanda nodded. "It would be nice to give her the good news in person." Then she sighed so deeply she shuddered.

"Everything is going to work out," Ava said.

"Four days ago I was worrying about what to wear to Sunday brunch before the horse races. Now look at me," Amanda said.

"I'll call Michael now," Ava said.

He sounded defensive and nervous when he answered the phone, and Ava couldn't blame him. The clock was ticking on Simon, and all Michael had to go on was Ava's assurances that she'd get the money. So she leapt right at him. "Michael, I've secured the money."

"Ava, that's great, how —"

"I called in some favours," she said. "You've heard of the Wong Group in Hubei?"

"Of course."

"They're advancing it. You'll have it for the first year interest-free. After that they're prepared to turn it into some small equity position in your company or convert it into a loan at no more than the standard bank rate. So that should buy you boys some time to build up the business — and give you the option of having a partner with some serious muscle."

"That's incredible."

"Well, it at least gets us past tomorrow, doesn't it."

"I haven't heard from Lok since yesterday, when we talked about the exchange."

"That's okay, you call him. Call him after you get the photo. Tell him you'll meet him tomorrow afternoon at two in the lobby of the Venetian, and that you'll be bringing him cash. That will make him happy."

"How will this actually happen, I mean — ?"

"The exchange?"

"Yes."

"Let's leave that for the morning."

"But if he asks, I have to tell him something."

That was a very good point, Ava conceded, realizing she hadn't given it a thought, and that Lok might find it strange if Michael didn't have something in mind, since it was he who had asked for the exchange in the first place. "Tell him that you'll be coming with me and a man by the name of Sonny Kwok. He can bring any two men he chooses. We'll meet directly in front of the check-in desk. They must have Simon with them. Simon walks to us, we slide the suitcase over to them, and then we turn and leave the hotel. Simple."

Michael didn't reply, and Ava thought, *Yeah, simple. Real simple. Too simple.*

"Look, Michael, I really have to go now. Let me know how it goes with Lok this afternoon. I'll keep my phone on."

"How was he?" asked Amanda after Ava hung up.

"I think you should get over there as quickly as you can."

"That was a hell of a story you spun. Where can I get some of that interest-free money?" May asked, smiling.

"Sorry, it just came to me. I thought throwing the Wong

Group's name into the mix added credibility."

"Sounded great to me," Amanda said.

"Well, if the day ever comes when we *do* do business together, you'll learn quickly enough that the word *free* doesn't exist in the Wong Group's vocabulary."

Amanda turned to Ava. "So now what?"

"You go home to Michael. He'll tell you about our chat and you'll pump him full of confidence. Please listen in on his conversation with Lok, and make sure he calls me when it's over. If it goes okay, then you grab the MTR and head for Sha Tin."

"How about me?" May asked.

"Keep in touch with your driver and call me the moment he reaches Macau. I'm going to go to my room. I still have things I need to finish."

24

IN HER TEN YEARS WITH UNCLE, AVA HAD PRIMARILY worked solo. She was accustomed to and comfortable with the rhythm of her own thought processes, of adjusting to strange countries, of encountering countless strangers and finding a way to bend them to her will. She lived mainly in her own head, driven by a pattern that came as naturally to her as breathing: link A to B and then B to C, and keep going until you get to the end. It wasn't complicated. People were what made things complicated. Clients who wanted to know about every inch of progress. Thieves who thought they could talk their way out of anything.

When she needed help — not Uncle-type help but hands-on, by-her-side help — she normally went to Derek. Dependable, loyal, ask-no-questions Derek. And even then he was in and out in a day or two, arriving at the tail end of a job when she needed to persuade the target more forcefully. The same was true with Carlo and Andy the few times she'd used them. She had a specific need for them to fill: get in, get the job done, get out.

At the end of the morning meeting, when Amanda joined the group, Ava had found herself looking at the assembly and thinking, *How the hell did I get myself into this?* It wasn't enough to have Michael to worry about; she had Amanda, May, Carlo, Andy, three other guys, and Sonny all depending on her, and their collective weight was stifling. And the two women were the largest burden. At least with the guys she could give them an order without worrying about hurting their feelings. With May, and especially with Amanda, she found herself having to choose her words carefully, and that was no way to get work done.

After she graduated from Babson College, Ava had worked for three months for a large accounting firm and quickly discovered it wasn't for her. She was a crummy employee, she admitted, not good at taking direction, particularly when she thought it was misguided, and she usually thought it was. And she knew she wouldn't have been any better as a manager, because she wouldn't have been able to trust her employees to perform tasks capably. Her mother complained that she was a perfectionist. "I'm harder on myself than anyone," Ava would reply. "And you think that's a good thing?" her mother would answer.

Maybe not, Ava thought, but she was who she was, and she'd found the job that let her express that.

Less than twenty-four hours to go, she thought as she opened her hotel room door, *and then things will be back to normal*. In the meantime, all she could do was tolerate the distractions, keep moving ahead, and execute the plan.

She put her phone on the nightstand and then fell on top of the bed. She closed her eyes and thought about the house. It was now so familiar that she almost felt she'd been inside. In her mind's eye she could see the truck crashing the gate, the SUVs tucked in behind and careering into the courtyard, the men jumping out and running to the door, Carlo with his ram leading the way.

There's no reason it won't happen that way, she thought. *Sometimes things do go smoothly.*

Her phone rang, and she looked to see if it was May or Carlo. It was Uncle. "Hi," she said.

"Where are you?"

"I'm in my room."

"I thought you would be busy getting organized."

"I am organized. I'm waiting now."

"I just called to wish you good luck."

"Thanks."

"Call me the moment it is over."

"I will."

"Do you have everything you need?"

She thought, *He doesn't know about Sonny*. Before she could catch herself she said, "Sonny is coming with me."

"I am not surprised."

"I don't think he wanted you to know."

"Then I do not."

"I'm going in at dawn," she said. "You should hear from me by seven."

"Be careful."

"I always am."

She looked at the clock on the table. It was just past eleven thirty. If she hustled, she could get to Victoria Park before the lunchtime crowd. Off came the business wear and on went the running gear.

It was another beautiful day. *Almost surreal actually*, she thought when she got to the park. *Is this God's way of giving me something to enjoy on my last day?* She got in two quick laps and then one moderate one before she was forced to slow to a crawl. She carried her phone in her hand while she ran, looking at the screen anxiously, fearful of missing a call. The first one didn't come until she was on the MTR headed back to Central.

"The boat is in Macau," Carlo said. "No problems."

"Then head over as soon as you can. Unpack everything, make sure the weapons are clean and primed, and store them in a dry, safe place. You might as well drop off the megaphone while you're at it; no point taking it to the hotel. Tell your cousin we'll be at the boat tomorrow morning at five thirty to do the pickup, and tell him I'll bring money with me."

"You got it."

"And then check into the Kingsway and call me when you're settled. I imagine I'll be there around dinnertime."

"I'll take my two men with me when I go. How about Andy?"

"Leave him and Sonny alone until I hear about the truck. I don't want to jinx myself."

"See you tonight then," he said.

Ava stepped out of the MTR into the crush of lunchtime Hong Kong. She hadn't eaten breakfast and still had no appetite. She looked up towards the Peak, in the direction of the Mid-levels. It was a quarter to one. Michael should have his photo by now; he should have called Lok. She'd give him until one, and if she hadn't heard from him by then she'd phone.

When she got to the hotel, she showered and changed back into her business clothes. She packed her carry-on bag: white New Balance runners with black and orange trim, white ankle socks, her black nylon training pants and jacket, the balaclava, black bra and panties, black T-shirt, and her toilet kit. Still no call from Michael. *Five more minutes*, she thought.

The phone rang just as she was reaching for it. "Michael, is everything okay?"

"I think so. I got the photo right on schedule but I had trouble reaching Lok. When I finally did, he didn't react very well to our exchange proposal."

"He was happy about getting cash, I bet."

"Oh yes, he had no problem with that, but he wanted nothing to do with the lobby of the Venetian," Michael said without any noticeable concern. In fact, he was calmer now than at any time since her arrival in the city.

Lok's reluctance was understandable, she thought. "What did you work out?"

"I didn't agree to anything — I mean, finalize anything. I told him I'd have to speak to my people."

My people? Ava thought. "Your people are listening," she said.

"He suggested that we meet in the square in front of St. Paul's Basilica. He said there's a lot of public parking nearby. We come in one car, them in another. We park where we can and then contact each other. Lok wants the suitcases in the trunk of our car so they can check them without attracting a lot of attention. If the money's there, we'll do the exchange at some midway point between their car and ours."

Yeah, sure, Ava thought. He'd want someplace open where he could position as many men as he wanted. If she'd had any intention of meeting with him, she never would have agreed to the arrangement. As it was, all she wanted him to think was that at some time on Friday afternoon, somewhere in Macau, Michael would be there with the money. "What do you think?" she said.

"It seems fine to me."

"Then call him back and tell him he's got a deal."

"Just like that?"

"Exactly like that."

"Okay."

"Now, can I have a word with Amanda?"

"She's just left. She's heading to Sha Tin to spend the night with Jessie."

Ava's phone beeped with an incoming call. "Michael, I have to go. I'll call you first thing in the morning and we'll finalize our Macau arrangements," she said, switching lines.

"The truck is in Macau," May said.

"Fantastic. Are you ready to leave?"

"I am."

"Meet you downstairs in ten minutes."

Ava phoned Andy and Sonny. The message was the same. "We're a go. See you in Macau."

25

MAY LING HAD CHANGED CLOTHES AND WAS NOW dressed in black slacks and a black raw linen blouse. Her mood was also different. She was quiet, almost withdrawn. After getting monosyllabic replies to some simple questions, Ava retreated into her own silence.

They were on the hydrofoil and halfway to Macau when May said, "I'm incredibly nervous."

"Me too," Ava said.

"You don't look it."

Ava gazed out the window at the churning sea. "Inside I'm doing flip-flops. I work hard at staying positive, but doubts always creep into my head. And the longer the wait, the more they occur to me."

"And what can go wrong here?"

"I don't want to talk about it."

"Is that you being superstitious?"

"Maybe."

May said, "When Song called me to say he'd arrived in Macau, this situation became very, very real to me. I mean, before that I understood what we were doing, but it was outside me. When I talked to Song, I thought, 'We're actually going to Macau, and we're actually going through with this. I've brought a truck and a driver all the way from Wuhan to start what could be a mini war.'"

"We're going to Macau to save a man's life — that's what you need to think," Ava said. "It will be over soon enough."

"What are your plans when we land?"

"I'll pick up our SUV and then we'll locate Song and drive to the house. You did tell him what is expected of him?"

"I did, in detail. His only worry was damaging the truck. Have you thought of that?"

"Of what?"

"The truck. What if it gets disabled?"

"We'll leave it there. The driver can ride back with us. If the authorities get involved, you tell them it was a stolen vehicle. I'm sure the police in Wuhan will back you up."

May Ling looked thoughtful and Ava knew she had something else to say, but both fell silent again.

This was Ava's fourth trip to Macau in four days, and she wondered if the immigration officer would comment. He barely glanced at her passport as he waved her through. Ava led May towards the car rental area.

The company had put the two SUVs aside for her. She did the paperwork and left her credit card number for both. All Sonny had to do when he arrived was show his driver's licence. As she turned to leave, May said, "I was thinking, maybe I should rent a car for myself."

"Why do you need a car?"

"You were just going to leave me at the hotel?"

"That was the idea."

"What about the second truck driver?"

And then Ava realized she hadn't thought about their accommodation. "Geez, I forgot about that. We need to get them a room at the hotel."

"I know them, and they won't leave the truck. Besides, it has its own sleeping quarters."

"Then surely he won't mind being on his own for a few hours after we leave."

"I was thinking that if I rented a car," May said slowly, "he could drive me out to Coloane with you in the morning. I really don't want to stay at the hotel by myself. I mean, I've come this far and I would like to see this through."

"You aren't seriously suggesting that you come to the house with us?"

May flicked her hand at Ava. "Of course not. I just want to be close at hand. When you were going over the map this morning, you pointed to where the main road meets the side road that leads to the house. We could park there at the intersection, act as lookouts. I mean, Ava, you wouldn't want to be in the house and have someone unexpectedly drop in on you. Geng — that's the other driver's name — and I can watch the road and give you a warning if anyone turns up."

She's going to be pissed at me if I leave her at the hotel, Ava thought. "Let's decide after we go to Coloane. I want to make sure there's a place to park the car without attracting unnecessary attention."

"Fair enough," May said, in a way that suggested she knew she had prevailed.

"Now call Song and find out exactly where he is."

May phoned him as they walked to the SUV. "They're at Fisherman's Wharf. The truck is parked outside the Rocks

Hotel and they're inside having some lunch in the café."

"Tell them we'll be there in five minutes."

Ava drove south, following the seacoast on her left. The road ran right onto the wharf, which was still a real working place. She passed about thirty fishing boats moored in the harbour, their nets and buoys and traps littering the area. The hotel was at the far end, a five-storey structure that looked a couple of hundred years old.

"There they are," May said as they parked, pointing to two middle-aged men emerging from the hotel. Dressed in jeans and T-shirts that were stretched across their big bellies, they were alternately smoking and picking at their teeth.

The two women climbed out of the SUV. "Hi, I'm Ava," she said, extending her hand as she walked towards them. The men didn't look her in the eye, their handshakes tentative.

"I'm Geng," one said. Song didn't say a word.

"We're going to drive to Coloane so you can see the job you have to do in the morning. We'll take my SUV," Ava said.

"Are you sure about Song?" Ava asked May as they walked to the car.

"They're intimidated, that's all. And a bit shy around the big boss and her friend."

"I hope that doesn't carry over into the way he drives."

"It won't, and by the way, there's the truck."

It was parked against the far wall of the hotel, the top of its red cab almost reaching the second-floor window. The front was flat and had a grille at the bottom topped by another grille with VOLVO slashed diagonally across it.

A sheet of red metal separated the upper grille from the window, which was topped by a metal awning. If there had been a driver inside the cab, Ava wasn't sure she would have been able to see him. "What a monster. I've never seen anything that size," Ava said.

"I think it should do the trick," said May.

The two men hung back when they reached the car, unsure about which seats to take. "Sit in the back," Ava said.

Ava took the Macau–Taipa Bridge out of the city to the causeway. The men were quiet. May tried to engage them in conversation, asking about the drive from Wuhan, and then gave up when all they seemed able to say was "No problem."

"My God, this is really beautiful. Who would have thought this existed here," May said when Ava reached southern Coloane and started the drive along the coastline, the sea shimmering to their right, the peak and the head of A-Ma looming on the left.

Ava drove past the turnoff to the house and stopped on the shoulder. She pointed back. "That's the road we're going to take," she said. "It's curvy for the first bit, but the last hundred metres are relatively straight. When we get to the end, you'll see the house and the gate. The problem is, there's two hundred metres of open space between the end of the road and the gate, so we can't hang around too long. When we're finished, we'll climb the peak to visit A-Ma. From the top you can get another view."

While Ava was speaking, May was looking around. "There seems to be all kinds of room to park a car and not attract attention. I mean, we could be here to watch the sun come up over the sea."

"Seems to be," Ava said.

She did a U-turn and drove down the side road. Both men in the back leaned forward. The route was more winding and narrow than she remembered. *Maybe it's the difference between driving a Toyota and an SUV,* she thought. She couldn't go more than thirty kilometres an hour, and she realized that the truck would have to drive even more slowly. When the road straightened to the right, she eased the car up to fifty but then had to brake when they neared the opening.

"I'm going to creep forward," she said.

"Why don't we get out and walk to the end," May said. "We can hide behind those trees. No one should see us."

"Great idea," Ava said.

The four of them moved forward, hugging the treeline to the right. From their vantage point they could see three-quarters of the gate, its left side blanketed by the wall. They stood there for several minutes. Then Song said, "If I come down this road at any speed and then take the fastest direct run at the gate, I'm not going to be able to hit it dead-on. I'll hit it at an angle, on the right side there, and there's a chance the truck — the back end of it, anyway — will smash into the wall. Remember, this isn't a family car that I can turn and spin any way I want. Once the truck is up to speed I don't have much control."

"You would still take down the gate, right?"

"I think so, but Madam Wong said the plan was for you to follow me in your cars."

"Yes."

"My fear is that the back end will hit the wall, and if it does, the truck could block the way into the house. You might not be able to drive through. Look," he said, picking up a stick. In the sand he drew an outline of the wall and the gate and then dragged the stick to the point of impact. "See, if I hit it there, the right side of the truck hits the wall. When it does, it will bounce left, like that."

Ava looked at his crude drawing. It made sense, and a feeling of apprehension crept into her belly as she tried to figure out the consequences.

"Song is right," Geng said, looking at May. "The truck would hit the wall and end up wedged in the gate. You would probably have to leave it there, and that is a very expensive vehicle."

"I don't care about losing a truck," May snapped. "All we care about right now is the gate."

"Are you sure it would be wedged in?" Ava asked.

"It could jackknife, roll over, anything. I can't be sure exactly how it would react, except that it probably wouldn't be something you would want," Song said.

"What would you suggest we do?"

"The best thing is for me to hit the gate flush in the middle, head-on."

"How would you do that?"

He drew another line in the sand. "I would have to take a hard right from here and then manoeuvre my truck around until it was facing the gate."

"How long would that take?"

"A couple of minutes."

"But then you're running at it from a standing start. What kind of speed can you generate?"

"I don't know for sure."

"Then you need to guess."

"Sixty kilometres an hour, maybe a bit more."

"Is that fast enough to take the gate down cleanly?"

Song hesitated and looked at his driving partner. Geng nodded. "We think so," Song said.

"What are you going to do?" May asked.

"I don't know yet," Ava said. "Tell me, Song, how much noise does that truck make? I mean, if you have to spend a few minutes manoeuvring it into place?"

"It's a truck," Song said.

"And you're outside in the middle of nowhere, with no other sounds," Geng added.

"Shit," Ava said. "Well, I'm going to have to think about this."

"It's all the same to me," Song said. "I'll do whatever you decide."

"Thanks," Ava said. "Now, do you want to go up to the peak?"

"I don't need to. I've seen everything I need to see," said Song.

"Okay, we'll head back to Macau."

She backed the car up the road to the main highway, her mind now on the gate. When she reached the junction, May tapped her on the arm and pointed towards the sea. "I could park a car there on the shoulder and then sit on the seawall. It would be a nice way to start the day."

"All right, May, go rent a car."

There was no more talk about the gate on the drive back to Macau, although Ava could hear the two men whispering in the back and see their hands moving to form various angles.

They dropped off Song and Geng at the truck, May telling them to be ready the next morning for a five-thirty departure. Then she added, "No drinking, no women, no gambling."

Ava drove to the ferry terminal, where May could rent a car, and then headed for the Kingsway Hotel. As she pulled into valet parking, Carlo and his two friends were getting out of a taxi, their bags in hand. Ava joined them and they walked into the lobby together. Carlo had a phone pressed to his ear. *Sonny*, he mouthed.

Ava held out her hand and Carlo passed her the phone. "It's Ava. Where are you?"

"On the ferry. Andy and his brother-in-law are with me."

"I made all the arrangements for the SUV. All you have to do is show them a licence."

"Thanks, and Carlo just told me that he and I are bunking together."

"So you should be set."

"We're having dinner together — the guys."

"I won't join you."

"Carlo said you wouldn't."

"I need head space. I can't switch on and off as quickly as you can."

"You don't have to explain."

No, I don't, she thought. "So I'll see you in the lobby at five," she said.

"Five."

She handed the phone back to Carlo, who promptly closed it.

"Have you been to the boat?" Ava asked.

"We just came from there."

"And?"

"Perfect."

26

AVA SAT AT THE HOTEL ROOM WINDOW, LOOKING OUT over Macau. The sun had set an hour before, but she could hardly tell night from day as the neon signs and klieg lights of the hotels and casinos flooded every square inch of the territory. She could see all the way to Taipa, to the Cotai Strip, to the City of Dreams, its pod-like shopping complex glowing like a spaceship. It seemed a lifetime ago that she'd walked through its doors with Michael and Simon to meet Kao Lok and Wu. Now she'd be walking through another door to meet them again. Strangely, she had only the vaguest memory of their faces. Lok's teeth were all that came sharply to mind when she thought about him. With Wu, it was the mole with its curly hairs.

May had called her when she checked into the hotel. Ava begged off dinner, explaining, as she had to Sonny, her need to be alone.

When she first got back to the room, she had sat at the small desk with her notebook open. She drew a diagram of the road, the courtyard, the gate, and then retraced the lines Song had marked in the sand. She had to make a decision, and the problem was that each of the options available to her carried its own set of risks. How to weigh them?

She started off by listing them and ended up with a multitude more, almost equally divided between the two. She thought of her breezy presentation to the men that morning, of her confidence about smashing through the gate. The one thing she had to have was certainty, she thought, certainty that the truck would bring down the gate and penetrate the courtyard.

Making a diagonal run from the side road to the gate would give them maximum power and speed and would be the most time-efficient. And Ava was worried about time. Every second after the moment when Lok, Wu, and their men knew they were under attack was crucial. Every second Ava and the guys were outside the house gave those inside more opportunity to arm themselves and organize resistance.

But what if the truck hit the wall, as Song had projected, and flipped over? What if it blocked the gate, made it impassable for their SUVs — hell, made it impassable for them even on foot?

So, option two: Song takes his time, a couple of minutes, and lines up the truck properly to ram the centre of the gate. If the gate collapses when he hits it, there isn't any barrier for the cars and they're at the door within seconds.

Song had estimated he'd get up to sixty kilometres an hour and that velocity would be enough to get through the gate. But he hadn't been sure, and neither had Geng. What if he couldn't get up to sixty? What if he did and it wasn't enough to do the job?

And then there was the noise issue. Just how loud was the truck going to be? While Song was moving it back and forth to get into position, would the people inside the house hear him? If they did, it would be a disaster. By the time they got into the house they'd run smack into seven or eight guns aimed at the door.

She'd called downstairs to the restaurant and ordered a plate of pad Thai and a bottle of sparkling water. She ate at the desk, her eyes flitting over the diagram, her lists, her comments. When she was done, she had moved to the window and had been there since, thinking and debating. There was nothing satisfying about coming to a decision between two evils.

It was nine o'clock when she finally stirred. She wasn't tired but she knew she should try to sleep. She showered and changed into panties and a T-shirt. Then she emptied the rest of her bag and laid out on the sofa the clothes she'd be putting on in the morning. There was an alarm in the room. She set it for four thirty and then called downstairs for a wake-up call for the same time, though she knew she probably wouldn't need either.

Ava had left her computer at the Mandarin, and her cellphone had been off since she'd got on the hydrofoil in Hong Kong. She turned it on and listened to messages from Uncle and Amanda. He was once more wishing her luck. She had arrived in Sha Tin and was walking to Jessie's. They would both have to wait to hear from her.

She crawled into bed and pulled the covers right up to her chin. *I won't sleep*, she thought, but she began to perform a bak mai *kata*, a standard series of exercises, in her mind. She did it in slow motion, trying to picture every little detail. She wasn't halfway through before she drifted off.

Ava dreamt, as she often did, about her father. This was different, though, from the usual theme of missed airplanes, hotel rooms that couldn't be located, cab drivers who never took her where she wanted to go. Her father was in a restaurant, sitting at a table with two strangers. He ignored her when she walked in. One of the men was holding a gun under the table against her father's leg while the other was insulting him. Ava asked him to stop, and the man spat at her and cursed her. The gun went off; her father collapsed to the floor, holding his leg. Ava pulled a knife from her bag and was about to attack when her alarm went off and the phone rang. *What a way to start the day*, she thought.

She made an instant coffee and drank it so quickly it scalded her mouth. She made another and carried it to the bathroom. She washed, brushed her teeth, fastened her hair with the lucky ivory chignon pin, and put on her gold crucifix and Cartier Tank Française watch.

She dressed slowly, making sure there were no wrinkles in her socks and that her black T-shirt was tucked tightly into her black training pants. She tied her runners with a double knot. Then she turned towards the bed and eased onto her knees. With her hands pressed together in front of her face, she began to pray.

She prayed to Saint Jude, the patron saint of lost causes, and asked him to help her get through the day. She prayed for the safety of her men, that she would find Simon alive and well, and that no unnecessary harm would come to Lok's men or his servants.

It was ten to five when she walked into the lobby. Everyone was already there. Carlo and Andy and their men were outside smoking; Sonny and May were standing together just inside the door. Ava gave a little wave and then went to the front desk. She checked out, signed all of the bills, and handed the girl her valet ticket.

"How did you sleep?" May asked when Ava joined them.

"Surprisingly well."

"I don't think I slept for more than half an hour at a time."

May was wearing her black slacks and blouse from the day before. "You fit in quite nicely," Ava said, pointing to the men, who were uniformly dressed in black. She hadn't specified what they should wear; she imagined Carlo and Andy had made that decision. Sonny was wearing a dark blue mock-turtleneck shirt and black slacks. "We look like we're going to a funeral."

"I wish you wouldn't say things like that," May said.

It took a full ten minutes to get the two SUVs and May's rented Nissan to the front door. Ava put Carlo and his men in her car, leaving Sonny with Andy and his brother-in-law.

"We're going to Fisherman's Wharf. We'll meet at Carlo's cousin's boat. May will get the truck and the driver, then off we go," Ava said.

It was a relatively tight schedule, and Ava had planned it that way. There was nothing worse than waiting, and she didn't want to give any of the men time to start thinking about what could go wrong. She'd done enough of that for all of them.

The wharf was a few minutes from the hotel, the boat moored near the entrance. Carlo directed her to it, and when she got near she saw a man sitting on a capstan.

"That's him," Carlo said.

The guns were stashed on the deck under a tarpaulin. Each man took his own, checking the firing action, the ammunition. Ava picked up her Kahr. It was an incredibly light gun, one of the most accurate she'd ever fired. "Put the ram in our car and distribute the handcuffs," she told Carlo.

She heard the truck before she saw it: a low rumble, disquietingly powerful. Then it rolled into view, filling their line of vision. "Fuck me," Andy's brother-in-law said. "I've never seen a truck that size."

Song looked down from the cab, his position so high that Ava couldn't see his shoulders. She saw him stare at the guns and blink in surprise. They were well armed, she knew. Andy's brother-in-law and one of Carlo's men had Uzis. Carlo's other guy wielded a Koch machine gun. Andy carried a Heckler. Sonny's Cobray was a match for any of them. Only she and Carlo had pistols, but they were both semi-automatic and in tight quarters just as effective.

"Follow me," she yelled at Song.

They clambered back into the cars. Getting their weapons into their hands had given the men a bit of a buzz.

"So where did you have dinner last night?" she asked Carlo as they pulled out of the wharf, Sonny behind her, May following him, the truck in the rear.

"We went into old Macau, to an animal restaurant."

"What did you eat?"

"Bat and some raccoon," he said, and turned to his friends. "What did you think of our meal last night?"

Ava smiled. It was her ploy to talk about anything other than the job, to calm the men's nerves, distract them. Carlo had obviously picked up on it.

The men talked about the dinner and other memorable meals for the entire trip to Coloane. Ava was happy to listen to them.

It wasn't quite six o'clock when they reached the highway that ran along the sea. Ava stopped short of the turnoff, parking on the shoulder. The others lined up behind her. She got out of the SUV and motioned for everyone else to do the same. Then she walked over to the seawall and sat down. They gathered around, waiting for Song to lower himself from the truck. "Don't rush — we can't afford to lose you," she yelled at him.

When he joined them, she said, "This is Song, and you obviously know what he does. He came here with me yesterday and looked at the gate. He had some suggestions and I think I'm going to follow them, so we have some slight changes to our plans," Ava said calmly. "Instead of making a direct diagonal run from the end of the side road to the gate, we've decided that Song will position the truck so that it can run straight through the gate. What that means for us is, instead of following him immediately across the courtyard, we're going to hang back until he's ready to charge. Then we'll tuck in behind and follow him down and in. After that, we follow the plan as we discussed in Hong Kong."

She didn't ask if there were any questions and she wasn't interested in any comments. "Okay, back to the vehicles, and everyone get their balaclavas on."

Ava walked with Song back to the truck. "Maximum speed, right?" she said.

"My foot will be on the floor."

"And don't take all day to get into position. That truck is so damn loud."

"I figure I'll drive straight right from the roadway, make a hard left, go down about twenty metres to straighten up, and then back up and I'm ready to go. I thought about it all last night."

"How did you know I'd make that choice?"

"It's the right one."

Ava said, "Then why did it take me so long to get to it?"

"You don't drive trucks for a living."

"Song, once you're through the gate and we're past you and in the courtyard, I want you to leave. Turn the truck around and head back to Macau."

"No, I can't. I'll go back out to the highway and wait with Geng and Madam Wong."

She watched him climb the stairs back up to the truck's cab, and knew there was no point in arguing. He wouldn't leave May alone.

May had stood off to the side while Ava was talking to the others. Now she drew near. "I guess I'll go sit on the wall."

Ava checked her watch. Five minutes to dawn. The sun was already starting to tease its way above the horizon. She looked out to sea and then stepped back, startled, as a brilliant streak of green shot across the point where water met sky. "Good God, did you see that?"

"A green flash!" May said. "I've read about them, and I have a friend who lives in Borneo who goes down to the beach every night at sunset to try to see one. They are rare, really rare. That has to be a good omen, Ava."

Ava felt the opposite, and she didn't know why. "I'm going to have my cellphone on, May, but don't call me unless it really is necessary. And don't time us. I have no idea how long this will take. When it's done, it's done."

"Good luck," May said.

27

SONG LED THE WAY DOWN THE SIDE ROAD, THE TRUCK going no faster than twenty kilometres an hour. Inside the SUV there wasn't a sound. When Song got to the end of the road, he stopped and Ava's heart leapt. Then the truck started moving again, hard to the right. To her it sounded like a freight train.

She eased the nose of her SUV into the open courtyard area. Song had already turned the truck to the left and was slowly rolling downhill. Then he braked and started to climb back, the truck straightening beautifully. She moved farther into the courtyard. He leaned out of his cab and stuck out his hand, giving the thumbs-up.

"Here we go, boys," she said as she turned into the yard, Sonny on her tail.

She looked down at the house. The sun hadn't entirely peaked yet. The house was still in shadows, and Ava couldn't see a single light on inside.

The truck revved and lurched forward. Ava swung in behind. She looked at her speedometer as they headed for the gate. Forty, fifty, sixty, seventy, eighty...

When the Volvo hit the gate, steel pipes flew in all directions. Song swung the truck hard to the left, braking madly. Ava drove straight towards the front door, Sonny now alongside.

She could hear the alarm inside the house before she got out of the car. The gate had been wired. *Fifteen seconds*, she thought.

Carlo ran at the door, the ram on his hip. He hit at the locks. Nothing. He hit it again. Nothing. Sonny leapt forward and grabbed the ram, moved back about five metres, and charged. The door cracked. He kicked it, and then kicked it again, until it fell back into the house.

Ava was the first one through the door, her eyes locked on the second floor in the direction of Lok's bedroom. She saw him run out in jockey shorts and a white undershirt. She aimed her gun at him and yelled, "Don't move!" She glanced quickly to the left, looking for Wu. His bedroom door was open but he was nowhere to be seen. Sonny swung his gun from side to side, his eyes searching, a worried look on his face.

Carlo and Andy and their men had charged into the house right behind them, fanning out into the lounge area, the men staying low, their guns trained on the door to the wing. Shots rang out, and she heard two screams.

Ava kept her gun on Lok. "Don't move!" she yelled again, trying to be heard above the alarm.

He looked down at her, and then his eyes flicked to the left.

Ava turned in that direction and saw Wu standing in the kitchen doorway with a gun in his hand. Without thinking, she jumped left and low towards a brown couch, her instincts screaming that he would have to bring his hand across his body to shoot at her. She felt the bullet rip through her right thigh.

She hit the floor hard, her elbows and knees taking a beating and her thigh searing with pain. She couldn't see Wu but she knew he would come for her. She crawled around the couch, staying low, trying to catch a view of the kitchen. The doorway inched into sight, but Wu wasn't there. Then she saw a bare foot. The first bullet caught him square on the ankle bone. He collapsed, exposing his shin. She shot him again.

Sonny ran past her and she heard his Cobray fire three times.

She looked up. Lok was gone, his bedroom door closed.

Sonny came to her and said, "He caught you in the leg. You're bleeding like hell."

"Go talk to Carlo, find out what's going on over there."

"Let me look at your leg."

"Sonny, talk to Carlo first."

He looked down at her.

"Go," she said.

She grabbed hold of the edge of the couch and pulled herself up. She reached for her waistband and slid her pants down. Her legs looked ridiculously pale in contrast to the brown couch and the blood that was running down her leg. "Shit," she said. She glanced over to where Wu had been standing. Only the top half of his body was visible behind another couch. It lay in an expanding pool of blood that was seeping from a hole in his chest and from at least two bullet wounds to his head.

Sonny and Carlo came back in a rush and then retreated when they saw her leg. Ava had never felt so naked in her life. "How are you doing over there?" she said to Carlo.

"It's under control. We shot two of them. One's dead, the other half-dead. The rest of them ran back into the wing."

"How many of them?"

"We saw five in total, so I guess there are three left."

"Get the ram. I need you and Sonny to get Lok out of his room and to turn off that damn alarm. Then tell Andy to talk the rest of Lok's people out of the wing. If they won't come out, he'll have to go in and get them."

"You've been shot," Carlo said.

"So?"

He paused. "I'll go talk to Andy."

Sonny stood over her. "You're bleeding badly."

"I don't think it hit bone. Have a look."

He bent to one knee, held her leg, and twisted it. "I think you're right. It looks like it just hit flesh."

"Go to the kitchen and see what you can find to wrap it."

He left and she waited. *It's gone well so far,* she told herself.

Carlo came back and said, "Andy will try to talk them out."

"Ten minutes, no more. If they aren't out in ten minutes, he goes in."

"Okay, boss."

She could see that Carlo was looking everywhere but at her. "I'm wearing underwear, for God's sake," she said as Sonny came back with some dishcloths.

"It's all I could find," he said.

"Wrap the leg," she said.

He had to knot two of them together to get them completely around the leg. "Now what?" he said.

"I want you and Carlo to flush out Lok. Break down the door and get that fucker out of there. When you do, have him turn off the alarm," she said. "Then handcuff him and come and get me."

She sat back down on the couch, her naked leg stretched in front of her. She turned to watch Sonny and Carlo climb the stairs and walk along the mezzanine to Lok's room. They flanked the door, Sonny rapping it with his knuckles and yelling at him to come out. They waited and then Sonny yelled again. She saw him nod at Carlo, and they moved together with the ram held between them. Then the door opened and Lok stood there in jeans and a Burberry shirt. Sonny reached for him, grabbing him by the shirt collar, and took him back into the room.

It took a minute for the alarm to stop its deafening screech.

Sonny bounded down the stairs and came over to Ava. "He's cuffed."

"I don't think I can walk. You'll have to carry me up."

"Put your pants back on," he said.

She stood up and bent over to reach for them, and the pain shot down her leg. It felt as if every nerve ending were on fire. She grimaced as she slid her pants back up.

"Better," Sonny said.

"Now carry me."

He picked her up, cradling her against his chest. As he climbed the stairs she could see Andy standing at the entrance to the wing, yelling. "You have five minutes to surrender," he said. "If you come out with your hands over your heads, you live. If we have to come in and get you, we'll be firing." He waited and then repeated the same message. *Don't be stupid*, she thought. *Come out.*

Sonny and Carlo had put Lok on his bed, his wrist attached to the bedpost. Ava looked around the room.

There was a big-screen television tucked into a corner with a floral-patterned easy chair in front of it. To the side there was a desk, covered in paper. Next to the door was a card table with four wooden chairs around it. "I'll sit in the easy chair," she said.

Sonny put her down as gently as he could, but there was no escaping the pain. "Put him on one of those wooden chairs and then turn it to face me," she said.

Carlo undid the cuffs attached to the bed, grabbed Lok by the nape of his neck, shoved him over to the chair, and locked the cuffs to it.

Lok stared at her. There was an initial hint of confusion in his eyes that quickly turned to rage. Ava felt sweat gathering inside the balaclava, and she decided to peel it off. Carlo and Sonny followed suit. "You bitch," Lok said.

"Where is Simon To?" she asked.

"You did all this for that stupid fucker?" Lok snapped.

"Where is he? You know there's no point in not telling me."

He stayed silent, glaring at her. "The room next door," he finally said.

"Is it locked?"

"No."

"Carlo, go check," she said.

They waited, Sonny standing alongside Lok, aching for any excuse to do him harm. Lok kept his attention on Ava, who was trying to find a position that would minimize the pain in her thigh.

Carlo hurled himself back into Lok's bedroom. "He's there. Taped hand and foot, and he's pissed himself more than once. Otherwise he's fine."

"Did you cut the tape?"

"Not yet."

"Geez, Carlo, do it now."

"Yes, boss."

After Carlo left, Ava said to Lok, "Wu is dead, and your other men are either dead or will be if they don't come out of their wing."

"Fuck you," he said.

"And the police aren't coming."

His face showed no reaction but she saw a shadow move across his eyes as he began to calculate the truth of her words. Then the rage in them returned, and she knew he didn't believe her. "The alarm has been disconnected at the police station," she said. "They have no idea we're here. So no one is going to come to your rescue."

He shook his head from side to side.

"I'll tell you what," Ava said. "We'll wait another ten or fifteen minutes, or however long you want. The thing is, I want you to co-operate with me, and I think you're smart enough to do that if you know help isn't on the way. I mean, if it's just you, me, and Sonny, alone and intimate for the next hour or so, you know you're going to do what I want anyway. But I don't want to waste time, and I don't particularly want to watch Sonny crush your balls and cut off your cock."

"Ava?"

She turned and looked at the door. Carlo had his arms around Simon To, helping him walk. To was shaking, tears running down his cheeks. His face was drawn, pale, fear still dancing in his eyes. Even from a distance she could smell him. "Hey, Simon," she said.

Carlo started to lead him across the room to her chair. "Let's not do this now," Ava said. "Carlo, take him to the bathroom and put him in the shower. Then go to Wu's room and get some clothes for him; they're about the same size. And then take him downstairs to the kitchen and get him a glass of water or something. Wu is on the ground near there, so Simon, if you're squeamish about dead bodies, close your eyes when you go past. We'll come down when we're finished here."

As Carlo and Simon turned to go, Andy burst past them into the room. "They came out, all three of them. We've gone through the wing and that's all there are."

"Are they handcuffed?"

"We're doing it now."

"Tape their ankles and mouths as well."

"Okay, boss."

"And, Andy, one more thing. There's an elderly couple in the middle bedroom on this floor. They're servants. Get them to come out. Don't be rough with them, but I still want them handcuffed and left with the others downstairs. Then you come back here."

"How are you feeling?" Sonny asked when he saw her wince.

"Not bad, considering."

"What are we going to do with him?"

She said to Lok, "I've got Simon, and now I want Simon's money returned."

"Fuck off."

Ava checked her watch. "Ten minutes already and no police. How long does it normally take them to get here?"

Lok glared at her.

She heard crying in the hallway. Sonny stuck his head outside the door. "Andy has the servants," he said.

"So that leaves you," Ava said to Lok, and then turned to Sonny. "I have a pair of handcuffs in my jacket. Take them out and attach this asshole's ankle to the chair leg. Then go downstairs to the kitchen and see what you can find in the way of utensils. A large, sharp serrated knife would be good, a meat cleaver even better. And see if you can find a hammer." She smiled at Lok. "Andy is handy with a cleaver, and I've heard stories about how proficient Sonny is with a hammer."

Lok didn't resist as Sonny chained him.

"When you come back, bring Andy with you," she said.

28

LOK WATCHED THE BIG MAN LEAVE AND THEN SPAT IN
Ava's direction.

"I want the money," Ava said.

"I don't have it."

"Bull."

"I spent it."

"Not all of it, you didn't."

"I don't have it."

"I don't know why you guys always insist on doing things the hard way. I mean, I'm not stealing it from you or anything. It's our money, and all I'm asking you to do is return it. If you think about it that way, it might be easier, you know. You need to get into the right frame of mind."

"Fuck off."

"That's fifteen minutes now, and still no police," Ava said, showing him her watch.

The house was so quiet now, she could hear the shower running in the bathroom next door.

"There's no computer in here. Do you have one somewhere else?"

He shook his head.

"How do you do banking, then?"

He ignored her, and Ava began to contemplate just how she was going to get her hands on the money. If there wasn't a computer, an online transfer was out of the question, and so were electronic instructions from Lok to the bank. She shifted in her chair again, the pain centred in her upper thigh now radiating downwards. Even resting the back of her knee against the chair was uncomfortable. *How the hell am I going to get back to Hong Kong?* she thought, and then caught herself. She had to get the money first, and then get out of the house. She'd worry about Hong Kong later.

Sonny entered the room with Andy at his heels. He carried two utensils: a meat cleaver and a stainless steel mallet. He laid them out on the table. "How do you want to start?" he asked Ava.

Ava pulled herself up from the chair, balancing on her good leg. "Hold my arm. I want to hop over to that desk," she told him.

The pain was excruciating, and if the distance had been more than three hops she would have succumbed to being carried again. She sat down, her leg extended, and began opening desk drawers. She found the banking information in the bottom one. There was a stack of thick files, one for each of Lok's businesses. She pulled out the Ma Shing Realty Corporation file and extracted the bank statements. They were from the Macau branch of the same bank Michael and Simon used. As of two weeks ago there had been more than HK$100 million in it. She opened other company files, looking for another $50 million. She found thirty of it in the Kwan Lok Entertainment Company and just over ten each in the Beautiful Lady Spa and Deluxe Spa. "I didn't know whorehouses and massage parlours were so profitable," she said.

"Fuck off," Lok said.

The chequebooks for the companies were under the files. She put them on the desk.

"Andy, Lok says there isn't a computer in the house. Have a quick look around and confirm that, will you?"

She twisted in the chair. "He might have to write some cheques, so whatever you do, don't hurt his writing hand," she said to Sonny.

"When do you want me to start?"

"We'll wait until Andy comes back."

She saw Lok glance at Sonny, and for the first time there was recognition in his eyes that she was serious. "Twenty minutes, and no police. I told you, we arranged to have the alarm disconnected," she said.

Carlo stuck his head in the door, Simon standing behind him. "We're heading downstairs."

"Simon," Ava called.

He took a couple of steps into the room. His face had already recovered some colour, and his eyes weren't full of panic and confusion anymore. Wu's clothes fit him badly; the jeans were so long he had rolled up the bottoms, and the blue San Miguel T-shirt was too tight. "You put a hundred and fifty million into this development, right?"

"Yeah."

"I thought so. Okay, head downstairs and get a drink and make yourself something to eat."

She began to think about Lok writing cheques. On the surface it wasn't the best idea — one phone call and he could cancel them. Except if he was tied up, like everyone else in the house, he wouldn't be in a position to make the call. How long could she count on that being the case? Maybe the whole day, maybe two days, maybe only an hour and a half? It was a complete gamble.

One thing she did know was the bank that everyone dealt with. That bank was on the hook for the 150 million, and if she could deposit the money today and instruct their branch manager to retire the loan, it would be very hard for Lok to undo that deed. One of the things Ava admired about Hong Kong banks was the way they looked after their own interests. If it came down to a choice between paying off a troubled loan and returning all the money to Lok, Ava had no trouble believing that the bank would stiff him.

Andy strolled into the room. "No computer anywhere."

She leaned forward, the effort causing her to grimace. "I want you to write four cheques: one on the Ma Shing account for a hundred million, another from Kwan Lok for thirty million, and the other two for ten million each. Make all the cheques payable to the Millennium Food Group. And on the note line at the bottom I want you to write 'repayment of monies advanced for Macau property investment.'"

He didn't react immediately, and for Ava that was a positive sign. She could almost see his mind whirring as he thought about how fast he could cancel the cheques.

"I'm going to give you another minute and then I'm handing you over to Sonny," she said.

He looked at Sonny and then at the hardware on the table. He had to know who Sonny was. And he had to know what Sonny was capable of.

"If I write those cheques, will that make us square?"

"Yeah, square, but I'm still going to leave you tied up like everyone else downstairs, and I need you to agree not to cancel those cheques."

"I just want you and those idiots with the noodle shops out of my life."

"Write the cheques, honour the cheques, and you'll never hear from any of us again. Try to screw us over and we'll be back. And next time Sonny won't be just a threat — Sonny will be your reality."

"Okay, I'll write them," he said.

"Undo the cuffs on his wrist and bring him here," Ava said, pushing back from the desk to make room for Lok.

He shuffled over, dragging the chair with his ankle. He was close enough that she could smell a hint of baby powder, and when he lifted his arm to reach for a pen, she saw traces of it in his armpit. *How peculiar*, she thought.

"Make them out to the Millennium Food Group."

"I know."

She stood on her good leg, watching over his shoulder. He took his time, following her directions precisely. When he was done, she said, "Now, that wasn't so hard, was it."

Sonny stood to one side, his arms folded across his chest. "Andy, take Lok into the hallway for a minute. I need to talk to Ava," he said.

Lok's head jerked up. Sonny ignored him. "Take him out now. I'll tell you when to come back."

Andy took hold of the back of the chair and dragged it to the door while Lok struggled to keep up with it.

Sonny closed the door behind him. "We can't leave Lok," he said to Ava.

"I know."

"We need to kill him."

"I have been thinking about that."

"And?"

"I don't know what other choice we have."

She was standing at the desk, her hand pressing down on it to support herself. She saw the determination in Sonny's eyes. "I was thinking the same thing," she said softly.

Sonny nodded. "I was hoping you'd see it that way. And this has nothing to do with those cheques. However this turned out today, he and Wu had to die. The other men downstairs don't matter; they'll forget about this as soon as they get out of here. But not those two. They'd come after us, and they have the money and the guts to succeed. I'm too old to have to worry about things like that."

"I know."

He walked over to the desk. "Do you want to sit?"

"No, I'm okay."

He gave her a rare smile. "I'm relieved. I thought I was going to have to argue with you," he said. "And I have to tell you that even if you'd disagreed with me, I was going to kill them anyway."

Ava knew he was saying that for her benefit, trying to make her feel she really had no part in the decision. "How do we do it?" she asked.

"A bullet in the head is the quickest and surest way."

"You'll need to get my gun. I left it downstairs on the couch," Ava said.

"No, no, I'll do it," Sonny said, reaching for her arm.

"There's no way that's going to happen," she said, pulling back. "This is my job, my decision, and my responsibility. I know it has to be done, and I've decided I'm the one who's going to do it. So, Sonny, please, go downstairs and get my gun."

"Uncle always said you were tougher than any of us."

"I don't think of myself as being tough. I think of myself as being responsible."

He backed away from her. "I'll go downstairs and get it. Andy needs to handcuff both of Lok's wrists. You don't want him flailing about."

Sonny left, and a moment later Andy was back in the room, pulling Lok with him. "Handcuff his wrists, both of them," Ava said, and then turned to Lok. "We'll leave you here for someone to find you. Hopefully it will take a day or two."

He looked uncertain, and Ava wondered if he suspected what the real plan was. He had to, she decided. It was exactly what he would have done if their positions had been reversed. He struggled a bit as Andy cuffed him.

"Thanks, Andy. Now you can go downstairs and start getting our group ready to leave. We should be out of here in a few minutes."

As soon as Andy walked out, Lok said to Ava, "Even if I get freed in the next few hours I'm not going to cancel those cheques, you know."

"I believe you."

"I mean it."

They looked at one another, each trying to decide who was telling the bigger lie.

Sonny walked into the room, his Cobray in one hand, Ava's Kahr in the other. He went to her and handed over the gun. "You'll have to support me," she said.

He slipped his arm around her waist and she put a hand on his shoulder. It was two hops to Lok, the pain getting worse now that the shock had begun to wear off.

Lok looked up at them, his eyes filled with fear. "We made a deal," he said, his voice cracking.

"Sorry, it has to be this way," Ava said, raising the gun and placing it against his temple.

"We made —"

She squeezed the trigger and then staggered back, shocked by the noise and by the explosion of blood. She fell against Sonny, her head against his chest. "Let's get out of here," he said, bending down to pick her up in his arms.

When they appeared at the top of the stairs, she saw Carlo and Andy and the other men below looking up at her. They had all heard the shot; they all knew what had happened. Simon stood in the kitchen entrance, his mouth wide open.

Sonny carried Ava down to the ground floor. The three men and the servants were sitting against the wall on the far left side, their hands cuffed behind them, ankles and mouths taped. Carlo had pulled the dead body behind a couch in the den. The guy who was wounded lay on the same couch. It looked like he had a bullet in his leg and another in his side. Carlo had cuffed him and taped his mouth but left his ankles free.

On the other side of the room was what was left of Wu. Ava saw that the body had stopped bleeding.

Ava was about to tell the men to gather their things when her phone rang. She pulled it from her pocket and saw May's name on the call display. "We're leaving the house now. We'll see you in a couple of minutes," Ava said.

"A police car's just turned onto the road that leads to the house," May said.

Ava felt sick, her stomach burning. "How many cars?"

"One."

Ava looked at her watch. They had been in the house for almost half an hour, so this couldn't be in response to the alarm. And they would have sent more than one car if they knew what was going down. This had to be a patrol vehicle doing a regular check, she reasoned. Not that it lessened the problem if they decided to come into the house. And why wouldn't they, with the gate smashed in and the front door demolished?

"You have to reach General Feng, May. You have to get in touch with him and tell him to arrange to get that car the hell away from here."

"Right away."

"And then call me back."

"How did things go?"

"May, call the General," Ava shouted.

Sonny looked at her.

"A police car is coming," she said.

"Shit."

"Yeah, exactly. I'm sorry, Sonny, this wasn't supposed to happen."

He shrugged.

Andy was at the front door looking out onto the court-yard. "There's a police car with two cops in it outside the gate, Ava."

"I know," she said.

"What are we going to do?"

"What are they doing?"

"Looking and talking. I don't think they know what to make of it."

"Have you seen them reach for their radio yet?"

"No, not yet."

"Put me on the couch, please," she said to Sonny. When she was settled, she said, "We need to buy some time."

"What do you want to do?" Sonny asked.

"I think you should go outside and talk to them, Sonny. Tell them Mr. Lok had an incident during the night, but it's over now and things are back to normal. Thank them for dropping by."

"Will they believe that?"

"What else do you suggest?"

She could feel the tension in the room, every man's imagination starting to run wild. She felt her own panic, and struggled to contain it. She had to stay calm, she told herself; at the very least she had to look calm. "Go, do the best you can," she said.

He dropped his gun on the couch next to her and headed for the front door. Andy moved aside and then slid back to follow Sonny's progress. "Tell me what's going on," Ava shouted to him.

"Sonny's waving at them and he's walking across the courtyard slowly. God, he's got balls," Andy said. "He's reached the cops and is pointing back at the house. They're listening...One of the cops is talking now and Sonny is doing the listening...They're shaking hands, and Sonny is heading back."

"Have the police left?"

"No, they're still outside, and it looks like they're arguing. One of them is pointing inside the vehicle."

He wants to call for backup, she thought.

Sonny took his time coming back. When he came into the house, he walked directly over to Ava. She could tell by his face that it hadn't gone very well. "Carlo and Andy, get over here," she yelled. And then softly to Sonny, "Wait for them."

They gathered around her. "What happened?" she asked.

"You were right, it's a regular patrol. They're really shook up by the gate and the door, but they know who Lok is, so they're not surprised that this kind of shit went down. I told them that we were fine and there was no need for them to get involved. The problem is, they don't know me and they asked to talk to Lok. One of them wanted to come into the house, and I said Lok didn't want any visitors. So he asked me to send Lok out. I said he was sleeping. At that point he told me to wake him. When I said I didn't want to, he said he was going to phone the precinct office and request backup. I told him I'd wake Lok, and they backed off."

"Fuck," Carlo said.

"How much more time do you think we have?" Ava asked.

"Five, ten minutes, no more than that," said Sonny.

"What do we do if the cops come into the house?" Andy asked, looking at Ava.

"I don't know about you, but I have no desire to spend two or three months in a Chinese prison waiting for them to put a bullet in my head," Ava said. "If the cops come, we resist."

"What if they wait for backup?" asked Carlo.

"We resist harder."

"It's the only way," Sonny said.

"How will your men feel about this?" she said to Carlo and Andy.

"If you had said anything different we would have had a problem."

"Okay, so we know where we stand. Andy, go back to the door and keep your eyes on them."

"We could try to rush the two guys out there now," Carlo said.

Sonny looked down at Ava, disapproval on his face.

"We couldn't get across the courtyard fast enough," she said. "Let's be patient, huh? May Ling is trying to work her brand of magic. Give her a chance."

Simon had ventured out of the kitchen again. Ava didn't know how anyone could look more out of place. "Simon, I want to talk to you," she said.

The cocky man she'd seen in the Millennium videos was gone. The angry man who had accompanied her on the first trip to Macau was gone. "They told me you were shot," he said when he drew near. "I can't tell you how sorry I am about all this."

Ava reached into her jacket pocket and pulled out the four cheques. "These cheques cover the money you advanced to Lok. Get them into a bank as fast as you can . . . Now, it could get hairy around here in the next fifteen minutes or so, and I don't want you anywhere near it. So stay close and pay attention to me. The moment I yell your name, I want you to get upstairs as fast as you can and get into one of those bedrooms. Don't concern yourself with anything going on down here. If your door opens and the police come charging in, tell them exactly what happened between you and Lok, and leave us out of it. You don't know who we are or why Lok and us were having a go at each other. You're just an innocent bystander. Got that?"

"I think so."

"Simon, I've gone to a lot of trouble for you. I don't want you to do anything but agree with me and do exactly what I say."

"Okay."

"Now this may all come to nothing, but I've never believed in ignoring the worst-case scenario."

"Do you want me to go upstairs now?"

"No, not yet. I'll tell you when."

"They're talking again," Andy yelled from the door. "One of them sure as hell wants to call this in."

May, where are you? Ava thought, reaching for her phone. She got a busy signal. A busy signal was good — or bad. She didn't know anymore.

Sonny hovered. "How's your leg?"

"I haven't thought about it in the past five minutes."

"That's good."

"I guess."

He looked towards the door. "If the two of them decide to come into the house, we can probably take them out without having to hurt them."

"I don't think there's a chance in hell they're going to come in here alone. They'll call this in and wait for backup."

"That's different."

Andy jumped back from the door. "One of them is reaching for the car radio."

"Here we go," said Sonny.

Ava struggled to her feet. As she did, the makeshift bandage around her thigh slid down to her ankle. She pulled up her pant leg, exposing the dishcloths, which were completely soaked in blood.

"We need to get you out of here," Sonny said, kneeling down and removing the cloths.

"It isn't as if I'm not willing to go," she said.

"The guy on the radio is getting in the car. The other one is staring at the house," Andy reported.

Ava's phone rang. She leapt at it. "Yes."

May was almost breathless. "Those policemen should be leaving soon. Feng spoke with his contact at the Security Force. He told him that the PLA has an interest in the house. I had to call Chao to get to Feng, and Feng had to make several calls himself before getting to the right man. Ava, I'm sorry it took so long."

"The other cop's getting into the car...he's closed the door...The car is leaving!" Andy yelled, doing a little dance at the door.

"Bless you, May," said Ava.

"Did everything else go okay?"

"We'll see you in a few minutes, but yes, it went well enough."

"You have Simon?"

"Yeah. We'll see you in a few minutes."

Sonny had gone to the other side of the main floor with Carlo. Ava saw him talking to the people they had cuffed and taped. She felt faint for the first time, and with the bandage removed her thigh felt colder, less sticky, the blood almost tickling as it trickled down her leg.

"Simon," she said.

He ran from the kitchen.

"We're out of here."

Sonny carried Ava to the SUV and laid her in the back seat. "I'm going to drive this one, you handle the other one," he said to Carlo.

Carlo, Andy, and their three men bundled into the second car. Simon sat up front with Sonny in the other. "She's bleeding badly," he said.

They sped up the road to the highway. When they reached it, Sonny paused as if expecting the police to be waiting in ambush. Instead all he could see was May, Song, and Geng standing beside their vehicles, their backs resting against the seawall. Sonny drove the SUV parallel to them and rolled down his window. "Let's go," he said.

May stared into the two vehicles. "Where's Ava? I don't see her," she said.

"In the back."

May opened the door and gasped.

Ava tilted her head back. "Listen to Sonny."

May turned and shouted to Geng, "Drive my car." Then she climbed into the SUV, lifting Ava's head clear before placing it on her lap. "There's blood seeping through your pants," she said.

Those were the last words Ava remembered hearing.

29

SHE WOKE IN A FOG, INTRAVENOUS IN HER ARM, A dull pain in her thigh, needing to pee, alone in a small room that contained only her bed. It took several minutes before she began to make sense of things. She raised her head and looked around. "Hello," she shouted.

She expected to see a nurse, but instead a small, wiry man with a thick moustache, dressed in jeans and a T-shirt, came into the room. "I'm Doctor Hop," he said.

"Where am I?"

"Macau."

"Which hospital?"

"The Hop Ling private medical clinic."

"I need to pee."

"The washroom is right over there. Let me help you up," he said, leaning forward so she could use his shoulders for support.

She sat on the toilet for what seemed an eternity, peeing in fits and starts. Her leg ached like hell, worse than when she'd been shot, and she wondered what they had done to it.

"What day is it?" she asked Hop when she came out of the washroom.

"Friday."

"What time?"

"Two in the afternoon."

She could hardly believe time had moved that slowly. "Where are my people?"

"They're close by. I'll call them when I think you are ready to see them."

"When will that be?"

"Later today, maybe. You need to get a bit more rest and some more fluids into you."

"What did you do to my leg?"

"The bullet was embedded in muscle, quite deep — and you have lots of muscle. I had to make a large incision to get at it."

After the doctor left the room, Ava slept again. No dreams, no sense of time or place, her body and mind floating in abstraction.

It was dark when she woke again, the room still strange but her mind quickly registering the name Hop Ling. She was in Macau, in a clinic, and they had taken the bullet out of her leg. "Hello," she shouted.

No one came, no one answered.

She jiggled her leg and felt nerve endings burn. She wouldn't be jogging for a while, she knew. She swung her good leg over the side of the bed, put both hands down, and forced herself to sit up. The pain made her yelp. "Hello," she cried.

Her head was surprisingly clear. She knew exactly where she was and remembered exactly what had happened up until the moment May got into the SUV. But where was everyone?

She lifted the corner of her hospital gown to look at her leg. All she could see was a bandage that seemed too big for the wound, and what looked like a full roll of tape holding it down.

The door to her room opened and Hop walked in with a short, middle-aged woman in a nurse's uniform. He looked at his watch. "You slept really well — it's nearly nine o'clock."

"Still Friday?"

"Yes."

"Where are my people?"

Hop said, "He is nearby; let me phone him. Now I think you should lie down again."

She lay on her back, memories of that morning dancing in and out of her head. It hadn't gone exactly as planned, but then, when did it? "Thank you, Saint Jude, for Sonny," she muttered, and then wondered if Saint Jude would appreciate being thanked for the deeds they had done. "And thank you for May Ling."

Hop swung the door open and held it back for Uncle. In the dim light he looked older than she could ever remember seeing him. He came to the bed, reached for her hand, and then bent over and kissed her on the forehead. "I have never seen you like this before," he said. "Quite the day."

"I don't remember anything after we left the house."

"Sonny called me from the car and told me what happened. He did not think he could get you past Immigration in Macau or Hong Kong. I told him to bring you here. Hop is a friend, a good man in an emergency and someone who knows how to keep his mouth shut."

"How long does he think I'll have to stay here?"

"Up to you and how you are feeling. You lost a lot of blood, but he tells me he has replaced it and it is now just pain management on your part."

"I want to get out of here as soon as I can."

Uncle said, "I have a bag in the outer room with clothes in it. May talked the Mandarin into letting her into your room."

Tears welled in her eyes, and she felt a surge of uncontrolled emotion. She closed her eyes, trying to shut it out. "I shot Lok."

"I know. Sonny told me."

"I executed him. I put a gun to his head and pulled the trigger."

"Ava, there was no other choice," Uncle said, gripping her hand tighter. "I spoke to Sonny yesterday before he left and reminded him what kind of men Wu and Lok were."

"I have never killed anyone in cold blood. Before it was always—"

"You or them? Well, let me tell you, I do not think this was any different in reality."

"I'm supposed to be an accountant," she said, her voice cracking.

Uncle grinned at her, and despite herself she found a small smile tugging at the corners of her mouth. Then she began to cry in earnest.

He held her hand, wiping her tears with a tissue.

"Could you get my clothes, please? And I'll need someone to help me get dressed."

"There is a nurse outside. I will get her," he said.

The same nurse who had come into the room with Hop

returned, bringing the bag with her. She emptied the contents on the bed.

Ava sat on the edge of the bed, gathering the willpower to stand. Finally she put her hands on the nurse's shoulders and slid to the ground. Pain burst along the entire length of her leg. She winced and groaned.

"You need to move," the nurse said. "The pain will ease the more you use the leg."

Ava nodded. She put on the black T-shirt herself, forgoing a bra, and then handed her panties to the woman. "I'm sorry, but you'll have to help me with these."

The nurse knelt down, put Ava's feet into the panties, and then slid them gently up her legs. She repeated the process with her track pants.

Ava leaned back against the bed. "Do you have crutches?"

"I'll get them," the nurse said.

A few minutes later, Ava hobbled out to a small waiting room, where Hop was chatting with Uncle. "Take me home, please," she said.

Hop handed her an envelope. "Tylenol 3 — take one whenever you need it. There is no virtue to being in pain when it isn't necessary."

"I have a car waiting outside," Uncle said to Ava, and then turned to Hop. "I was pleased to find that you are still here after all these years."

"I provide a service that always seems to be in demand in Macau."

30

A MERCEDES-BENZ S-CLASS WAS IDLING AT THE HOSPI-
tal entrance. Ava eased into the back seat next to Uncle. The
front passenger seat had been pushed all the way forward
so she could stretch out her leg completely.

As the car pulled away from the clinic, Ava turned to
Uncle and said, "How did the rest of the day go for everyone else?"

"All hell broke loose for a while."

"Why?"

"The cops went back to the house, and when they saw
your cars were gone, they went in. They did not expect to
see three dead bodies. It went all the way up the line, and
the police chief called General Feng. The chief said they
had not agreed to that kind of action and was ready to put
out an alert to stop the SUVs — they had written down the
plate numbers when they were at the house. Feng called
May to warn her. She was in the car with you and Sonny,
and Sonny decided to get you to the clinic and then park
the vehicles somewhere safe until things got resolved. That
was a good decision. It would have been too dangerous to

go anywhere near the ferry terminal."

"How did it get resolved?"

Uncle shrugged. "The same way it always does in Macau. Favours were exchanged, and sometime in the next few days money will change hands. We will have to pay Feng and the Macanese police. May is going to put up half, and I committed to the rest."

"My brother, my problem, my money," Ava said. "I don't want you or May to pay a penny."

"You were not available, so we handled it. We will sort it out later."

"So everyone got back to Hong Kong?"

"Almost in time for lunch."

"Thank God."

"I think the fat little blond man was more inclined to say 'Thank Ava.'"

She shifted her weight and pain shot down her leg. "Simon got to Sha Tin?"

"Yes, the girl Amanda called May after he arrived there. He told her you were shot and she was out of her mind with worry. May calmed her."

"I couldn't have done any of this without May."

"She went to Hop's clinic with Sonny late this afternoon. They wanted to stay but Hop would not let them. No room, he said. He did not want them to know exactly who he was or what he does. They will be waiting for us in Hong Kong."

The terminal was coming into view when she thought about what Uncle had said to her at the clinic about Wu and Lok. "You ordered Sonny to go to Macau with me, didn't you."

"I suggested it to him. He thought it was a good idea."

"You told him to make sure Wu and Lok died, didn't you."

He held her hand, his index finger tapping gently. "I have known men like them all my life. It would have been foolish not to get rid of them. I am getting old, Ava, but I am not a fool. And neither are you. Without Sonny, without me, you would have made the same decision."

Lok's face, with its twisted mouth, gnarled teeth, and desperate eyes, filled her mind. What had he said? *We made a deal.*

Ava turned away from Uncle and looked at the jetfoil terminal, lit up like the City of Dreams. She was an hour from Hong Kong, less than a full day's journey from Toronto.

Time to go home, she thought.

COMING SOON
from House of Anansi Press
in February 2013

Read on for a preview of the next thrilling
Ava Lee novel, *The Scottish Banker of Surabaya*

REVENGE WAS NOT AN EMOTION SHE WAS ACCUS-tomed to managing.

In the course of business there were times when things came unstuck and she found herself on the wrong end of an outcome. But in her mind it was still business, and the people who were causing her grief were simply exercising their own right to do business as they saw fit.

This was different. He had made it personal, more personal than she could have imagined possible.

She lay in the dark, cold despite being wrapped in a thick duvet, and she thought about the day that was about to dawn.

She was going to get him. She was going to hurt him. The thought of it didn't bring peace. It ran unchecked in her mind, bouncing from pain to pain.

She prayed she would be calmer and in control when the moment came. It might be brutal revenge she sought, but she still wanted it to be quiet, and private.

IT WAS THE FRIDAY BEFORE THE LABOUR DAY WEEK-end, the last weekend of Canadian summer, and Ava Lee woke with the realization that her two months of relative seclusion were about to end.

She lay quietly for a moment, listening for the sounds of birds that greeted her every morning through her open bedroom window. She heard the leaves rustling and lake water lapping against the dock, and she knew the wind was up.

She moved her legs and felt a burning sensation in her right thigh. Two and a half months before, she had been shot there during a house invasion in Macau. She had flown back to Canada two days later on crutches that had evolved into a cane and then a limp. Most mornings she felt nothing in the leg, only to have the pain reappear randomly, burning and throbbing; it seemed to twitch, to be almost alive.

Ava was a debt collector. It was a job often fraught with peril, and over the ten years she had worked with her Hong Kong partner, Uncle, she had been stabbed, kicked, punched, hit with a tire iron, and whipped with a belt.

None of them had left a permanent mark; none of them revisited her like the muscle memory of that bullet.

She pulled down the sheets and glanced at her leg. The doctor in Macau had done a good job getting the bullet out of her thigh and treating the initial wound, but he was no cosmetic surgeon. Her girlfriend, Maria, had gasped when she first saw the raw red scar, which eventually turned into a less ugly long pink worm.

She slid from the bed, slipped on her Adidas training pants, and left the bedroom. She walked softly down the hallway so as not to disturb her mother and went into the kitchen. The hot water Thermos she had brought from her Toronto condo sat ready on the counter. She opened a sachet of Starbucks VIA instant coffee and made her first cup of the morning.

The sun was well over the horizon, but she could still see the last remnants of morning dew glistening on the wooden deck. She opened the kitchen door and felt a slight chill in the air. She put on her Adidas running jacket, slipped her iphone into a pocket, grabbed a dish towel, tucked her laptop under one arm, and, balancing her coffee, walked across the wet grass to the dock.

Ava started every morning on the dock with her coffee and her electronic device. She wiped the dew from the wooden Muskoka chair and eased herself into it. One broad arm held her coffee, the other comfortably accommodated the phone. She turned it on.

It was just past nine o'clock, and the emails from the part of her world that was beginning its day were first in line. Maria had emailed at eight. I have a seat on the Casino Rama bus leaving the city at 4 this afternoon. I should be at Rama by 5:30. Do you want me to take a cab to the cottage?

Ava started to reply and then realized Maria would be at her desk at the Colombian Trade Commission office by now. She called her direct line.

"Hi, honey," Maria said.

"I'll pick you up in front of the casino hotel," Ava said.

"Your mother is staying at the hotel again?"

"Yes."

"She doesn't like me."

"That's not true."

"She never wants to be in my company, and when she is, the only two things she ever says to me are that I have nice manners and that I look good in bright colours."

"Those are compliments."

"I make her uncomfortable."

"No, *we* make her uncomfortable. Although we've never discussed it, I know she can't stay in the cottage when you're here because she wouldn't be able to stop herself thinking about what's going on in our bedroom. She's very Chinese and very Catholic, and as understanding as she tries to be, there are limits to what she can handle. Is your very Colombian, very Catholic mother any different?"

"No," Maria said softly.

"So I'll see you tonight. The weather forecast for the weekend is fantastic."

Ava returned to the emails. Her sister, Marian, had sent one of her typical newsy emails. The girls go back to school on Tuesday. New uniforms for them this year. I bought them over a month ago, and when I did I couldn't help but remember how Mummy always left doing that until the very last minute, and how we ended up in long lines that took hours to process and were lucky at the end to find uniforms in the right size.

Ava sighed. Her mother and her sister had personalities that didn't mesh well, and the relationship grew even more contentious when Marian married an uptight *gweilo* civil servant who was incapable of understanding a woman like Jennie Lee.

And I can't believe that she actually stayed at the cottage with you for two months, Marian wrote. She came to our cottage in the Gatineaus once and barely lasted the week. She said she didn't like blackflies, squirrels, raccoons, horseflies, mosquitoes, dirt roads, and cold lakes.

Give the girls a hug for me, Ava replied. I'm sure they'll have another great year at school. As for Mummy, well, she initially came to the cottage because she knew I needed her help, and she stayed because I stocked the fridge with Chinese food, brought in Chinese cable TV, told her to invite her friends from Richmond Hill to play mah-jong, and most evenings I drive her over to Casino Rama to play baccarat.

The cottage was on Lake Couchiching, near the town of Orillia, about an hour's drive from Toronto's northern suburbs and only fifteen minutes from the casino. She had discovered it online, surprised to find something that could give her the privacy she wanted and still be close to good restaurants and the services she was used to.

She worked down her email list, deleting most of them until she got to the part of her world that was ending its day. There were emails from Amanda Yee, her halfbrother's fiancée, in Hong Kong, and from May Ling Wong in Wuhan. Amanda was worrying about wedding dates and venues, two subjects Ava had no interest in. May Ling's message was long and colourful.

Ava had met May Ling as a client. Their early relationship devolved into mistrust and anger, but fences had been mended and May had been supportive and indeed integral to Ava's success in Macau. The two women were now friends, and perhaps becoming more than just friends. May's emails were chatty, full of news about her business and other things going on in her life. She asked questions, sought advice, but mainly wrote to Ava as if she were writing in a diary. The first few times that May became intensely personal, Ava had been taken aback. She didn't need to know, she thought, about May's fears, the details of her marriage and sex life. Then she became accustomed to it and even found herself — tentatively — sharing more of herself with May. They had not been and never would be physically intimate, but there was an emotional connection. May Ling, a Taoist, said it was *qi* — the life force — flowing between them.

About once a week May would phone. She was smart, tough, and funny and could buck up Ava's spirits in no time. It was during one of those calls that May had asked Ava if she would be interested in joining her business. She and her husband, Changxing, were the wealthiest couple in Hubei province and among the wealthiest in China. It was time for them to make some North American investments, she said, and they needed someone to spearhead the initiative.

"I wouldn't be a very good employee," Ava said.

"A partner, then," May said.

"I have a partner, and I have a business."

"Ava, you know that Uncle can't keep doing this for much longer, and I can't imagine you would want to do it without him."

For ten years Ava and Uncle had been partners in the collection business. They had met when both were separately pursuing the same thief and had bonded almost at once. He was now in his late seventies or maybe his eighties — Ava didn't know — and he had become more than a partner. He was a mentor, almost a grandfather, and the most important man in her life. And that was the source of her dilemma. She was tired of the stresses of the job, fed up with the kind of people she had to pursue, and she was beginning to wonder how much longer her luck could hold out when it came to dodging bullets and knives.

As she mended, she had waited for the urge to get back to work to return. It hadn't. She then began to ask herself if it was possible that it never would.

During her recuperation Uncle had stayed in constant touch by phone. He didn't discuss business or ask when she was coming back; his only concern was her health and her family and friends. He did talk about May Ling, whom he knew well. He had urged Ava to make up with her when their relationship went sour, and his judgement of May Ling's character had proven to be correct.

"The woman has *guanxi*, influence, and could be a very powerful ally for you in the years ahead. You need to stay close to her," he said during one call.

Ava didn't know if Uncle knew about May's offer, and she wasn't about to tell him. "I have a business partner," she said.

"Yes, one who is not going to be here forever."

"I have a business partner," she repeated.

"I am not suggesting otherwise," he said.

Ava thought that over time she could grow as close to May Ling as she was to Uncle, sharing the kind of closeness where trust is absolute and forgiveness is never necessary. The chance to do real business, to build a company, was an attractive proposition. Ava was an accountant with degrees from York University in Toronto and Babson College, just outside Boston, and liked the idea of using her education for something other than locating and retrieving stolen money.

But no matter how she spun things, it all came down to one fact: she couldn't leave Uncle. He loved her, she knew, and she realized that she was the daughter — or, more likely, granddaughter — he had never had. She loved him in return. Neither of them had ever mentioned the word *love*. Their relationship was built on things that were never said, and never needed to be said.

Ava finished her coffee and weighed the options of having another or starting her workout regime. At the beginning of her second week in the north, Ava had begun to exercise again. She started with a walk/jog cycle in the mornings and rapidly extended the distances and increased her pace. In the afternoon she would go down to the lakeside and do bak mei drills in slow motion, as she had been taught. Only a handful of people in Canada practised this martial art. It was taught one-on-one, traditionally passed down from father to son, or in her case from teacher to student. It wasn't pretty to watch but it was effective, designed to inflict the maximum possible damage. Ava had become adept at it.

"Ava, do you mind if I join you?"

The voice startled her. She looked up and saw her mother standing to one side with a cup in each hand.

"I made you another coffee," Jennie Lee said.

"Thanks. I'm surprised to see you up this early."

"I couldn't sleep."

"Is something bothering you?"

Jennie passed a coffee to her daughter and then sat in the other Muskoka chair, ignoring its dampness, her eyes fixed on the lake. "I need a favour," she said.

Jennie was close to sixty years old, but even without makeup and with her face lit by the morning sun, she looked like a woman in her forties. "What is it?" Ava said.

"I'd like you to drive me to the casino at three o'clock."

"That's early, Mummy. Maria doesn't get in until five thirty."

"I know, but I need you to talk to someone there."

"Who?"

"Theresa Ng."

"Who is Theresa Ng?"

Jennie Lee took a pack of DuMaurier extra-mild king-size cigarettes from her housecoat pocket, lit one, and blew smoke towards the lake. "She is a baccarat dealer at Rama."

"Why would I talk to a baccarat dealer?"

"She has a problem."

"I'm not a counsellor."

Jennie took two more long puffs and then threw the cigarette to the ground. "She has a money problem."

"How do you know that?"

"I asked her why she looked so troubled."

Ava knew that her mother made friends as easily as other

people changed clothes. There wasn't a store she went into or a restaurant she ate at where she didn't ask the server or the sales associate what their name was and how they were doing.

"How does this involve me?" Ava said.

Jennie leaned her head against the back of the chair and then slowly turned towards her daughter. "Just because I never talk to you about what you do for a living doesn't mean I don't know."

"Really?"

"Yes, really. I've always had suspicions that you didn't make all that money you have by being a good accountant. I also found it strange that you work with Uncle, but I ignored all the rumours about his triad connections by telling myself he's an old man who's moved on to other things. But any doubts I had were put to rest after you went to Hong Kong and Macau and saved Michael's partner's life, and their business."

"Michael wasn't in Macau."

"Ava, please don't treat me as if I'm an idiot or can't handle the truth."

Ava sipped her coffee and stared out at the water, which was dotted with people quietly fishing from canoes and small boats. The jet skiers usually invaded the lake after lunch and then departed before dinner, leaving the lake to the fishermen again until dusk. "Macau was hard on me emotionally as well as physically," she said. "I don't like talking about it."

"Other people in the family, including Michael, have done enough talking for everyone to know what happened."

"And I'm sure it's been exaggerated."

"What, you didn't save the partner and the business?"

"I had help."

Jennie waved her hand dismissively. "You led; we all know you did. When your father heard the story, he couldn't handle his emotions. It was the first time I've seen him cry. And then I cried, because I knew you had not only saved Michael, you had saved the entire family. If you hadn't recovered all that money, your father would have emptied his bank accounts to cover Michael's losses. And then where would we be? His years of labour gone, and my security and that of the other wives and children completely at risk."

"I did what I had to do."

"You mean you did what you chose to do, and that's why I was so proud. You didn't care what other people said or thought. You decided for yourself what was important and you acted on it. When I was raising you and Marian, that was my prayer — that my girls would become women capable of being true to themselves."

"Some days that's harder to do than others," Ava said. "When it is, I often think of you and how you have persevered."

"Ava, you don't have to —"

"I'm not. I mean it."

"Well, it's true that my relationship with your father has tested me. When I married him, I knew what I was getting into: the second wife of a man who wouldn't leave his first. I thought I could handle it, but all of us being in Hong Kong was too much. So I moved us to Canada. That was my choice, Ava, not his. And once we were here, I re-established my marriage on a basis that suited me and was designed to look after you girls...I would have done anything to look after you girls."

Ava reached over and touched her mother's hand. "We know."

"And your father and I have somehow made it work for more than thirty years."

"I know it wasn't easy."

"No, it wasn't, and it isn't. I know what people, particularly non-Chinese, say and think about my so-called marriage. They don't understand our culture and traditions, and in their eyes I'm sometimes a mistress and sometimes a whore. I just pretend I don't hear them and I go about my business and my life, knowing that it is a life I chose and not one that was imposed on me."

"We're the same that way. Neither of us can stand being told what to do."

"Your father sees that as a blessing in you and a curse in me," Jennie said.

Ava closed her eyes. She wasn't up for a discussion about her father or the complicated family he had created — her mother and sister and her alone in Canada; her father with his first wife and four sons in Hong Kong; and a third wife with two young children in Australia.

"This Theresa Ng, she's a friend?" Ava said.

Her mother sipped her coffee and took out another cigarette. Ava saw her jaw relax. "By now she is."

"And you say she has a money problem?"

"Yes, and I told her you were good at sorting out that kind of thing, so she asked me to see if you would talk to her."

"Uncle and I don't normally take on Canadian clients."

"She's Vietnamese Chinese."

"But her problem is in Canada?"

"Yes, I think it is."

"Well, there are other options she can pursue here. She could get a lawyer, a good accountant, even a local collection agency. This is a country with laws that actually work."

"She wouldn't feel comfortable with them. Besides, from what I can gather, the problem she has is complicated."

"How so?"

"She hasn't given me any details. She just shakes her head and moans every time she starts to talk about it."

"Mummy, very honestly, I don't think this is a job for me."

Jennie Lee took a deep drag on her cigarette, and Ava saw her jaw muscles tighten again. "The thing is, I told her that you would talk to her."

"I wish you hadn't."

"Well, I did, and it's too late to undo it."

"Why?"

"She wasn't even scheduled to work today. She's driving up from Mississauga for the sole reason of meeting with you."

Ava sighed. "I wish you wouldn't do this kind of thing."

"I'm sorry, but all you have to do is listen to her and then point her in the right direction."

Ava put her hands over her face and rubbed her eyes in frustration. "You cannot tell anyone again that I'll meet with them. Uncle and I have our own way of operating, and I don't freelance."

"Does that mean you'll drive me to the casino early?"

"Yes, I'll drive you to the casino early."

"Thank you. And you will take the time to speak to Theresa?"

"Yes, I'll talk to the woman, but that's all. You didn't promise anything else, I hope."

"No."

"Good. Now, how large is this problem the baccarat dealer has?"

"Somewhere between three and thirty million dollars."

"What?"

"Like I said, she's vague about the details."

ACKNOWLEDGEMENTS

This is the fourth book in the Ava Lee series and, as always, I would like to thank Sarah MacLachlan and her team at House of Anansi for their support, with a special nod to Barbara Howson, Allison Charles, and the rest of the sales team.

Kudos to my agents Bruce Westwood and Carolyn Forde, who continue to work diligently on my behalf.

My thanks to Sandra Cunningham and Robin Cass at Strada Films/Union Pictures. They not only optioned all of the Ava Lee books, they also lifted my spirits with their enthusiasm, and then they went one step further by hiring the very talented Karen Walton to write the screenplay for the first book. Karen became one more woman in the Ava Lee circle for me to feel happily inadequate around.

This book, like the rest, is the result of the working relationship I have with my editor, the great Janie Yoon. I can't thank her enough for her insight, expertise, and advice.

Last, I need to thank my family, the entire large and very extended family of children, grandchildren, siblings, aunts and uncles, in-laws, cousins, nephews, and nieces, who — whether their last name is Hamilton or Laporte or Poirier or Field or Howell or Moniz or Burns or Hencher — rally behind every book.

IAN HAMILTON is the author of *The Water Rat of Wanchai*, *The Disciple of Las Vegas*, *The Wild Beasts of Wuhan*, and *The Red Pole of Macau*, the first four Ava Lee novels. *The Water Rat of Wanchai* was an Amazon.ca Top 100 Book of the Year, an Amazon.ca Top 100 Editors' Pick, an Amazon.ca Canadian Pick, an Amazon.ca Mysteries and Thrillers Pick, a *Toronto Star* Top 5 Fiction Book of the Year, a *Quill & Quire* Top 5 Fiction Book of the Year, and winner of the Arthur Ellis Award for Best First Novel. The fifth book in the series, titled *The Scottish Banker of Surabaya*, will be published in February 2013.